THE CIRCLE EIGHT

CALEB

Beth Williamson *writing as*

EMMA LANG

Published by Beth Williamson
Copyright 2013 Beth Williamson
Cover design by Croco Designs
Interior Layout by www.formatting4U.com

This book is a work of fiction. The characters, events, and places portrayed in this book are products of the author's imagination and are either fictitious or are used fictitiously. Any similarity to real persons, living or dead, is purely coincidental and not intended by the author.

For more information on the author and her works, please see www.bethwilliamson.com

ISBN: 978-0-9885666-1-3

Circle Eight: Matthew

"Book one in Lang's new Circle Eight series is a delicious tale of passion and betrayal. Opposites attract in this fiery tale, with memorable characters, fast-paced action and emotional rewards." — 4 Stars, Romantic Times Book Reviews

"Wonderful love story, featuring the well thought out theme, filled with mystery and heroic women and strong western men." — 5 Hearts, Romance Book Scene

"Go back to the days when Texas was a Republic in Emma Lang's first book of her Circle Eight series, Matthew. From its opening page, I became engrossed with the Graham family" — 4 1/2 Kisses, Two Lips Reviews

"MATTHEW is one of the rare novels a reader picks up and never wants to end. Luckily for all of us, this is only the beginning of The Circle Eight series." — The Romance Reviews, Top Pick

Circle Eight: Brody

"A hot, raw western romance. If you like 'em gritty, this one's for you." — New York Times bestselling author Kat Martin

"Lang has grabbed reader attention with her Circle of Eight series and continues to hold it with Brody, as a bold Texas Ranger meets his match in a determined rancher's daughter. Not only is Lang's latest a powerfully realistic western/adventure, but a sizzling hot love story as well..." — 4 Stars, Romantic Times Book Reviews

"Hotter than a habanero, and a thrill-a-minute action adventure to boot, "Brody" is a very intense romance read." — Red Room, Virginia Campbell

"Brody is a wonderfully well-written, good old-fashioned western love story. And when you get done, you'll definitely be anticipating which of the next Graham siblings will fall in love!" — 5 Stars, Affaire de Coeur Book Reviews

Dedication

To everyone who believed in me and supported me through the journey to publish CALEB. Thank you all!

A special thank you to Kim, who is my right-hand lady, keeping me on track and preventing my brain from exploding.

The biggest thank you to DH, my partner, my love, who held my hand and jumped with me.

CHAPTER ONE

May, 1840

Caleb Graham stared down at the incredible bosom in front of him, displayed like a banquet for a starving man. She leaned in to him and smiled, showing teeth yellowed by tobacco. Ah well, nobody was perfect, but unfortunately he couldn't take her up on her offer. He gently pushed her back and brought forth his most charming grin.

"Much obliged, Mary, but I don't have time for a quick poke. I have orders." He had been to the small town of Espejo before since it was part of his territory as a Texas Ranger. Mary had flirted with him—or offered her services if he was being honest with himself— each time he came to town. Its proximity to headquarters gave him the excuse to stop there more often than he should have.

One day he might take her up on it. Being a ranger was a twenty-four-hours-a-day job and he didn't get many opportunities to do much of anything but work. It had been nearly six months since he'd been home to see his family at Christmas. The Republic of Texas was a busy place for a man of the law. There were plenty of folks up to no good.

"Aww, are you sure, Ranger Graham?" Mary's soft breasts pushed into his arm and his dick twitched. Damn but she was well built.

"Yes, I'm sure. I got orders." The truth was, he was exhausted. He had brought in a pair of cousins who had burned down a school. While he was at headquarters, his commander gave him an "easy" assignment. Some blacksmith named Rory Foster refused to vacate government-owned property. Hopefully he wasn't a gunslinger pretending to be a blacksmith who would try to shoot holes in him.

It was an easy assignment as far as they went. Caleb had been shot, stabbed and almost hung throughout the course of the last four years. Kicking a squatter off a patch of land didn't sound too bad. Perhaps after he completed this assignment, he would sleep, a luxury he longed for. The memory of sleeping in his old bed at the Circle Eight, his family's ranch, teased him. Although that life wasn't for him, he did love his family, as crazy as they were.

"Maybe after your orders are done?" Mary's hand crept down and caressed his balls with practiced ease. Oh yes, she was obviously gifted in the bedroom arts. His dick twitched again and he sincerely contemplated putting off his assignment for twenty-four hours. It wasn't as though he shirked work ever. He was as relentless with himself as he was with the men he chased.

It was tempting. Incredibly tempting.

His sense of duty and honor, however, stood between him and a day of debauchery with the nicely endowed Mary. In the end, he wouldn't give in to what she offered. Caleb devoted himself to the job as a Texas Ranger and he would not falter, even if he ached for a soft woman and a warm bed.

"Maybe." He kissed her cheek, earning a few catcalls from the men standing outside the livery.

Mary shook her head. "That one was for free 'cause you're a good kisser. One day I'm going to find out if the rest of you is as pretty as your face." She squeezed his dick for good measure then sashayed away.

He stood there for a moment until the blood stopped pounding through him. Or at least until he could walk without a hitch in his step. The woman had gifted hands, that was for sure. He adjusted the saddlebags on his shoulder and proceeded into the livery to pick up his gelding, Justice. The horse had been with him all four years, a gift from his oldest brother, Matt, when he left to join the Rangers.

The quarter horse had a big heart, a long stride and could run like the wind. He'd proven himself over and over during the last four years. He was a loyal companion who didn't complain, at least not in words, although he did occasionally express himself with a nip to Caleb's ass.

Caleb stepped into the shadows of the livery and headed for Justice's stall. As a Texas Ranger, he had to take excellent care of his horse. Without it, he was a dead man. He took the responsibility seriously and always paid for the best feed and stabled the gelding whenever he could. Espejo's livery was run by a crotchety old man named Edgar McGee. He had some questionable hygiene habits, but the man knew horses like the back of his hand.

McGee stood by the stall, his skinny frame silhouetted in the morning sunlight behind him. His wiry silver hair stood on end and Caleb wondered if the man even knew what soap or a hairbrush was.

"Come to get your horse then?" McGee smacked his lips as though he was still tasting breakfast, which was possible since some of it hung on his scraggly beard.

"Yes, sir." Caleb opened the stall door and Justice immediately shoved his head toward Caleb's pocket. "Whoa, boy, anxious are you?" He pulled out the sugar cubes he'd snatched from the restaurant and fed them to the spoiled gelding.

"You shouldna give him too much of that. Make him fat." McGee farted as he spoke. The man was not one to hold back.

"I know how to take care of my horse." Caleb made quick work of saddling the horse. Justice tapped his right front hoof on the ground as though he was anxious to leave. So was Caleb, although this easy assignment wouldn't last long. He would take his time getting back to headquarters. After such a long stretch without a day to himself, perhaps it was time he took a breath.

He paid McGee and led the horse out of the livery. The sun shone brightly in the clear sky. It was going to be hot, the promise of summer in the air. He swung up into the saddle and headed out of town. It was no good to be in one place for very long. He'd left the Circle Eight to get away from roots—they had strangled him when he lived with his family.

Now he was always moving, always looking for the next challenge. He wasn't a fool heading face first into danger, but he didn't shy away from it either. The last time he was home he argued with Matthew about how often he did make it to the Circle Eight. It wasn't as if they needed him. There were six other Grahams, plus Hannah, Matt's wife, and Brody, Olivia's husband. Not to mention Eva and her two sons, Lorenzo and Javier, who worked as ranch hands.

The Grahams didn't need him and he convinced himself he didn't need them. He could only take them in spoonfuls, nothing more than a few days. Getting stuck at the ranch during Christmas for a week drove him to hide in the barn with a bottle of booze.

3

Truth was, he was only twenty miles from home. He should turn that direction and pay them a visit. Whoever the blacksmith was, his eviction could wait a day. Guilt was an unwelcome visitor but it had taken up a perch on his shoulder.

Although he told himself to head north, Justice turned east instead. The damn horse seemed to read his mind. A stop at the ranch would appease his family. That was the only reason he was riding that direction.

The morning passed quickly with no more than a few critters for company. The sun was high in the sky when he turned by the big banyan tree that marked the edge of the Circle Eight. A shout in the distance told him he had already been spotted.

Sure enough, a little streak of lightning on a horse raced toward him. Catherine, the youngest girl of the Grahams, pulled her horse to a halt, kicking up dust and rocks. Caleb waved his hand in front of his face to clear away the cloud.

Catherine was eleven, full of piss and vinegar, determined to be the most hellacious teenager that ever lived. Her blonde hair had been chopped off and she wore trousers all the time. At Christmas she had spent her time brooding that he never visited and then pouted when he left. Now she wore a grin as wide as Texas. If that girl ever started dressing like a female, she would be the most beautiful creature on earth. Her blue eyes sparkled with mischief.

"Well, look who decided to come for a visit." She turned her horse back toward the house. "Thunder has been waiting to challenge that sorry gelding to a race. Ready?"

He shouldn't race her. Hell, she shouldn't race at all. She was supposed to be a young girl, not a wild creature, but her behavior told a different story.

Caleb grinned. "Loser has to rub down both horses."

"Deal." She leaned forward in the saddle and flicked her gaze back to his. "Go!"

She kneed her horse into motion and soon was a blur. Caleb was behind her, noting that her lithe, long form was at one with the animal. His little sister was quite a horsewoman, put the rest of the Graham women to shame. He came within six feet of her, the pounding hooves and the heat from the horses surrounding them. The thrill of the race made him laugh. She turned to glare at him and he stuck out his tongue.

4

"Jackass." With that, she found an extra burst of speed and the horse pulled ahead of his, way ahead.

Damn, the girl beat him by at least ten seconds. He was astonished to find his sister had that kind of skill and a horse with that type of speed. Plenty of yelling and exclamations split the air as the horses galloped into the yard. His family was noisier than hell, never quiet even when they slept. The Grahams were a group of snorers.

Nicholas appeared from the barn and the lanky twenty-year-old broke out into a wide grin when he saw Caleb. Then he scowled at Catherine. "You're supposed to be exercising him in the corral, not by racing hell for leather, stupid."

"I won, I won, I won!" Catherine ignored Nicholas's acerbic remark and pranced around as though she'd just won the county fair.

Caleb dismounted and shook his brother's hand. It surprised him how much his younger brother favored Matt. He had the same wavy brown hair and brown eyes, even had the same build without the muscle. Matt had ten years of hard ranching and the bulk to go along with it. Nicholas was bigger than he had been six months earlier. The spring was the hardest on a cattle ranch, with the cutting and culling of the herd.

"I won, I won, I won!" Catherine crowed again.

Caleb wanted to spank her. Nicholas shook his head at her antics. "Brat."

"You would know." She rode off behind the barn, leaving another cloud of dirt behind. Catherine hadn't even stopped long enough to say hello or talk to him. All she'd wanted was a race and a victory—he'd handed her both. Ah well, it was a short visit anyway. At least he could say he had seen his youngest sister.

"I've got to unsaddle my horse before dinner. Need a fresh one for the afternoon. Not all of us have a horse like yours." A wry grin split Nicholas's face as he walked back toward the barn. Caleb followed. "What brings you by? You staying for a visit?"

A pinch of guilt made Caleb frown at the horizon. He pushed away the unwelcome thought and focused on the fact he had orders. His life belonged to the Republic of Texas—there was no disputing that fact.

"A quick one. I've got orders and a hard ride to get there. It's about two hundred miles away." Caleb breathed deep when he stepped into the barn. The familiarity of it all sent an arrow through him. The

5

dented bucket still hung on the bent horseshoe nail on the wall. The pitchforks, one with a bent tine, stood beside it waiting for mucking duty. The smell of fresh hay and horse filled the air.

"Damn. Liv will pitch a fit when she finds out you were here and she missed you." Their older sister lived with her husband, Brody, on his farm fifty miles away.

"Don't tell her." Caleb walked deeper into the barn, taking note of changes in the midst of the sameness and familiarity.

"Hmph. We are talking about Olivia. Our sister? You think she won't find out from one of the girls?" Nicholas snorted. "Unlikely. You'll have to endure a tongue lashing the next time you see her."

Caleb shrugged, knowing no matter what he said, Olivia would talk his ear off for not visiting more often. When she found out he stopped when she wasn't there, she would probably explode into a thousand pieces of suffering sisterhood.

"Is everybody coming in for dinner?" Now that he was here, he wanted to see everyone. His gut told him it was because he missed them but his head told it to shut up. There were other things in life than the Graham family and the Circle Eight. The wide world offered so much, he'd barely had a chance for a small taste of it over the last four years. Most of that had been the shit on his shoes—he wanted more.

"Should be. It's tortilla day so Eva should have fresh beans to go with them." Nicholas's stomach yawned and he grinned. "Talking about it makes my gut do a dance."

Caleb returned the grin. "I've dreamed about those damn tortillas and the spicy beans she stuffs in them."

"Then you came on the right day." Nicholas clapped Caleb on the shoulder with enough force to make him move forward. Damn, he was getting to be a real man with enough force to move Caleb's bulk.

The dinner bell rang and memories of how many times he'd rung it washed over him. Things never changed on the Circle Eight. He didn't know if that was good or bad, but he was glad he had made the detour to come home.

Home.

As the two of them started for the house, he thought about what "home" was to him. For years it had been whatever spot he found to lay his head. Yet somewhere deep inside he had obviously retained the thought that the family ranch was still home. Caleb loved his family,

God knew he did, but he couldn't stay here forever. He needed the taste of the world on his tongue.

He didn't have a woman like Hannah or two young 'uns underfoot like Matt. Nothing to tie him down and that was fine by him. Coming back twice a year to the madness and mayhem was enough. For now, it was more than enough.

Little girl squeals rang in the afternoon air. Caleb spotted the Matt and Hannah's twins, Margaret and Meredith, chasing each other around the big oak tree beside the house. It had been his mother's favorite spot, where the flowers grew the most beautiful and where two weddings had taken place. It held a bit of magic and the three-year-olds obviously knew it.

"Hey, peach pits, what are you doing over there?" His nickname for the little girls with the auburn hair never failed to make them smile.

Their squeals reached a fevered pitch when they spotted him. Sixty pounds of pure joy ran at full speed. He squatted down and they flew at him so hard they knocked him on his ass.

"Uncle Caleb! Uncle Caleb! Uncle Caleb!" They covered him with sticky kisses, yanking on his hair and his shirt until he had to crawl out from under them.

"I give up." He stayed on his knees until he caught his breath, then got to his feet. That's when he spotted his pistol on the ground and Meredith reaching for it. "No!"

She started and jumped a foot in the air. Then she started crying.

"Ah, hell, Meredith, I'm sorry. I didn't want you to get hurt. That's dangerous, honey." He slipped the pistol back in its holster and picked up both girls, one in either arm.

"You cussed. Mama says no cussing." Margaret stuck her thumb in her mouth and eyeballed him with the suspicion of a sister protecting her kin.

"I know. I'm sorry." He had apologized more to the girls just now than he had in a year. "Let's go have dinner. Eva made tortillas and beans."

The girls were easily distracted by the promise of the treat. Nicholas opened the door and Caleb carried the twins into the house. Then the real noise began. Screeching, yelling, cursing, back slapping and chastising all hit him at once. The Graham clan was known for their noise level and it grew every year, with each child they hatched.

"Caleb, what the hel—in the world are you doing here?" Matt smiled and took Meredith. His oldest brother had a few more lines around his eyes from life on the ranch, but living there suited him as he'd never looked happier. At twenty-seven, he was the oldest Graham, responsible for the entire brood, including his own little group.

"I had orders in this direction. I was over in Espejo and thought I'd stop by for a visit." Caleb set Margaret down and hugged Matt briefly. "It's good to see you." To his surprise, Caleb meant it. For so long he had resented his brother, lived in his shadow, under his rule, especially after their parents were murdered nearly five years ago. Now that Caleb had his own life and was his own man, he no longer had any hard feelings for Matt.

"Caleb Ezekiel Graham." Hannah, Matt's wife of four years, was a beauty in her own way, with glossy brown hair and expressive brown eyes. She was also extremely pregnant.

Caleb's mouth dropped open. "You're having another one?"

"If you came around more than twice a year you might know that." She swatted his arm and then pulled him into a hug. The babe in her belly picked that moment to kick him. "See, the baby agrees with me."

Caleb laughed and hugged her back. They hadn't started off as friends when Hannah married Matt, especially since it was a marriage of convenience. Yet he quickly discovered how strong and incredible his sister-in-law was. She was one of a kind and he had nothing but love for her.

Two brown-haired teenage girls watched him from the other side of the table. At sixteen, Elizabeth had their mother's beauty and grace. She was also too smart for her own good, the quietest of the Grahams. Rebecca was wild at thirteen, not quite as wild as Catherine, but a close second. At least she was wearing a dress.

"*Hijo.*" Eva appeared at his elbow. The petite woman was much more than a housekeeper and cook. She was the heart of the family, the second mother they had known all their lives. When their parents died, Eva was there for them, kept their home together when they might have fallen to pieces.

Caleb found his throat tightening as he leaned down to hug her. She squeezed him surprisingly hard and he kept his touch gentle. The olive-skinned woman had aged gracefully, with beautiful black eyes and an elegance about her that few women had. She also always smelled good, like home.

Damn, there was that strange thought again. The Circle Eight hadn't been his home in four years. He had to stop thinking it was the place to go. There was no way he would stay or, God forbid, settle there for good.

"I missed you, *hijo*." Eva finally let him go and waved a finger in his face. "You stay away too long."

"I have a job, Eva, an important one. The Republic of Texas doesn't take a holiday." He looked around and wasn't surprised Catherine was missing. "Your angel baby whooped my as—me in a race. You need to get her out of those trousers and give her a sewing needle."

Six females smacked him at once, on his arms, his shoulders, his back and even his knees. Exclamations of disgust preceded them leaving him alone. Finally. Too much family time made him break out in hives.

"Sit, everyone. It's time to eat," Eva ordered and they obeyed. Everyone sat down quickly, eager for the delicious treat ahead.

Caleb noted three empty chairs. One was obviously Catherine's. "Lorenzo and Javier?"

"They had to go into town today for supplies. They might be back in time but I made enough for everyone. Even unexpected guests." Eva raised one brow at him and emphasized the word guests.

Caleb didn't want to think he was a guest, but at the same time he wanted to stop thinking of the Circle Eight as home. He couldn't have it both ways.

"I get here when I can, Eva. I'm not avoiding you." He sat in Catherine's chair and hoped she appeared so he could make her try to move him. That would teach her to beat him in a horse race. Brat.

Everyone heaped their plates with hot tortillas, spicy beans and peppers. Eva was a traditional Mexican cook and her food was the best he had ever eaten, no exaggeration. The first bite of the stuffed tortilla made him groan aloud.

They all laughed and rolled their eyes. He didn't care. The food was damn good. He might dream about it later it was so delicious. He ate in restaurants occasionally, but most days his food was whatever he had in his saddlebags and could cook up over the fire. Once in a while he got a rabbit or squirrel to eat. Once in a blue moon, a rancher treated him to a steak dinner.

But this food was the ultimate treat. He stuffed himself until his stomach was nearly bursting. Then he scooped up the leftover beans on his plate, sat back and belched loud enough to shake the walls.

Meredith and Margaret rolled their eyes. "Ewww." Meredith seemed to be the outspoken sister.

"It's how I compliment the cook." Caleb grinned and caught the tortilla in mid-air that Rebecca had thrown at his head. "I see nothing has changed here."

"Things change every day." Rebecca got to her feet and Caleb noticed she had grown breasts. Well, damn. He sure as hell didn't want to notice that. "You are too busy to be here and see it." She stuck her nose in the air and started clearing the table, apparently done telling him what she thought.

Elizabeth got to her feet and looked at him, her green eyes very much like Matt's. She was the old soul in the family, the one Graham who seemed to see everything the rest of them missed. He didn't imagine the disappointment in her gaze though. She didn't have to say a word to tell him what she thought.

"You are not nice to your sisters." Eva mused. "Wait until Olivia gets here. She will do more than throw a tortilla."

Caleb shook his head. "I can't stay."

Eva's expression fell. "Will you stay for longer than a meal?"

"I only have a few hours. I have orders, Eva. I shouldn't have even stopped but I wanted to see you all." Caleb's tongue nearly tripped over his lies. Guilt gnawed at him but he pushed it aside. He had nothing to feel guilty about. Life was not centered on a small ranch in eastern Texas.

She stared at him, her gaze all-knowing and assessing. He forced himself not to squirm in his seat. For God's sake, he wasn't an eight-year-old boy in trouble for filching cookies.

"One day you will realize the importance of family, *hijo*. And then you will know what you have lost by running from here." With that piece of wisdom, she rose and helped the girls clear the table.

Nicholas, Matt and Hannah watched him, their expressions a mixture of curiosity and excitement. He sipped at his coffee, waiting for the inevitable questions. He remembered being Nicholas's age and having the same insatiable need to know more about Ranger Brody Armstrong, his brother-in-law, now retired to live life on a farm with

CIRCLE EIGHT: CALEB

the impossible Olivia.

"You killed any men lately?" The question burst from Nicholas's mouth and both Matt and Caleb laughed. Hannah smacked her husband.

"That's not an appropriate question for the dinner table," she admonished with a sideways glance at the twins, who were watching the adults as though it were the most interesting puppet show ever.

"Why don't you two go check on the kittens in the barn? We want to make sure they don't wander away and get lost." Matt's suggestion energized the girls into motion and in a blur of three-year-old energy they raced out the door. He grinned at Caleb. "The barn cat had a litter a couple weeks ago. They've been watching over it like a couple of mother hens."

"Now can I ask about the killing?" Nicholas sounded impatient.

Caleb shook his head. "Sorry, Nick, I ain't had occasion to kill anybody since the last time you saw me. Sometimes I get to knock them around a bit though." The critters he dealt with were usually too stupid to put up much of a fight after the first punch. More than a few occasions, he had to put them out to finish the job but he got it done, no matter what.

"Boring except maybe the punching part. I can do that anytime with my brothers though." Nicholas made a face.

"It's never boring, but I'd much rather use my fists than my gun. I don't like killing any more than the next man. Taking a man's life will haunt you for a mighty long time. Possibly the rest of your life." Caleb knew that firsthand, but he wasn't about to discuss it with his younger brother. There were better stories to be told, ones that didn't involve a river of blood and the stench of death.

"Listen to him, Nicholas." Hannah patted his hand. "Being a Ranger is dangerous work and definitely not one where you have a clean bed or a hot meal every day."

Nicholas patted his stomach. "I do have a liking for regular meals, especially ones Eva cooks."

"One day you will find a woman who will cook you tortillas instead of me." Eva ruffled his hair. "I won't be cooking for you when you're an old man."

"I ain't in no hurry to find a woman." Nicholas backed away from the table and Eva's touch. "Women are trouble, no offense to any of you, and with a house full of Graham females, there ain't no need to

11

add more. We're already outnumbered."

Hannah smiled. "I have a feeling this baby is a girl too."

"Dammit, that's another confounded female." Nicholas sidestepped Eva's smack for cursing. "I've got to get back out and finish my chores. With Javier and Lorenzo gone, I won't get finished until late anyway."

Caleb got to his feet. "You need a hand?"

Matt joined them. "We're checking all the calves we cut in March and counting the heifers that are pregnant."

"I can count." Caleb didn't know what possessed him to offer to help with chores. If he did go out with his brothers, it would be hours, full dark, before they finished. He didn't want to be there the entire afternoon but now that the words were out of his mouth, he couldn't get them back.

"Nah, we can manage. Will you be gone when we get back?" Matt caught his gaze, a bit of wistfulness in his eyes. "Off to bigger and better things?"

"Nothing is bigger than a ranch in Texas." Caleb grinned but he didn't feel it. "I have orders to evict a squatter on government property."

"Sounds riveting." Hannah rose to her feet with a groan. "I hope you will come back before this baby turns a year old."

Caleb pushed back the guilt her remark brought. "I will be back soon."

"Dare I ask for a date?" Hannah pulled Caleb into a hug and he allowed himself to hug her back.

"I'll be back this summer. Is that close enough to a date?" He had no idea what was in store for him in the next three months but he could try to plan on coming back to the Circle Eight.

"No, but I'll take it." Sadness painted her expression. "We miss you, Caleb."

He nodded, not knowing what to say. In a way he missed them but in other ways, he was glad to be out in the world on his own.

"You need to lay down, hija." Eva took Hannah's arm. "The baby will pop out if you don't get your rest."

"Pop out? The baby's going to pop out?" Matt's panic made his brothers chuckle. "Shut up, both of you. Not funny."

"*Pobrecita.*" Eva ignored the men and led Hannah to the master bedroom.

"Having the twins was hard on her but she's strong. Eva says there's only one baby this time but I worry." Matt stared after his wife, love and concern evident in his gaze.

"She'll be fine." Caleb didn't know if that was true or not but it seemed like the right thing to say.

"C'mon, Matt, we'd better get moving." Nicholas hugged Caleb briefly. "Next time stay for more than tortillas and beans."

Caleb punched his arm hard before his younger brother escaped out the door with a grin, slapping his hat on his head. Matt shook his hand with a serious expression on his face.

"Be careful out there. Don't forget you're part of the circle here. It's not whole until we're all together." What Matt didn't say was louder than what he did. His older brother walked out the door with less speed than Nicholas.

"He talks about Benjy sometimes." Rebecca appeared at his elbow, her gaze pensive. "I think he's hoping one day the smallest Graham will come walking up to the house."

Caleb rarely thought about Benjamin, the smallest brother who had disappeared five years earlier when their parents were murdered. While they had searched endlessly for him over the last four years, Olivia and Brody had helped other children. Yet the only information they had been able to uncover was that he was sold to a ranch in Texas.

The Republic was a big place, bigger than anyone really knew. A little boy with no family to protect him could disappear in a blink. Caleb had spoken to his Commander about looking for Benjamin twice, both times he had been turned down. Cold trails were low priority when there were dangerous situations to handle. Although the squatter wasn't dangerous, he could be if he was unwilling to vacate government-owned property.

"He feels responsible." Rebecca continued. "He's the oldest and we were all his to watch and then he let that awful Jeb Stinson on our ranch. I think Matt will always look for Benjy."

"You're likely right. He takes everything he's responsible for pretty serious." Caleb hadn't had a conversation with his younger sister in years. She was a thoughtful kid, pretty perceptive too.

"I think we all do." She turned to him and he saw just how beautiful Rebecca would be as a woman. She had their mother's heart-shaped face and blue eyes, with the rich brown hair nearly all of them had.

"The curse of being a Graham." Caleb grinned but she didn't smile back.

"We are your family whether or not you want to remember us. They all miss you, especially Matt. You need to remember that when you're off rescuing dirt from blacksmiths." With that, Rebecca disappeared from the kitchen, leaving him alone with Elizabeth.

"Are you going to yell at me too? Maybe you can make up for Liv not being here." Hell, why had he even come? He knew they would make it difficult.

She turned from the sink and shook her head. "No I wasn't planning on it, but I can if you like."

Caleb crossed his arms. "I'll pass on the yelling, thank you."

"Then dry the dishes now that you've run Rebecca off." She pointed to the stack of plates waiting. "Then you can go away with a soothed conscience because you helped out at least a little."

"Damn, when did all my sisters become so hard?" He chuckled and picked up the towel. "I'll help, Elizabeth."

Her mouth kicked up a little at the corner but she didn't smile. They stood together, doing the dishes side by side, until they were done and put away. Caleb was grateful for the quiet to end his visit. His family didn't disappoint him and he couldn't wait to be on his way.

CHAPTER TWO

Aurora Foster wiped the sweat from her brow with her sleeve and pressed the bellows again. The fire crackled and breathed from the intense heat. It was nearly hot enough to put the iron in the forge. She stirred the embers with the poker and pressed the bellows again.

The wooden flaps were open to catch the spring breeze. It floated through the opening, carrying away the smoke from the forge. The beautiful weather made for ideal conditions for a blacksmith.

She had twelve more tools to make for the Garza hacienda this week. Pablo Garza paid well and she desperately needed the money. Any day she expected someone with a gun and an attitude to appear on her doorstep and demand every last penny her husband owed. Damn the fool for dying and leaving her in debt. He was a good-hearted man but couldn't add two and two together.

She'd married Horatio after her parents had died when she was sixteen. She had been desperate and grief-stricken. Theirs had been a marriage of convenience but she'd grown to love him over the next five years. He supported her work as a blacksmith. Her father had taught her how to use the forge from the time she could hold the hammer. That was the moment she ceased answering to Aurora and became Rory, a blacksmith's apprentice.

Now she was as successful as she could be, given Horatio had died from a horse kick to the head without telling her what he'd been up to. He owed quite a few people and they all came to her doorstep with his marker in hand. Life had been hard the last year and there had been letters from the Republic of Texas too. Ones she didn't understand so she'd burned them.

Rory wasn't a genius, but she was smart enough to run a business and pay back the money her husband had borrowed. What she didn't know was what he did with all of it. They lived modestly. There were no luxuries to be had and she worked every day at the forge.

One day she might discover his secret, but if she never did, life would go on and so would she. The deadline for the tools loomed and she had to get at least three more done this afternoon. She adjusted the leather apron that hung on her neck—it had been her father's—and picked up the lumpy piece of iron with her tongs.

She plunged the iron into the forge, then pumped the bellows. After waiting the appropriate amount of time, she flipped the iron over and pumped the bellows once more. It became a rhythm to her, a dance she knew well enough to repeat without thought. The fire burned white hot and she closed her eyes for a moment to escape the heat.

Soon enough the iron was hot enough for her hammer. She pulled it from the forge with the tongs and grabbed her hammer. The ringing of the hammer hitting the iron and the anvil was as familiar as any other sound in her life. She used the cross peen of the hammer to lengthen the iron, crafting what would be a chisel.

Rory put it back in the forge to heat again, repeating the process over and over until she was satisfied with the shape and size of the chisel. She plunged the iron into the cold water, the hiss of the super-heated metal akin to an animal caught in a trap. The forging was done. Next would be the sharpening of the blade and the filing of the rough edges.

"Rory?" Eloise Jensen called out from outside.

"I'm out in back. Come on around." Rory pulled off her gloves. No doubt she was covered in soot but Eloise had seen her dirty before.

Eloise was a plump, round-faced blonde woman with merry blue eyes and consistently red cheeks. She had married Sven, the livery owner in town. He sent Eloise with horses to Rory to reshoe them all the time. Although Rory was not a true farrier, she took as much work that came her way. The horses didn't complain either.

"There you are." Eloise waved her hand in front of her face. "You're busy. I can come back later."

"No, no it's fine. I just finished a chisel. I can let the forge cool down for a spell while we have a visit." Rory didn't have many female friends. Many of the women in town and the surrounding ranches only dealt with her when they needed their pot handle fixed or if they needed a new kitchen knife. Otherwise they avoided her.

Rory accepted the fact women didn't understand why she would choose, and enjoy, blacksmithing. She had tried to explain it to the little girls she played with as a child, that the forge and the anvil called to her. The hammer was an extension of her arm. She considered herself an artist, and could see the finished product when she began with that lump of iron.

Aside from her choice of professions, Rory was not in the least feminine. She had muscles on her arms, back and shoulders, and wore trousers because they were a safer choice for a blacksmith. When she grew breasts, they got in the way of her hammer swing, and she'd been binding them down every day since then. She was usually dirty, with grimy nails, and her skin wasn't soft. The heat from the fire took care of that. Her hair was short as a man's and she wore a leather cap when she worked.

"I brought by some fresh milk, honey and bread." Eloise held up a basket.

"Bless you." Rory took a rag from the pile by the door and wiped off her face the best she could. "Let me wash my hands and we can sit and enjoy that treat."

Rory hung up her apron, took a clean rag and stepped out into the early afternoon air. The breeze cooled her overheated skin and she breathed in deep. It really was a beautiful spring day. She went to the well pump and took time to scrub her hands until they were red. As she dried them, she walked back to the small building she lived in.

The blacksmith shop was larger than the tiny house next door. It was the perfect size for one, and now that Horatio was gone, she enjoyed the privacy. Eloise waited by the door, her expression tight. The pleasant time Rory had imagined was not going to happen. There must have been a fight between Eloise and Sven or something equally as horrible. Sometimes Rory envied her friend for having a partner to rely on, and other times, she was glad to be a widow.

"What happened?" Rory opened the door and let her friend follow her inside. The small iron table and chairs sat to the left and very small kitchen to the right. In the center of the building was a large stove used both for heat and cooking. Her bed was in the back, nearly end to end as the building was no more than ten foot by ten foot square.

She sat in one chair and waited for Eloise. The blonde set a tablecloth from the basket on the table. She might not care that Rory was a blacksmith but Eloise was a woman who prided herself on cleanliness. The jar of milk, a small pot of honey and a sliced loaf of bread were soon laid out for their dinner.

Rory's stomach rumbled and she grinned. "It smells wonderful."

"Today was bread day. I made half a dozen loaves and I knew I wanted to bring one to you." Eloise pulled out two plates, a knife and two tin cups from the basket. She always brought everything required for a meal and Rory had come to expect it. One day she might actually make a meal for her friend of eggs, hash and corn bread. Although she wasn't a great cook, Rory was quite handy on that old stove and the frying pan she'd made for herself years earlier.

One thing she didn't make was bread. Never had the patience other folks had to knead and let the bread rise. She'd tried when she was first married but the bread was always harder than her hammer. She gave up and made quick breads like corn bread. That was hard to ruin in a frying pan.

Eloise served them each two slices of bread with honey drizzled on them, along with a cup of cool milk. Rory dug right in, taking a bit bite and closing her eyes as the sweet, delicious food danced on her tongue. That woman was an incredible cook.

"This is wonderful." Rory spoke around the bite in her mouth. "You are gifted in the kitchen, Eloise."

As expected, Eloise blushed, making her rosy cheeks a deeper pink. "I don't do anything special. I follow my mama's recipe, that's all." She nibbled on her bread and Rory waited for whatever was on her friend's mind to come tumbling out of her mouth.

Outside the birds chirped, the squirrels chattered and the cicadas buzzed. If she could have this every day, life would be perfect. Rory didn't know what lay ahead, but she would enjoy this moment, the good food and her good friend.

"I heard something today." Eloise finally started in on whatever she had gnawing at her.

Rory took a big gulp of milk. "That so?"

"I heard there was a Texas Ranger who rode into town last night." Eloise picked small pieces of bread and popped them in her mouth, chewing the tiny bits to mush as far as Rory could tell.

"Here? Hm, that's new. I don't believe we've ever seen one around these parts. I've heard of them of course." All she knew was what Horatio told her. They were all hard men who had fought in the war and now served the Republic with their guns. Men of the law who tried to keep their new country free of lawlessness.

"The thing is, I heard Sven talking to Mr. Stevenson, you know the man who owns the store in town? They were talking about this ranger and how he was here to find a specific person." Eloise finally looked up and met her gaze, pity shining in their blue depths. "One Rory Foster."

The bread turned to ash in her mouth and she could barely get the bite past the tightness in her throat. "Me?"

Eloise nodded. "Yes, he was asking where he could find the blacksmith shop and Rory Foster. That was just before I came out here. Sven sent him to the Bessie's for dinner and then promised him directions on how to find you."

She grabbed Rory's hand and squeezed tight enough to cause discomfort. Rory had no time to be surprised because fear raced through her.

"He'll be here within the hour? Is that what you're telling me?" Rory didn't know if she was going to vomit or shit her drawers.

"Yes, I'm sorry, Rory." Eloise was a good friend and she looked perfectly miserable to be delivering the news.

"I wondered who it would be." Rory pushed the plate away, the half-eaten bread taunting her with its sweetness.

"Who?" Eloise frowned.

"Horatio owed lots of folks money. I don't know how much or who, but they've been arriving over the last year with his marker. There were a few letters from Texas but I didn't understand them." She ran her hands down her face. "I've been paying back what I could and when I could. This ranger means that Horatio's stupidity will bite me in the ass once more."

"Rory, your language." Eloise wasn't really chastising. She was too upset for that; her words were said out of habit. "You can run. I'll help you."

Rory shook her head. "I won't run. This is my home, such as it is, and I can't pack up the forge, my tools and the two-thousand-pound anvil. I'm a blacksmith, Eloise. I can't make a living without it."

"What will you do?" Eloise wrung her hands together.

"I'll find out what the ranger wants and then convince him to be on his way." Rory would do anything she had to, including chasing off one of the legendary rangers. Nothing he said or did would get her to budge from her smithy. Nothing.

Caleb was pleasantly full of meatloaf and green beans, and even a piece of peach pie. The restaurant in the tiny town of Marks Creek was a treasure. He hadn't had such a wonderful meal outside of the Circle Eight. He was in a good mood, surprisingly good.

Not only had he located Rory Foster but he had directions to the smithy. The mission was by far the easiest he'd ever been sent on. Now he had to convince Foster to leave the property. Texas had plans for that particular parcel of land and they had let him squat there long enough. Caleb didn't know the particulars, and he didn't want to know. All he had to do was carry out his orders and then ride back to headquarters for his next assignment.

It should be as easy as the ride out to Foster's smithy. Regardless of what a good mood he was in, Caleb made sure his pistol and rifle were both loaded. He was about to evict a man of what was perceived as "his" property. There would be resistance, but if Caleb were smart, he would control the situation from the moment he stepped foot on the property.

The area was beautiful with rolling hills, a plump creek running freely and the kind of thick grass cattle could get fat on. It was clear why the smithy stayed when the Republic of Texas told him to leave. Caleb might have stayed too if he'd been smack dab in the middle of such rich land.

He followed the smell of smoke and rode up to a square building with a sign that read "Foster's Smithy" in faded red letters. It was a typical blacksmith's shop, with large windows controlled by hinged wood panels. The smoke and heat could get fierce inside the building. The windows were currently open offering him a clear view of the inside. There was an enormous stone forge inside and a large number of tools scattered around, not to mention an anvil that probably weighed more than a team of horses. It was a solid shop and a smidge of guilt pinched Caleb for arriving to take it all away from Foster.

He dismounted and finally noticed the tiny shack in the shadows behind the smithy. It wasn't quite a house, but it did have a door, one tiny window and a smoke stack, which meant there was a heat source inside, likely a stove of some sort. It must be where the blacksmith lived, modest as it was. There was great care taken in the actual smithy, which told Caleb the man might be more difficult to remove than he expected.

"Foster?" Caleb walked into the larger building. The forge wasn't fired up, the embers glowed orange. "Is anybody here?"

He hoped like hell nobody told the man there was a ranger on the way. If so, his job got even harder. Caleb kept his hand on his pistol as he walked around the building. Whoever the blacksmith was, he had skills. The iron work was top notch, even in the pieces that weren't finished yet.

"Who are you?" A woman's voice startled him from his perusal.

He turned to find a man wearing a leather apron and cap, and trousers that had seen better days. Caleb shook his head and frowned at him.

"Ranger Caleb Graham. Who are you?" He couldn't equate the husky woman's voice with the blacksmith. Was he hiding her in the apron?

"Aurora Foster."

The voice came from the man's mouth. The ground shifted beneath his feet as realization hit him. Sweet heaven above. Rory Foster. Aurora Foster. Holy hell. The blacksmith he was there to evict was a *woman*? When he got back to headquarters, he'd give his commander a piece of his mind about this particular assignment.

"You're a woman."

"I can see why you're a crack man of the law, Ranger." She raised one brow. "You're trespassing."

He swallowed his response to her sarcasm. She definitely wasn't a wilting flower, but the leather apron should have told him that. "You have that backwards, Mrs. Foster. You are the one trespassing. This property belongs to the Republic of Texas."

Her mouth twisted. "That's ridiculous. My parents settled this land twenty years ago. The Republic can go find someone else to harass." A very large, lethal looking sickle appeared in her hand from beneath the apron. "Now leave."

Caleb took a few moments to study her. Taller than the average woman, she also had muscles most women didn't. Honed, lean arms and long hands, a heart-shaped face with an upturned nose. The one thing that set her apart were the amber eyes currently staring holes in him. They were an unusual shade, like the colors of the embers in the forge behind him.

"I can't do that."

"Then I will make you." She pulled a huge cleaver out with her

21

other hand. The woman was a lethal weapon with all the blades she made.

Caleb decided to appeal to the woman's logical side, if she had one. Truth was, he was distracted by the way she looked and spoke. He'd had plenty of experience with females, but no one like Aurora Foster. "You're the blacksmith, Rory Foster. Is that correct?"

"Only my friends call me Rory. You can call me Mrs. Foster as you ride off my land." She ran the sickle down the edge of the cleaver. It made a screeching sound that made the hairs on the back of his neck stand up. Was she going to chop him into pieces?

"It's not your land."

"That's a pile of horse shit. This land belonged to my father and now it belongs to me." Her tone and her expression told him he had a hell of a fight on his hands.

"Females can't own property in Texas, Mrs. Foster. I'm guessing no one ever told you that. It's understandable that you think this is yours—"

"I don't think anything. I know." She stepped closer, her hands tightening on the weapons. "Now get out before I make you leave."

Caleb sighed. "I can't leave." He didn't want to pull his pistol on the woman. Hell, even the most aggravating female deserved respect. "Ma'am, this is my job. I have an assignment to remove an illegal squatter off land owned by the Republic of Texas. I can't leave until it's done."

She bared her teeth. "Get out of my smithy."

"It seems we are at an impasse. I'll go wait outside while you gather your things. We can ride to Marks Creek and get the legal paperwork in order." Caleb watched her hands, her strong, capable hands, as she edged closer with the sharp implements.

"I have work to do. I'm not going anywhere least of all to town. No one there for me and the legal paperwork means nothing." She threw her arm wide. "This is all I have. This is who I am. I can't leave either."

Well, shit.

Caleb wanted to be on his way, the blacksmith firmly off the property. However, that wasn't going to happen easily. The woman was fierce as hell, not giving even an inch.

He'd dealt with dangerous criminals, wily thieves, even murderous outlaws, but never with a woman like Aurora Foster. Rory was a man's name and she worked in a man's profession. She was stronger than expected. Now he had to devise a plan to get her out of the smithy and off the land. It sure as hell wasn't going to be easy.

Rory shook with anger. White-hot fury raced through her at the ranger's high-handedness. He thought to slide in and pull her home, her business, her life out from under her. The arrogant bastard was more handsome than any man she'd ever seen—too bad it was spoiled by the stupid, sorry jackass.

Her hands shook so hard, she clenched the tools until her knuckles cracked. She wouldn't use them on him, but he didn't know that. Years ago she discovered men took her more seriously when she was armed. Several of them had decided to cheat her out of what was due by physical intimidation. Now she used her height and her finely honed tools to protect herself.

She wanted to scream at him until he left, but it wouldn't do any good. That didn't mean she had to nearly bite her tongue off to keep from letting the dark thoughts loose. Her temper had been her downfall more than once. Keeping it now was the only option. The ranger would have no trouble convincing folks a woman carrying on like a crazy person deserved to be thrown off and thrown away.

Rory had fought too hard, given up too much, to simply lay down and let this man take everything from her. If he had to kill her, then so be it. She was willing to give up her life for what she loved.

"I've got work to do." She walked passed him, ignoring the scent of man that wafted past her nose.

"Work? You're going to work?" His dark brown eyes widened as though he was surprised. The man had ridiculously long lashes for a man. She wondered if he'd been teased about it.

"Yes, I have orders to fill. I work for a living." She stirred the embers with a poker.

"What am I supposed to do while you work?" He leaned against the post in the center of the building.

"You can stand there and play with your gun if you like. I don't give a damn." The coals sparked and glowed. She added a bit more coal from the bucket on the floor, then stirred them into the forge, like mixing a stew.

"You curse too? Ain't you a unique woman?" He watched her, which made her itch.

"I'd like to think so." She worked the bellows, raising the temperature of the forge slowly and steadily. To her consternation, the ranger watched her.

"Nothing you do will change my mind." He crossed his arms, emphasizing the broadness of his chest and shoulders. Damn the man.

"Nothing you do will change my mind," she threw back at him. "I was born here, Ranger, and I plan on dying here. How about you? Don't you have a home you love?"

He seemed startled by her question. Good. She at least put him off center once, which meant she could do it again.

"My home is none of your business, Mrs. Foster." He got his back up with that question. Curiosity told her to keep poking.

"Sounds like you have your own business to attend to. Why are you bothering me when your own home needs you?" She didn't even hear him move but suddenly he was beside her, nearly nose to nose.

"I am losing patience with you, ma'am. If you keep pushing, you're liable to end up belly down on the back of my horse." He sounded cold and furious, but completely in control. It frightened her, much as she wouldn't admit it to him.

"Dead or trussed up like a turkey?" she snapped.

"That's your choice. As long as you leave this property, I don't rightly care."

Red rage ripped through her and her temper finally grabbed hold of her.

"You son of a bitch! What right do you have to come in here and intimidate me? None!" She pushed him, catching him off guard so she was able to move him back a few inches. He was built like a brick wall, though, and she wouldn't be able to do it again. "Does your mother know you ride around pushing women out of their homes and call it your duty?"

He swallowed. "My mother's dead."

"Mine is dead too and this is all I have of her and my father. Do you know what it's like to lose both your parents in an instant? To have nothing but the dirt under your feet to call your own?" Her throat was tight with emotion and she knew her face was redder than a beet.

"Yes, I do," he said quietly. "I do."

His honesty deflated her anger in a flash. She hadn't expected that from him.

"My parents died in a fire." She could still taste the bile that coated her mouth when she found out they were dead. "I never got to bury anything but ashes. I have nothing but this. And you're here to take it away from me."

He looked as though he was going to say something but changed his mind then leaned back against the post, crossing his ankles.

"I won't leave." She turned her back on him and focused on her work. The tools wouldn't make themselves and Pablo Garza didn't forgive lateness. She'd lost money from him before when Horatio ruined one of the yokes she'd made and the new one was two days late. Garza was a jackass but he had money to spend.

For a few blessed minutes, she forgot about the ranger and focused on her work. The forge heated quickly, calming her frayed nerves a bit. She turned to pick up her tongs when a pair of long legs reminded her she wasn't alone.

"You know what you're doing with that thing," he observed.

"I hope so. I've been using it since I was seven." She picked up the tongs, annoyed to see her hand shaking. It had to be from anger because she sure as hell wasn't afraid of this man.

"Seven? Isn't that dangerous for a little girl?"

Rory snapped the tongs together in front of his face. "As opposed to not dangerous for a little boy?"

"That's not what I said." He uncrossed his legs, then recrossed them, calm as could be. "It would be dangerous for any child to be around a fire that hot, or all these tools."

"My father was a master blacksmith. He never put me in danger." She was annoyed all over again at his insinuation her father was not a good parent. "What he did was teach me a craft, turn me into an artisan by the time I was sixteen."

"Artisan? Big word."

She scowled at him. "I'm a big girl. Now if you don't mind, I have work to do. I gotta get these tools done no matter what orders you have stuffed up your ass."

To her surprise, he laughed, a gut-buster that echoed through the small building. She frowned. Why would he laugh when she was deliberately disrespectful?

"Are you touched in the head or something?"

He laughed again and smiled. Oh, that was a sight that stopped her cold. The man was perfectly devastating when he grinned. He was a right beautiful specimen of the male creature. She wasn't immune to a good-looking man but neither should she be noticing the ranger's handsome visage.

"I'd appreciate it if you didn't laugh at me." She pumped the bellows and tried not to look at him again.

"I wasn't laughing at you. You remind me of my sister."

Rory reared back as if he'd slapped her in the face. His sister? She reminded him of his sister. No need to be acting foolish around him because he was handsome enough to make her eyes hurt. No need at all.

"You'd throw your sister off her land, take away her livelihood?" Might as well throw back his own arrogance at him.

"Yep. I would. She's a pain-in-the-ass bossy woman who knows everything. Her husband is the only one who can control her." The ranger shook his head. "Bossy women have always been a problem for me."

"How sad for you." She pumped the bellows again, keeping her focus on the fire, watching for the perfect shade of white to put the iron in the forge.

He chuckled. "You know, I thought Rory Foster was a man. Imagine my surprise when he turned out to be a she."

His story kept getting better. Now she was like a manly, bossy woman who reminded him of his sister. She had no reason to be self-conscious.

"Sorry to disappoint you, Ranger. You can go back to your boss and tell him you couldn't find the man you were sent for." She plunged the iron into the forge and concentrated on creating the tool, not on the man standing four feet away.

He watched in silence but he watched. She had an itch she couldn't scratch because of it. The best thing she could do was show him what this meant to her. So that's what she did.

Caleb had no idea what he was in for when he rode out of Marks Creek in search of a blacksmith squatting on Texas land. She was nothing like he expected nor was she really like Olivia. Aurora Foster was as unique as the pieces of metal she crafted.

He wouldn't admit it, but she impressed him not only with the way she spoke to him but by everything she did. Hell, a woman blacksmith? Unheard of, even in Texas. She was strong, not only in body, but in spirit and heart. The woman was ready to die to keep her life and her business. There was a warrior inside her.

He knew what it meant to lose your parents, to feel adrift in a world without their guiding ways. They had more in common than he thought yet they were as different as the moon was from the sun.

As he watched her work a piece of iron, the heat from the forge made his face tight. She was graceful if that were possible. He'd watched blacksmiths before, men of course, and not one of them had the skill this woman possessed. She was one with the hammer and anvil, creating a tool from nothing but a lump of iron. Artisan was the right word for her. She was an artist.

It wasn't as though he could tell her any of that. No, she couldn't know he had even the smallest amount of admiration for her. That was a weakness he did not expose to anyone.

Yet for some reason he watched her work. The woman knew her way around a forge and it was a pleasure to see. He should have simply thrown her off the land and been done with it. Even if she was taller than average and packed muscles most women didn't, she was no match for him. He outweighed her by at least sixty pounds and six inches.

Caleb wouldn't tell his commander that he'd stood there and let the blacksmith carry on business as though the state of Texas wasn't waiting for the land. He didn't know what they needed it for but he knew what she wanted it for. Caleb couldn't feel bad for doing his job. Rory could find a new husband to support her—she didn't need the smithy.

After she plunged the long chisel into the water, a hiss of steam wafted toward him. She stood the tool up beside others on the floor, each one as finely crafted as the others. Then it appeared the process would begin all over again with another lump of iron.

"Stop."

She didn't even hesitate, pumping the bellows while the fire blazed.

"I said stop. It's time to let that fire die down and leave this place. Don't make me force you." Caleb gestured to the door.

"I have a job to do. Did you not hear me? I won't be going anywhere. Ever." She pumped the bellows in rapid succession, then threw a scoop of water on the fire.

Smoke filled the room in an instant, winding its way around him and making his eyes water. A loud bang was followed by another and darkness surrounded him. He was blind, coughing and disoriented. Then strong hands shoved him and he landed on his ass.

"Dammit, Rory."

"That's Mrs. Foster," she hissed in his ear.

He tried to make a grab for her but he only found air. "Fucking hell."

"Such language, Ranger Graham. I may have to report that kind of behavior." She snaked out the door, leaving a brief snatch of light before it disappeared. It gave him enough to follow her.

Ranger Graham got off the floor and prepared to chase his quarry.

CHAPTER THREE

Caleb wiped his eyes and blinked, the bright light of the day making it worse. He took off his hat and fanned his face, trying to clear some of the residual stinging. The woman definitely had a pair of brass balls.

He was finally able to focus without weeping like a girl. All he saw was his horse, happily grazing. Justice apparently didn't care that his master was attacked by a lady blacksmith with an attitude. There were no unusual sounds, no feet pounding, no hooves, and thank God, no laughter.

He didn't know what Rory hoped to do by dousing him with smoke. She'd run like a rabbit, leaving the very property she refused to leave. He was suspicious of her motives. Why would she do what she refused to do the last hour? It made no sense.

With more trepidation than fear, he walked around the side of the building then around the back. No sign of the confounded woman. He stepped into the tiny shack. The woman continued to surprise him. Her house was neat, organized, and full of the things she had obviously forged. There were no personal items beyond a few clothes on nails in the corner. It was a lonely little house, no more than a small piece of the house at the Circle Eight. Beyond it he saw the charred remains of something else. Grass had grown up around it but it had been a house at one time. Now there was only this shack, which at one time might have served as a smokehouse or storage for the smithy. It was better than sleeping on the ground each night and the house had a wooden floor. It wasn't the worst he'd seen, but it was definitely meager.

Unfortunately she wasn't in the house, or she'd managed hide in six inches of space beneath the bed. He left the shack and turned around to find Justice fifty yards away. Someone had untied him from the tree branch he'd secured him to. Smoke still poured from the

29

smithy, turning the visibility murky but he could still see the damn horse.

"Son of a bitch." He whistled and Justice stopped to look at him. The horse threw his head back and whinnied. "Get back here."

With apparent reluctance, the gelding trotted back to Caleb. It seemed the blacksmith wanted to play games. He could play too, only she wouldn't like his games. The warning of riding with her belly down on his horse wasn't an idle one. He'd done it before, he could do it again.

"You're making this harder on yourself." He spoke to the air around him, knowing she was nearby and listening. Why else would she have released the horse? "I will take you off this property one way or the other."

It was an implied threat. A ranger had to make plenty of hard choices but he would never cross the line and kill a woman. Unless she was shooting at him and even then, he would aim for a leg or a shoulder. The vivid memory of his mother's body still haunted his dreams. There was no excuse for what had been done to her—Caleb would not join the ranks of men who murdered women. Ever.

"The Republic has plans for this patch of land, Rory." He waited for the backlash for using her nickname again but only the wind spoke to him. "If it isn't me, then it's a group of rangers or possibly troops."

He had no idea if that was true or not but it sounded good. All he knew was Texas claimed it when Lowell Benson died and now this woman claimed to be his daughter. Or at least he thought she did.

"This land belonged to Lowell Benson, not Foster. You might claim this land but you don't appear to have a legal right to it."

Again the wind was the only thing that answered him.

"I will sit right here and wait on you, Rory. I've got a lot of patience. Had to with four sisters." He picked a likely spot to camp beneath a big oak tree right in front of the smithy.

Sooner or later, she would return. If he was right, the woman cared a great deal about her business and the building it sat in. She wouldn't let it be destroyed by the untended fire inside or the voluminous amounts of smoke leaking from its closed hatches.

All he had to do was outwait her.

The afternoon crept by while he waited, poking around her things. He knew she watched him but he couldn't spot her. Damndest thing ever. To find a woman like her was like a punch to the gut. She unmanned him with her frank and sneaky ways.

He would have shot a man in the leg. A flesh wound of course, but it slowed them down. No way he could do that with a woman. It went against all he'd been taught. Even if she cussed and swung a hammer, she was a female and deserved a measure of chivalry, or a flavor of it anyway.

When she sat down beside him, he had to tell himself not to react. It was damn hard. She was warm, hot even, with a firm body he could clearly see outlined in the trousers she wore. They were pulled tight on her ass and hips. There was a hell of a lot more curves than he expected.

"I'm sorry I pulled that dirty trick on you, Ranger. I was angry. Still am." Her tone was honest but tight with that anger she professed to.

"Understandable, but I'm an officer of the law for the Republic. I could arrest you for assault." He would do no such thing. It would embarrass the hell out of him but she didn't need to know that.

"Facing a dangerous person like me must be exhausting."

A chuckle crept up his throat and he managed to swallow it. "I have my fair share of perilous situations in this job, Mrs. Foster. You're not the first and you won't be the last."

"Hm, I'm sure that's true." She didn't sound as though she believed him. "I have a proposition, Ranger."

For a moment, perhaps two, he wondered if her proposition involved naked bodies and the promise never to tell what they'd done. Hot, sweaty bodies in the tall grass, firm curves and an afternoon of pleasure he would never forget.

"I want you to leave and forget you found me. Tell the government they made a mistake and this land belongs to me."

His fantasy about her curves in his hands was gone in a puff of reality. "Pardon?"

"The way I see it, you can't admit I bested you and I have nowhere to go. Leave now and no one has to know." She had a smug expression on her face, as though she had solved both their problems with her foolish notions.

"You didn't best me." He crossed his arms and gave her his best lawman stone cold stare.

"Yep, I did. You just don't have the balls to admit it." She got to her feet and brushed her trousers off. His gaze slid to that posterior, its round shape giving him all kinds of ideas of how it would feel if he took her from behind.

Caleb was surprised by the direction of his thoughts. A few days ago, he had Mary in his lap, her tits in his face. Yet he hadn't had one thought as lascivious as what had rolled through his head about the lady blacksmith. Maybe he should have found his pleasure with sweet Mary and he wouldn't be twisted up about Aurora Foster.

"I've got balls, big ones. You wanna see them?" He reached for his trouser buttons.

She held up her hands. "I've seen enough men's balls to last me a lifetime." Her eyes widened after the words fell out of her mouth, then, to his amusement, she blushed. That's when he noted her amber eyes, a deep shade that shone in the speckles of sunlight coming through the leaves.

"You've seen plenty of men's balls then?"

"No, but more than I ever need to see." She backed up a step. "Now I need you to leave."

"I ain't going without you. I will make sure you leave this property, pack up everything and find a new place to live." He gestured to the house. "I'll help you pack up." It was kind of him to offer, even she had to admit that.

"I'm not leaving." She backed up two more steps. "And I can guarantee you won't make me."

He chuckled. "You can't guarantee a damn thing, Aurora."

"You do not have my permissions to use my given name." She was now ten feet away from him and from the looks of her, ready to run like a rabbit.

"Don't disappear again." He still didn't get to his feet, confident whatever she did, he would be victorious in this little skirmish. Hell, he was an ex-soldier and a Texas Ranger. One lady blacksmith was no match for him.

"This is my land. It belonged to my father and now it belongs to me. You cannot make me leave." She reached the fifteen foot mark and he moved to stand.

Quick as lightning, she was gone into the shadows with nary a puff of dust to give away she'd even been there. He stared at the spot, stunned by the speed at which she moved.

Damn. This was going to take a lot longer than he thought.

Rory climbed up on the roof of the smithy and across the branches of the oak tree until she was perched above the ranger. He hadn't even thought to look up because she was female. Ha! She'd spent her entire life climbing this particular tree and knew it as well as she knew the forge. Wearing trousers had advantages she hadn't thought of and climbing trees was one of them.

Sitting up there in the branch wasn't so bad, although she would have to come down. She hadn't thought through her hiding very well and had no food, no water, no blanket and no privy. One of the four would drive her from the tree. Right about then, the privy was the likely winner. Her bladder spoke to her, told her it would appreciate relief shortly.

Damn.

She thought he would take time to search the area around the house and then give up. But no, not this ranger. He confined his search to the buildings then sat down pretty-as-he-pleased under the very tree she hid in. Damn ranger had no common sense. Weren't they supposed to chase their quarry? What kind of ranger sat down and waited?

Perhaps if she hadn't released the horse, he might have left. It was a childish thing to do but it gave her a peculiar sense of satisfaction to do it. The horse was stunning, more perfect than any equine she'd ever seen. Considering she had farrier duties on a regular basis, that was saying something. He was smart too, listened to his master and returned with only a whistle.

She envied the ranger for what he had. A steady job, an excellent horse, and four sisters. Four! Without siblings to play with, Rory had been a lonely child. Her parents had tried for more and the failure had weighed heavily on them. Her father had wanted a son to teach his trade to and had settled for a daughter instead. It didn't matter. When Rory showed aptitude, he taught her everything he knew. She was grateful to him for that. Otherwise she would truly be adrift in the world.

Rory tried to imagine what it was like to have four sisters and failed. It was usually quiet around her, except for the noise she made with hammer and anvil. No chattering girls, no squealing, no laughter, nobody. Envy pinched harder and she looked down at him sourly. He was probably bossy with his sisters too. Heavy handed and arrogant,

33

that's what he was.

She would wait until he fell asleep, no matter what her bladder insisted upon. Then she would sneak down and take care of him. How, she didn't know, but she had hours to find out. It was only the afternoon. The next eight hours would be time enough to figure out how to outsmart Caleb Graham.

Rory didn't remember giving in to sleep but she woke in a split second when she fell out of the tree. Her first thought was he would laugh since her grand plan to outsmart him was foiled by her own foolishness. Her second thought was she might die at his feet when she stopped falling through the branches. It was an ignominious way to die and she resented herself for letting it happen.

One broken branch speared her side, piercing the skin. She screamed as agony shot through her. By the time she hit the ground, her body ached from slamming into the hard oak. Blood poured from her side and she knew she was in serious trouble.

Caleb jumped to his feet the moment the first tree branch broke. He expected her to jump on him while he slept. What he didn't expect was her to come slamming down out of the tree, screaming like a banshee and bleeding like a stuck pig.

"Son of a bitch!" She rolled to her side. "Goddamn fucking tree!"

Caleb was momentarily nonplussed by the cussing. Then he found his common sense. She had fallen a good twenty feet or more and needed help. He crouched beside her and waited until she stopped to take a breath. She even threw out a few curses he'd never heard.

"What happened?"

"I fell out of the tree, you jackass." She pressed her hand to her side. Fresh blood oozed through her fingers.

"I realize that, Rory. What happened to your side? Was it a weapon?" He didn't want to touch her until she was aware of what was going on. Right now she was still ranting and caught up in the shock of falling.

"Damn branch gouged me. I think I left a few important parts up there too." She finally looked at him, her face a mask of pain. "I'm hurt really bad."

"I can see that. Will you trust me to help you?" He held up his hands. "I promise not to hurt you on purpose."

"This is your chance to bring me in belly down, Ranger." Her voice was rough but her meaning clear.

"I won't bring anyone in like that. You have my word on my mother's grave." His mind flashed to the idyllic spot beneath the big trees in the yard at the Circle Eight, where both his parents rested side by side. She must have seen something in his face because she nodded.

"It hurts. It hurts worse than anything I've ever done, even burning myself on the forge." She loosened her hands and blood flowed steadily from her side.

He got to his knees and took a closer look at the wound. It was a jagged hole at least an inch in diameter with bark and dirt caught in the gore. She had to be in agony.

"I need to rip your shirt to get to it." He needed to warn her.

"Rip it to shreds, just help me."

He tore the shirt open until he could see more clearly. The blood wasn't gushing but it was definitely still coming out in a steady stream. He pulled off his shirt and pressed it to the wound. She groaned and bit her lip.

"We need a doctor. That wound has to be cleaned and stitched. And we need to check for other damage inside." He squeezed her hand. "Is there a doctor in town?"

She shook her head. "No. The only doc within fifty miles lives at the Garza hacienda. It's about ten miles north of here." She winced and sucked in a shaky breath. "You don't have a shirt on." Her gaze traveled his chest and it made him want to go find a new shirt. It was the pain making her act that way, nothing more. There wasn't a possibility there should be anything between them. They were on opposite sides of the law and that was the end of it.

"Do you think you can ride ten miles?" He didn't want to move her, but if he left her here, she might die before he could return. The possibility was real enough to make his blood run cold. Her antics in the smithy and the tree weren't supposed to result in a life-threatening injury. Fate was a fickle bitch.

"I'll do whatever I have to." She waved a bloody hand in the general direction of the smithy. "First make sure the fire is low enough not to flare up and open the windows to air it out."

He frowned at her. "You want me to take care of your business before I save your life?"

"That building is my life." A few drops of blood stood out on her

35

cheek like macabre freckles.

"Fine, but I won't be as careful as you. We're getting on Justice and riding for the Garza place." He put her hand on the shirt. "Hold the pressure here while I do your bidding."

She snorted. "I don't think you've ever done anyone's bidding."

Caleb wasn't about to tell her she was right. Damn woman already knew she was. He hesitated for only a few seconds before he sprinted for the smithy. The fire was still burning but it was low. He doused it with a bucket of water, knowing she would have to clean out most of the ashes to start it up again. That would slow her down for a while.

After he pushed open the windows again, he propped them open with the wooden planks she'd used. Ingenious really. With the hinges on the flap, she could open and close them easily. Even without glass, the windows were efficient. He left the building and ran back to her.

Her eyes were closed and he thought perhaps she'd passed out. However, as soon as he knelt beside her, her eyes flew open. They were glassy with pain and were an even more remarkable shade of amber up close. Flecks of a darker shade swirled in the depths.

"Did you check the fire?"

"Shut up about the fire, Rory. I'm going to pick you up and it's going to hurt like hell." He slid his arms beneath her knees and neck. "Are you ready?"

"No but that doesn't matter. You sure you can pick me up? I ain't a lightweight." She appeared to be serious.

"You are a ridiculous female. Shut up about everything now." He scooped her up fast so she didn't have time to spout anymore nonsense.

She groaned and made a funny little sound like a kitten yawning. He got to his feet with the now unconscious woman in his arms. He had to get her to the Garza hacienda but he had no idea how to get there, only that it was ten miles north.

Shirtless, he walked over to Justice with the unconscious, bleeding woman in his arms. It wasn't the first wound he'd seen but it bothered the hell out of him. Perhaps because she was a woman.

He didn't have time to be soft. The woman truly needed a doctor and he had to move. Justice was well trained, standing by patiently, no matter the coppery smell of blood. Although he didn't want to do it, he had to set her belly down on the horse. He vaulted into the saddle and then picked her up, rolling her over until she lay across his lap.

Her head lolled as he started off. He could only head north and hope to find the hacienda with the doctor. If he didn't, he'd have a dead woman in his arms within twelve hours. The blood hadn't soaked through the shirt but she was pale as hell. That might have been caused by the fall or the loss of blood. He didn't know which and it frustrated the hell out of him.

There was a trail of sorts through the tall grass. It appeared wagons rolled through pretty regular. He followed the well-worn path at a trot. He really wanted to gallop but was afraid the jarring of the horse might cause more damage than the additional time to get where he was going. She was pretty torn up from the branch and more injuries were the last thing she needed.

"You need to wake up Rory. I don't know where the hell I'm going." He jiggled her a little and her hat fell off but she didn't respond. No doubt when she woke up she'd be annoyed he lost the ugly thing. He wasn't about to stop for it.

Without the leather cap, her appearance softened. She looked more like a female, with soft brown hair the color of a fawn's pelt. Too bad it was cut short. Women should have long hair. It looked nicer. He would be sure to keep that opinion to himself or she might throw one of her hammers at him.

"You finished ogling me?" Her words were slurred but she was awake.

"Nope. It's the first time you haven't been talking at me. Good Lord, woman, but you could talk the bark off a tree." He looked down into her eyes. "I hope I'm going the right direction but you passed out before you could give me details on how to find the Garza ranch."

She tried to sit up and gasped. "Shit."

"That's another thing. You sure as hell cuss a lot for a female."

"Oh why don't you shut up, Ranger. Hell, man, I can't imagine the outlaws you chase are on their Sunday best behavior."

She had a point yet he didn't concede it. If she was mad, she wouldn't pass out again.

"I found a trail back yonder, maybe fifty yards from that big tree in your yard. I've been following it and hope like hell it's the right direction." He didn't see anything that told him there was a big hacienda nearby.

"It's the right way. Stay on the trail until you hit the creek, then follow it north about a mile. There's a bridge across that leads into the ranch. There will be men at the bridge with guns. Don't shoot them. Mr. Garza protects his property." Her face relaxed and she snuggled into his chest. "You have nice skin."

"Jesus." He regretted not putting on another shirt. The woman was out of her mind with pain and that made her spout nonsense. "I won't shoot anybody unless they shoot at me."

"That's a good policy." She put one blood-crusted hand on his arm. "Can I call you Caleb? It's such a nice name."

He choked on his own spit. "You are really going to regret everything you just said. Probably want to throw yourself in the forge to purge it from your memory."

She giggled, startling him. "Your lashes are ridiculously long, did you know that? Do you feel a breeze when you blink?"

He shifted her in his arms, wondering if it were possible another woman had taken her place in the tree. Where was the tough Aurora Foster who had kicked his ass a few hours ago? The silly girl who had taken her place put him completely off balance. He knew what to do with a stubborn woman, but a flirty one? He had no clue.

"Don't make me tell you to shut up again. Stop talking now. You need to save your strength."

She stuck out her tongue. He shook his head and kept quiet. The blood loss or the knock on the head from falling out of the tree made her foolish. Either way, she would regret what she said if she remembered it. He regretted it already and it wasn't coming out of his mouth.

The easy assignment to push off a squatter had turned into a strange battle with an unusual woman and now a life-threatening situation. A ranger was prepared for anything, but this went beyond any of that. For God's sake, she was flirting with him. He had no idea how to respond to it. She was the least feminine woman he'd ever met.

Lights flickered in the distance. Even with her ramblings, it appeared he had headed in the right direction. Soon she wouldn't be his problem any longer. He would make sure whoever Garza was, he didn't allow her to return to her property. Somehow he would get word to his commander and they could come in and do what they needed to. Caleb would make sure her things were taken care of, as much as he could. The forge and anvil weren't going anywhere unless they had a team of twenty mules to use.

"What happened?" Her eyes rolled toward him, glassy and unfocused.

"You fell out of the tree." He kneed Justice into a faster pace, eager to get to the doctor and help the woman. She was getting worse by the minute.

"Who are you and why are you naked?"

He sighed. "Ranger Graham and I'm not naked. My shirt is busy stopping the blood from leaking out of your body."

"I'm bleeding?" She tried to move and a groan of pain burst from her mouth. "Oh shit that hurts."

"I'm sure it does. We're almost there, Rory." He had seen the wound and it was likely excruciating for her. She was tough, no matter how crazy she acted.

The armed sentries were waiting by the bridge, just as she predicted. Two large men with rifles lounged against the pillars holding up the fantastically intricate wooden bridge. Who would build such an elaborate looking structure to cross an eight-foot creek?

They straightened and held positions as Caleb and Rory rode up. He touched the brim of his hat.

"Evenin' fellas. Ranger Caleb Graham. I've got Aurora Foster here and she's wounded. She tells me Mr. Garza has a doctor here."

"Aurora? You mean Rory?" The man on the right chuckled, his pockmarked face breaking into a gap-toothed grin. "Her name is Aurora?" That must have been the funniest thing he'd heard in a while, a knee slapper.

"I don't think you understand the situation here. She's bleeding to death and you're laughing." Caleb couldn't keep the annoyance out of his tone and it didn't go unnoticed.

Pockmarked man stopped laughing and straightened up. The man on the left hadn't even blinked when they rode up. He gestured to Rory.

"Did you do this?" Heavily accented English told him the man in the shadows was Mexican. Interesting considering the war had only been over four years.

"She fell out of a tree and a branch did it."

The Mexican nodded. "She tell you Señor Garza has a doctor?"

Apparently Caleb was going to be questioned before entering the sacred ranch property of this Señor Garza. That told him whoever this man was, he had enemies. He obviously had a lot of money to spend, given his outlying property was protected by sentries and a wooden bridge that belonged in a fancy park in a big city.

"Yes, she did. She's also out of her mind from blood loss. I'd rather she live to tell her the story herself." He shifted her weight and she moaned, a tiny hiccupping sound that was pitiful and bothered the hell out of him.

"Where is your shirt?" The Mexican stepped closer to the horse.

"It's pressed up against her side to stop the blood. It was all I had. Now do you have a doctor or not? I'm a Texas Ranger. I mean Mr. Garza no harm." Caleb spoke through clenched teeth but he kept his tone even. No need to spook the hired muscle with the temper that simmered, now beginning to boil.

"*Sí*, we have a doctor. I will walk you to the house." The Mexican turned to his gap-toothed companion. "Stay here."

Finally they were going to cross the damn bridge. It made Caleb think of a child's tale and he wondered if Garza was a monster that lived beneath it. Fanciful foolishness but the entire situation was strange.

The Mexican walked and Caleb had no choice but to follow on Justice at a slow pace. Apparently sentries didn't warrant a horse of their own to ride. It took fifteen minutes to arrive at the intricately crafted wrought iron gate and stone wall that protected the house. It was a goddamn fortress.

Caleb's opinion of Mr. Garza reached a level of full alert. Whoever this man was, he was dangerous and rich. The sentry opened the gates after unlocking the large screw lock. Caleb wondered if Rory had made both the lock and the gates. Either way, the man had protection everywhere. The hairs on the back of Caleb's neck stood up. He was about to ride into the lion's den.

"Go up to the main house. Señor Garza will be there." The sentry stayed at the gate and watched as Justice picked his way across the courtyard. There was a fountain in the middle of it, with water cascading down the sides. That was something nobody in Texas ever wasted—water. They rode toward the largest house Caleb had ever seen.

Two stories high and stretching at least two hundred feet across, the structure was made from stone with enormous wooden doors, wrought iron décor protecting large glass windows. It was a palace, not a house.

He rode Justice up to the largest door, one made of a dark walnut by the looks of it, stretching six feet across and eight feet high. Hell, the damn horse could ride through it. The door opened and a man stepped out wearing an outfit made entirely of white. He glowed in the light from the torches and lanterns around the courtyard.

"*Buenas noches.*" The stranger puffed on a cigar. He sported dark blond hair but his eye color was indecipherable in the semi-darkness. He was shorter than Caleb, with a slender build and delicate features. A very handsome man, almost pretty. His thick mustache highlighted prominent cheekbones and aquiline nose. He didn't appear to be Mexican but that didn't mean a thing. Many hacienda owners married Texans and vice versa. He could be the product of one Mexican parent and one Texan parent.

"Evening. Are you Mr. Garza?" Caleb knew the answer to the question already.

"*Sí*, I am Pablo Garza." The man puffed on the cigar, the orange tip glowing in a brief circle on his face. "Who are you and why are you on my land?"

"Ranger Caleb Graham. I'm here to ask for help for Auro—Rory Foster. She was injured falling out of a tree and she says you have a doctor here." He waited while the other man processed the information.

"Did she finish the tools she was making? I need them in a few days to start my next project."

Caleb had no interest in finding out what his next project was. "I didn't think to take any tools with me. She was bleeding and I thought her life more important than her business."

"Ah, that's why you are a ranger and I am a *patron*." He flicked his right hand and two burly men stepped through the door. "Take Señora Foster and put her in the blue room. I will take Ranger Graham to the doctor's quarters."

The men approached Justice and Caleb reluctantly handed over his bundle to them. She made another pitiful sound that cut right through him.

"Careful. A branch went through her side and she's already lost too much blood." He could hardly believe his reaction to her injury. No explanation came to mind. He had only known her less than a day. Why would he care? He sure as hell shouldn't.

Caleb dismounted and secured his horse to the hitching rail in front of the house. It even had an iron ring to use, no doubt made by the lady blacksmith whose sticky blood coated his chest and hands.

"You perhaps have a shirt to wear, Mr. Graham?" Garza gestured to Caleb's undressed state.

"In my saddlebags, yes. I need to wash up first so I don't ruin that shirt too." He put his hands on his hips, wondering what this dapper blond Mexican man was up to in his fortress. The lawman inside him sniffed the air, sensing all was not as it seemed.

"Of course. I shall take you inside. Please follow me." Garza turned toward the massive door.

Caleb grabbed his other shirt from the saddlebags and followed Pablo Garza into the depths of the enormous house.

Rory floated in and out of consciousness. Each time she kicked her way up from the depths of the sea of darkness she swam in, excruciating pain sent her back down. She looked for anything to anchor herself to but found nothing except air. Her side burned and her stomach roiled. She didn't know where she was or what happened. She cried out for help, the smells and sights unfamiliar and frightening.

A warm hand covered hers and another touched her forehead. "Who are you fighting now, Rory? Let the man help you."

The man was familiar but she didn't know who it was. He spoke to her as though her knew her and the rumble of his deep voice calmed her. She squeezed his hand and he chuckled.

"This woman will never cease to shock me."

Rory kept her eyes closed but tears leaked from them anyway. She was embarrassed to know she wept. Even if she was in pain, she never cried.

"Let me take a look at the wound." Another man spoke softly near her ear. "From the looks of her, she's lost a great deal of blood."

"I kept pressure on it and used my shirt to plug it." The first man tried to take his hands away but she held on tight. Whoever he was, she needed him. "She ain't letting go. Can you do it yourself?"

"Hold onto her. This is going to hurt."

Rory wanted to tell them to stop and leave her alone but her mouth wouldn't work. A groan sounded in her throat and he tightened his grip.

"Hang on, Rory. I'm here."

A ripping sound and then it felt as though someone was peeling her skin off. She groaned louder and more tears fell. Cool air bathed her heated skin. Fingers probed her belly and pain shot through her.

"Easy, now miss, I am trying to help you." The soft-spoken man sounded calm. Of course he was, it wasn't his belly that burned like it was on fire. "I need to clean this, but I think it would be better if we gave her something before I did that."

"You mean laudanum? Are you sure that's necessary? She might not want it. I know I don't cotton to it." She didn't like it. The first man was smart.

"As a physician, I recommend using it."

"And as her friend, I ain't gonna let you."

Rory had a friend? A friend who spoke for her and protected her and held her hands. She didn't know who he was but she would accept him as her friend. She turned her face toward him and tried to say without words that she was grateful.

"You'll have to hold her down then." The doctor sounded doubtful.

"I can do that. Let's get a move on, doc. That blood ain't gonna stop itself." Her new friend leaned down and spoke in her ear. "This is going to hurt like a bitch, Rory. You're gonna try to buck me off but I'm hanging on tight."

Fear flitted through her but she was in a hazy world of pain and confusion. Her friend pushed down on her shoulders and she whimpered. Then the true agony began.

Cool liquid that should have felt good burned like it was acid eating through her skin. She screamed and tried her damndest to move away from them, but they continued the torture. The doctor poked her with a stick or other sharp instrument, then wiped at the raw flesh.

Tears flowed freely down her cheeks as she sobbed for mercy. She hadn't experienced such helplessness, such deep terror, for a very long time. Not since she'd been a child and had fallen down a well, breaking her arm. This was worse, much worse. Now two men held her down while they tortured her.

If she'd had a gun, she would have shot them dead and enjoyed watching them bleed.

"You've got to settle down, honey. He's almost done." Her supposed friend spoke to her again.

"Fuck you. Fuck both of you. Let me go before I kill you." She tried to summon the strength to break his grip but he was too strong and she was too weak.

"She knows how to curse." The doctor didn't sound amused, at least that was something. "I am almost finished, miss. I am sorry this is hurting you."

"Hurting me? You're sawing me in half, you rat-faced son of a bitch!" She managed to lift her right leg and connect with something.

"Kicking me is not going to make this quicker. If I am unable to function, you will surely die from this wound." The doctor was well-spoken but he was also someone who liked to inflict pain.

"I don't care. Stop it!" She screamed until her throat was raw.

"I'm going to use alcohol to finish. This will hurt worse, young lady." The doctor spoke as if he'd just told her she needed to do her laundry on Mondays.

"Don't you fucking touch me," she hissed through clenched teeth. "Don't you dare."

"Hold onto her tight."

"I'm sorry, honey," her friend whispered in her ear.

The gurgle of the liquid as it left the bottle echoed in her ears, then the excruciating agony hit her and she was certain he was sawing her in half. She screamed with every fiber of her being, certain she was being flayed alive. It went on and on, until she thought she would die from the pain.

Blessed darkness swallowed her and she gratefully sank into its depths.

Caleb had to wipe his own brow before he wiped hers. Holy hell. The woman had a set of lungs that would rival any banshee. She fought like a wildcat too. He could barely hold her down. The doctor at least looked like he knew what he was doing and cleaned the wound thoroughly.

Now she was unconscious, thank God. She'd almost made his ears bleed with her wailing. He'd never heard such a noise coming from a human before. Aurora Foster never did anything like a regular woman. She wasn't wounded like one either.

The doctor was stitching her up with care, tiny stitches from the inside out. The blood had slowed to a trickle, which meant the doc did something right. He was pleased to see the care the old man took with a stranger. In his line of work, he didn't see a lot of human kindness. The doc obviously lived at the Garza hacienda. While a big ranch had consistent flow of minor injuries, and occasionally wounds like Rory's, why would Garza need a full-time doctor?

The entire place spoke of secrets. Caleb had to listen close enough to hear the whispers. With Rory screaming it might be hard to catch it all but he was listening real close. A shadow moved near the door. Caleb glanced up to see a skinny boy scooting away down the hall. Probably a curious ranch hand's child wanting to get an eyeful of blood. The ranch had an air of something dark, nearly sinister. Caleb's instincts were screaming like a battle-seasoned warrior.

"You work here long, Doc?" Caleb dipped a cloth in the basin of water and squeezed out the water. He wanted to wash the blood from Rory's skin.

"Oh, a few years. I had a practice in town but my hands got to painful to catch babies anymore." He had little hair on the top of his head, but white tufts grew from the sides, his ears and his eyebrows. No taller than Caleb's shoulder, he stooped over as he worked, his back in a permanent curve.

"Mr. Garza needed a full-time doc?" Caleb rinsed the rag, leaving a pink residue behind.

"No, but he was kind enough to give me a place to live and I patch up the occasional injury. Your lady's wound is the most exciting thing I've seen in a spell. Things are pretty ordinary around these parts." The doctor didn't meet Caleb's gaze when he spoke, as though he was practicing lines he had memorized. Caleb didn't believe the old man for a minute. He knew a lie when he heard one, but the question was, why did this skilled doctor feel the need to prevaricate?

"That was mighty kind of him." Caleb kept his tone noncommittal. "I know Mrs. Foster appreciates your help even if she didn't appear to."

"I'm sure she was out of her head with pain. That's common when folks get wounded. I won't pay it any nevermind." The doctor threaded himself a fresh string of catgut and continued to stitch up the hole in Rory's side. His hands were steady as a rock. There was not even a hint of shakiness. Whatever the doc's reasons were for working for, and living with, Pablo Garza, they had nothing to do with his incompetency in medicine.

"Much obliged. I do have some money I can pay you with."

Caleb had little but considering the amount of time and effort expended by the doctor, he deserved compensation.

As expected, the doctor waved his hand in dismissal. "No need. I have everything I need. Mr. Garza is a generous man."

Generous to those who were loyal to him and ruthless to those that weren't, that was probably the truth. There were far too many strange goings on within the first hour of being on the Garza ranch. Caleb wondered if the doctor might slip up and give away some details that could prove useful.

"Then you're a lucky man." Caleb wiped the bits of blood from Rory's hands. She had strong fingers that were callused but long and tapered, still feminine. That surprised him considering what she did every day. Her fingernails were caked with dirt, but he took the time to clean them, and he didn't know why.

The doctor finished stitching her up and then peered at his own handiwork. "She is very strong. She has a good chance of recovering if a fever doesn't catch hold."

Caleb rinsed the cloth in the basin, leaving behind a pinkish tinge. "When would a fever hit?"

"Within the first day I should think. Possibly two. She shouldn't be moved for at least a week." The doctor gestured to a fresh pile of bandages. "After she is clean, you can wrap her, but not too tightly. If she starts to bleed again, send someone to fetch me."

The doctor got to his feet with a groan. "I'm afraid I need to rest now. I'm not as young as I used to be."

Caleb watched the old man shuffle out, looking like someone's grandfather. He would reserve judgment on just how benevolent the doctor was.

"Now it's you and me, Rory." He should feel uncomfortable with a half-naked, bloody stranger. Her face was relaxed, making her look very young and accentuating the softness of her skin. Her cheekbones were high, framing a heart-shaped face he hadn't seen beneath the leather cap. Her hair wasn't merely brown. In the light from the lantern, bursts of red and gold shone in the strands.

Caleb shook his head to dispel the image. He had no call to be thinking of Rory Foster as a woman. She was a blacksmith and a squatter. It wasn't his fault she was injured. The confounded woman had climbed the tree and fallen out on her own. He wasn't going to feel guilty.

Except he was.

He had to take off what was left of her shirt. The damn doctor had cut it open to patch her up then left it hanging on her like a rag. Caleb would have to see what lay beneath the tattered garment. He reached for the buttons, refusing to accept his hands shook. It was a trick of the light, nothing more.

The buttons were smaller than those on a man's shirt and he fumbled to push them through the holes. He finally got them undone and opened her shirt.

"Holy shit."

She had bindings around her breasts, well-used ones by the look of them. He untied the knot beneath her arm and tried to unwind them. Unsuccessfully. With her lying on bed, there was little chance he would move her to a sitting position to get them off, not to mention the possibility he would tear her stitches.

There was no help for it. He would have to cut the bindings. No doubt Rory would rip a hole in the ceiling when she found out. She must have used them for years and it didn't appear as though she had money to buy much. Her clothes were threadbare and her house meager. The woman was barely getting by, probably enough to keep herself fed and nothing more.

He would make sure she got new shirt and bindings. Her trousers, another curious thing about the woman, were stained with blood but with some effort they might come clean.

Caleb was stalling. Once he cut the bindings, there would be nothing between Rory and him but air.

He pulled the knife from the scabbard in his boot and carefully sliced through the fabric. The old bindings nearly fell apart in his hands and soon they revealed the smoothest, creamiest skin he'd ever seen. Her breasts were marked from the tight bindings but they spilled out as though they had been gasping to be released.

Her nipples were the color of a blush pink rose, a sweetly feminine thing he didn't expect from a woman he hadn't thought of as female. Oh, she sure as hell was as womanly as he had ever seen. Not many had breasts the size of Rory's. She might have kept the bindings on to work without injuring herself.

Regardless, he found himself staring at a half-naked, unconscious woman who was still sticky with her own blood. His brother Matt would kick his ass if he'd caught him.

"Sorry, Rory." She couldn't hear him but he still apologized. It was rude and uncalled for to take advantage of her.

Caleb cut the rest of her shirt off and slid the pieces out from under her. Then he put the blanket over her upper half to give her some modesty. If she woke up right about then, he might lose a tooth from her right hook.

He cleaned the blood from her stomach, sides and her lower belly. For that he had to unbutton her trousers, amused by the men's drawers she wore. She was the only woman he ever met that tried her best to look like a man.

The shadow of her pussy hair came into view and he jerked, jarring her. She moaned and he stopped, frozen in place with guilt. She didn't wake up, which was lucky for him. He let out the breath he didn't know he'd been holding, then finished cleaning her as quick as he could.

The bandages were easy compared to the rest of the clothing foolishness he had waded through to get her cleaned up. Her wound looked clean, with barely any blood leaking from the tight stitches. He secured the bandage and then sat back, sweating as if he'd run around the Garza house a few dozen times.

Rory Foster had turned his life sideways in the single day he'd known her. She would be dangerous to be around for a long time, not that he had any plans to.

He glanced around the small room they were in and there was little to see. A small washstand sat against one wall, a pitcher sitting on top that he had used to fill the basin with clean water. There were a few nails in the wall but nothing hung from them. If he could find that boy he'd seen earlier, he might be able to ask him if there were any female clothing to be had. Yet the hallway was as empty as the room.

Without any other options, he would have to use his clean shirt. It's what he would do for his sisters, that was the only reason. Rory meant nothing to him, no matter how intense their time together had been.

He took off his shirt and managed to get her arms in the sleeves and button it up. Although Caleb was a big man, the buttons strained against the large breasts that were now unfettered. He licked his lips as he looked down at her, his masculine senses pulsing with awareness. If he were honest with himself, her breasts were lovely, the most beautiful he'd ever seen. They had also been inches from his face.

48

Damned if his dick wasn't joining in the fun by twitching along.

He refastened her trousers, then arranged the blanket over her. Sweat rolled down his bare back and he decided he needed to wash himself up now. He threw the pink water out the window into the darkness of the night, then rinsed it with a bit more before he was satisfied. After he poured fresh water into the basin, he used a clean rag to wipe himself down.

Although the water was tepid, it felt good. His stomach was tied into knots over the last twelve hours. What he really needed was a whiskey, a bottle maybe. He also hadn't eaten in hours, which had to be the reason he was shaking.

A breeze blew through the open window and his skin pebbled. He closed his eyes and let his body cool down. Whatever happened, he had to leave the Garza ranch as soon as possible. Staying with Rory might have been more dangerous than digging for information on the patron.

"What am I going to do with you, lady blacksmith?"

"Do with me?" Her voice was husky and startling. "What have you already done to me, you son of a bitch?"

EMMA LANG

CHAPTER FOUR

Rory's gut burned as though she had caught on fire again. It took her a few minutes to focus and realize where she was and what happened. The ranger had been washing up, the lines of his half-naked body were beautiful—honey-colored skin stretched over muscle, bone and sinew. Mother Nature had created a gorgeous creature, one who had brought darkness to her corner of the world. If he hadn't come to her property, she wouldn't be lying there in agony, nor would she be wearing someone else's clothing.

It took her a full minute to realize not only was she wearing a different shirt, but her bindings were gone. Gone! What the hell had the ranger done to her? She tried to move but the pain stole her breath and she closed her eyes again until the wave passed.

"What am I going to do with you, lady blacksmith?"

"Do with me?" Her anger with the man was alive and well. "What have you already done to me, you son of a bitch?"

He whirled around, his eyes wide. "You're awake."

"You're observant." She narrowed her gaze. "What have you done with my clothes, all of them?"

He had the grace to look embarrassed and his gaze flitted to the floor. "The doctor and I had to cut everything off you. The blood had soaked through most everything. I, uh, we left your trousers on but they're in need of a lot of soap and water."

"You stared at me naked?" She wasn't about to let him off easy. No sir. He was the cause of her pain and he was going to pay for it.

"I didn't stare. I helped the doctor and cleaned the blood off you." His jaw tightened and she knew he wasn't being entirely truthful.

"Whose shirt is this, Ranger?" She knew the answer but she asked anyway.

"Mine. I couldn't leave you, ah, without something to wear." He pointed to a bloody ball of fabric on the floor. "I need to rinse out my other shirt."

She remembered how he had used it to staunch the blood from her wound. He had sacrificed both shirts for her. Rory didn't want to feel grateful to him. After all, he had destroyed her clothes. Plus he had seen her naked, which bothered her more than the clothes. Her breasts were the bane of her existence, always in the way and bothersome. Men constantly stared at them when she was a teenager, never taking her seriously as a blacksmith. She bound them, cut her hair and wore trousers. From then on, they considered her neutral and her business picked up.

Now Caleb had seen her secret, viewed her at the most vulnerable moment possible. She was sick to know she was unconscious the entire time too. If she had a gun, she might have shot him for it. All of that discomfort was on top of the burning pain in her side and stomach. If she didn't know what misery meant before today, she knew it now.

"The doctor wanted to give you laudanum but I told him no." Caleb met her gaze from across the small room. "I thought it should be your choice."

Rory stared at him, surprised by his considerate gesture. "I had laudanum once when I broke my arm. It made me puke for days."

A silence settled, the sounds of the ranch disappeared. With each moment that passed, the air grew awkward and uncomfortable.

"I treated you like you were one of my sisters and only did what I had to do." He looked down at his feet. "The doctor was gone by the time I cleaned you up and put the shirt on."

She didn't know whether to be horrified she was alone and naked with him or glad it had only been him. "I kind of remember the doctor. He had white hair."

"Yup, he knew what he was doing to. With seven, er, six brothers and sisters, our housekeeper Eva has a hand at doctoring us up. She had to, considering the amount of cuts, bruises, broken bones and gashes we all had." It was the most words he'd spoken to her. She wondered if he was nervous. How curious that would be.

"Seven or six?" She frowned at him. "Don't tell me you don't remember how many, or are you lying about your family?"

His expression changed in an instant. His jaw tightened and his eyes hardened. "I suppose I had that coming. There are eight of us, but my youngest brother was kidnapped five years ago, the same day my parents were murdered."

Rory forgot about her own problems in the face of his bald statement. What must it have been like to not only lose your parents, violently, but to lose a brother? She didn't think it possible to empathize with the ranger, but she'd been wrong. Losing her parents had been agony, but they had died in a house fire, a senseless accident. Caleb had lost his to someone else's evil deeds.

"I'm sorry." The apology was softly spoken but she meant it. Hopefully he could see that.

"Nothing for you to be sorry about but I appreciate the sentiment." He looked away, his throat moving as he swallowed. "Are you hungry? I haven't eaten since breakfast. My belly is rubbing on my backbone."

The abrupt change in subject was understandable. No doubt the topic of his family tragedy made him uncomfortable. She would have trouble talking about her parents' deaths too.

"I don't know if I'm hungry but I'm definitely thirsty." Her mouth tasted like dirty water, something she wasn't going to share with him though.

"I am going to see if I can rustle up some food and drink." He pointed at the basin. "There is a bit of water in the pitcher but there isn't a cup to use."

She shrugged. "I can drink from the pitcher for now. If you find the kitchen, Bernadette is the cook. She usually has goat milk, which I would want. It's Friday so it's tortilla day too."

He started. "Tortilla day?"

"She makes tortillas once a week. I try to make all my deliveries on Friday because she makes the best tortillas in Texas." Sleep tugged at Rory and her eyelids weighed at least five pounds apiece.

"Best tortillas in Texas." Caleb repeated what Rory said, his brow furrowed. He stared off into space, and she wondered where he'd gone.

"Ranger?"

He cleared his throat and brought the pitcher. "I'm going to go find a place to rinse out my shirt and then find the kitchen."

53

Up close, he took her breath. She watched his muscles ripple as he lifted the pitcher to her mouth and held her neck so she could drink. The water leaked out from the sides of her mouth but she barely noticed. Caleb Graham was stunning. She hadn't been in such close proximity to a man since Horatio died, much less a half-naked man.

"Rory?" He frowned. "You still there?"

She yawned to cover up the foolish reaction to his good looks. "I'm tuckered out. I think I need to sleep."

"Probably the best thing. How's the pain?"

The pain? She had forgotten all about it for that brief snatch of time he was within inches of her. The ranger was a human pain cure.

"Bearable." She shrank back into the pillow, needing to breath, to get a little distance between them.

"I'll be back as soon as I can." He got to his feet, his expression concerned. She didn't want to think the ranger was concerned about her. He was the enemy, the man who came to throw her out of her house, out of her business. It didn't matter if he'd saved her life. He was not her friend nor was she ready to throw her anger with him away simply because he was godlike beautiful.

No, sir, Rory was not done fighting Caleb Graham.

Caleb closed the door behind him and let out a breath he didn't know he'd been holding. Rory had looked at him as though he'd been a meal and she was starving. It made his body tighten and his gut flip flop. For a second or two, he thought about kissing her, licking the water from her chin.

Absolute lunacy.

He walked down the dimly lit hallway into a large open area that held a huge table with at least a dozen chairs. Garza never did anything small scale. Caleb wound his way around the table and into the next hallway. There were glass chandeliers with golden glass hanging and the ceiling had to be twenty feet high. This house was truly more of a palace than he first suspected.

The hallway led to the kitchen. It was another enormous room with not one but two stoves on one side, plus what appeared to be a bread oven beside them. An island with a stone top, bigger than the dining room table, dominated the center of the room, holding a flickering lantern. Two wooden sinks were separated by a large counter of six-inch-thick wood. A pump handle sat on the right-hand sink, which meant no water hauling was required.

A doorway on the left opened up to a pantry the size of the bedroom Rory currently slept in. From what he could see, shelves of staples, along with barrels of others, filled the pantry. Ham hocks, bacon and other meats hung from hooks in the ceiling.

This was a kitchen large enough, and stocked enough, to feed an army. A big army. This was ten times as much food as the Grahams ever hand on hand for a ranch of twelve people. How many men did Garza have on his payroll? Caleb had suspected the man was up to something and this kitchen proved he was on the right track.

He went to the sink with the pump handle and proceeded to rinse out his shirt. At this time of night, there was no one there to help him, or yell at him, for using it. It took a good ten minutes to get the worst of the blood off. It would be stained for sure but he might be able to wear it in the morning if it dried overnight.

Caleb squeezed out the excess water then shook the shirt. It looked horrible but it would have to do. He laid it on the side of the sink and then went in search of food. The pantry was certainly the place to find vittles.

He found a container with the famous tortillas and took a stack, then pulled a can of peaches and a can of beans. That should be enough. He wrapped the tortillas in a cloth and tucked them in his pocket, then put the cans in his other pocket.

As he was about to grab his shirt to leave the kitchen, he remembered Rory's request for goat's milk. There had to be some sort of cooling system in the kitchen, given the amount of money spent on the house, he had no doubt Garza kept his dairy cool to last longer.

Caleb turned around and noted a small door in the corner beside the bread oven. He walked over and unlatched the small handle and pulled it open. Cheese and buckets of milk with cheese cloth over the top filled the small steel-lined cabinet. Cool air washed over him and he wondered how they kept it cold. He took a bucket, found a glass on the shelves above the sink and poured a nice full drink. As he put the bucket back in its place, curiosity got the best of him and he squatted down to peer inside. Huge chunks of ice lay beneath burlap sacks, wisps rising from them. There had to be two dozen chunks of ice. Big ones. There didn't appear to be anything Garza did in small measure.

Awareness prickled the back of his neck. He was no longer alone in the kitchen. His hand crept to the butt of his gun and he slowly got to his feet, as though he had all the time in the world and no worries. He latched the cabinet and turned to pick up the glass of milk.

He whirled and squatted, gun pointed at the sneaky person who had crept up on him. The boy with brown hair he'd seen from the back earlier squeaked and threw his hands over his face. Caleb was a fool but at least his senses were working properly. The child couldn't have been more than ten, gangly, at the stage before puberty hit and started to fill in the skinny parts.

"Sorry, I didn't mean to scare you. You shouldn't creep up on folks like that." He holstered his gun and picked up the glass. His heart still pounded but he breathed in deep, willing himself to come out of battle mode. The boy meant no harm, probably just curious who was in the kitchen. "What's your name?"

The boy slowly lowered his arms, peering at Caleb over a pointy elbow.

"I'm a Texas Ranger, name's Caleb Graham." He watched the boy's eyes widen and awareness slid over him. There was a familiarity about the color of his eyes. Caleb's heart thumped harder, pushing blood past his ears. The world tilted beneath him and recognition made time stand still.

It couldn't be. *It fucking couldn't be.*

"Benjy?"

The boy's arms fell down to his sides and his face turned paler than the milk. There was no mistaking it now. Caleb had found his lost brother, Benjamin Graham.

The trained Texas Ranger, who had killed men, showed no fear in the face of imminent danger, dropped to his knees with a sob and pulled the boy into his arms. He hugged him hard however the boy was stiffer than a board, unmoving. Caleb pulled back and stared into eyes so much like his mother's it spooked him.

"Benjy, do you remember me?"

The boy's eyes couldn't get any wider or they would pop out of his head. He nodded his head slightly.

Caleb smiled, his eyes stinging. "We've been looking for you for almost five years, Benjy. We never gave up though." Although he pushed it out of his mind, Caleb had nearly given up. Finding his youngest brother was a shock of biblical proportions. He would never give up again.

He took a look at Benjy, noting the hair neatly trimmed, the high quality clothes and leather shoes. Someone was taking good care of him and Caleb suspected it was Pablo Garza. Perhaps the *patron* was the rich landowner who had purchased Benjy in Mexico from the caudillo he and his brothers had killed.

"Do you live here?"

Another nod.

"Can you speak?"

This time a shake of his head.

There were a thousand questions Caleb wanted to ask him but if the boy couldn't answer them, now wasn't the time to ask. He had to plan how they would leave the Garza hacienda with no one noticing a boy by his side. Then there was Rory. He couldn't leave her there alone and unprotected in a house full of danger and deceit. Now that Caleb knew exactly what kind of man Pablo Garza was—one who would buy a child from a whorehouse.

"We need to get out of here. Come with me—"

"Marcello? Are you in here?" A tiny redheaded woman walked into the kitchen. She wore a voluminous nightdress so he couldn't tell much about her shape. Her kinky curls were poking out of a nightcap. Her eyes widened when she saw Caleb, still shirtless of course. She looked at Benjy. "What are you doing in here, Marcello? You know Papa doesn't like you to wander alone."

Marcello? The bastard had made Benjy change his name too? Caleb swallowed back the angry words that crowded his throat. He would not be so polite the next time he met up with Garza.

"I needed some help, ma'am, and the boy offered to assist. I'm Ranger Caleb Graham." He gestured to the glass of milk. "I was getting something for Rory Foster. She was injured and the doc patched her up. Are you Bernadette?"

The woman's expression lost its panic. "Yes, I'm Bernadette. Rory's here? I didn't hear about that. The poor dear. Let me make you up a tray for her." Her gaze flickered to the shirt still hanging on the sink.

"I had to use my shirt for the blood. Much obliged you had a sink for me to rinse it in." Caleb tried to keep a polite face but inside he was shouting with fury. He grabbed his shirt and looked as unthreatening as he could.

"I like a man who can take care of his own laundry." Bernadette stepped further into the kitchen and Caleb saw she was probably in her forties and had a lot of living on her face. Perhaps Garza had a hold of her life too. She busied herself around the kitchen, gathering a tray, a plate, then slicing ham and bread. The tortillas were added and some kind of pepper with a can of beans.

Although wound up tight, Caleb's stomach picked that moment to yowl loudly. Bernadette frowned at him and added more ham and bread to the plate. She put the glass of milk on it along with the tortillas, wrapped up with the beans and peppers, and two cups of coffee. It was enough food for three people. He intended to wrap all the food and take it when they left. Sure as the sun would rise, Caleb was leaving the Garza ranch with Benjy and Rory. He would not leave anyone behind.

"Let's bring this to Rory. Where is she?" Bernadette tried to lift the tray but Caleb stopped her with one of his best smiles. She didn't have to know it wasn't genuine. It had the desired effect and she tittered as she stepped away. "A gentleman, I see."

They started to walk out of the kitchen when she turned to Benjy who hadn't moved the entire time. "Go back to bed, Marcello. You dare not let Papa catch you."

Caleb wanted to scream at the woman but she wasn't to blame. The idea that Garza was pretending to be Benjy's father made his blood boil.

"Rory wanted to see him to say hello," Caleb lied through his teeth. "I'm sure it won't hurt to give her a few minutes to visit. It might help her heal faster."

Bernadette looked at Benjy dubiously. "I suppose that's true. A visit always helps along folks who are laid low. All right, I'll let you come along but don't tell your Papa. He would be unhappy with me."

The unlikely trio made their way back through the house, down the hallways and through the dining room until they reached the small room Rory lay in. Caleb gestured to the door and Bernadette couldn't disguise the surprise on her face. Wherever Garza stuck them, it wasn't normal. That put Caleb's instincts into screaming mode. Was he hiding them or keeping them in a location where no one could find them?

Caleb waited for Bernadette to open the door, his fear for Rory as real as the tray in his hands. He'd been away for fifteen minutes. Anything could have happened to her. Although she might not agree with it, he was responsible for Rory.

58

He was able to take a breath as soon as he spotted her in the bed, watching them. She smiled when she saw Bernadette, which widened when she saw Benjy.

"Marcello and Bernadette! It's nice to see friendly faces."

It didn't miss Caleb's attention that she knew his brother as Marcello. The boy had obviously been there at the Garza ranch for some time. Possibly five years. Caleb carried the tray to the bed before he did something stupid like throw it. Anger warred with the urge to run like hell with Rory under one arm and Benjy under the other.

Rory reached for the glass of milk then winced and her arm dropped. Caleb picked up the glass and held her neck while she sipped, then gulped the creamy liquid. Her throat worked as she swallowed and he had the stupidity to notice that her neck was graceful. He then compounded it by wiping her chin with his fingers when he pulled the glass away.

Her gaze dropped to his chest then back to his face. He saw a flash of heat in the depths of her amber eyes, and then it was gone. Something was brewing between them and he was helpless to stop it.

"You should eat something, Rory." Bernadette gestured to the heaping tray of food. "Today was tortilla day."

"I know." Rory smiled wanly. "I wish I had the appetite to eat them."

"You should rest and let yourself heal." Bernadette patted her hand. "You'll be hungry when you wake. Now it's time for Marcello to go to bed before he gets in trouble."

Caleb's gut clenched at the possibility of losing sight of Benjy. "I could use his help for a few minutes."

Bernadette turned to him in surprise. "What could he help with?"

"I need to wash up and I thought he could keep Rory company for a few minutes." He hoped he looked honest as lies tumbled from his mouth.

"Of course he can. Can I help?" Bernadette looked at Rory.

"No, you've already done enough. I know it's late for you and you have to be up before the sun." Rory yawned. "Marcello will probably just watch me sleep for ten minutes." She managed a chuckle.

Caleb wanted to kiss her.

"You are right. I went into the kitchen when I heard your ranger in there." Bernadette frowned at her charge. "Ten minutes and no more."

The boy nodded and stood stoically while the housekeeper ruffled his hair—the hair that matched Caleb's. Funny how neither of the women noticed.

Bernadette said her good-byes and left the room. Caleb waited until he couldn't hear her footsteps any longer, then waited another thirty seconds before he spoke. He kept his voice low.

"Rory, do you know this boy?"

She frowned. "Of course. It's Marcello Garza, Pablo's son."

Caleb expected it but the bald statement hit him like a slap to the face. "His name is Benjamin Graham." He bit off the words like whispered cannon balls.

"Pardon?" She glanced at Benjy then back at Caleb, then repeated it. Her eyes widened. "This is your missing brother?"

"Yes. It was providence we came here for help. I would have never found him otherwise. Garza has this place locked up like a fortress." He blew out a frustrated breath. "I about shit my drawers when I saw him."

Benjy sat down on the opposite side of the bed, still silent and watchful.

"I can't believe it but it's right there. I can see the resemblance." She shook her head. "I knew folks with money were different but stealing someone else's child? That's not right."

"No, it's not right. Even if Garza wasn't the one who took him, he kept him from his family for almost five years." Caleb had to tamp down his temper as his voice lowered back into a growl.

Rory turned to Benjy. "Do you remember your family?"

Benjy nodded and looked at Caleb, his expression much older than an ten-year-old's.

"He's never spoken as far as I know. I thought he'd been someplace to help him before he came here." She shook her head. "I'm sorry, Benjamin. I could have helped."

The boy shrugged as though it meant nothing, but it meant quite a lot. This woman, who was ready to lay down her life for a forge and a patch of land, was genuinely sorry for not seeing that a mute boy didn't belong at a neighbor's ranch. For all intents and purposes, she could not possibly have known, especially considering Benjy didn't speak.

"You can help now." Caleb waited until they both looked at him.

"We're leaving here tonight. All of us."

Rory's brows rose. "Tonight?"

"I can't leave him here a minute longer and I sure as hell won't leave you here to face Garza's wrath when he discovers what I've done."

"Have you asked your brother what he wants?" She gestured to the boy. "He's old enough to make that choice."

"No, I haven't. It doesn't matter what he wants. He's coming home with me." Caleb sounded foolish to his own ears. "That's not true and I'm an ass for even saying it." He closed his eyes for a moment before he looked at his little brother, really looked.

Benjamin's gaze was solemn, wise as though he had lost his childhood years ago when he was kidnapped. However, behind the serious expression, Caleb saw a glimpse of something, a spark buried deep.

"Do you want to leave with us and go back to the Circle Eight? The circle isn't whole without you there, Benjy." Caleb's voice wavered a little as emotion swept through him. He hoped the boy wasn't going to refuse or the ranger would be guilty of kidnapping.

Benjy stared at him, then cocked his head before he turned to look at Rory. She took his hand, her face taut with pain and stress. Caleb was sorry she'd been injured but if she hadn't, he wouldn't have found his brother. Life was scraping the bottom of the barrel right now but he would be forever grateful to have meet Rory Foster.

"Benjy?" Caleb took his brother's hand, which he didn't pull away, thank God. "Catherine kicked my ass in a horse race last week. She's gone wild without you there to keep her in line."

Mention of their sister made that spark in Benjy's eyes grow brighter.

"Will you come home with me?" Caleb's rough whisper was full of hope and raw emotions.

Benjy nodded and Caleb had to swallow the tears that threatened. He had found the missing link in the family's circle. Now all he had to do was find a way to get him home.

The ranger seemed to have a fire under his ass. He packed up all the food and used a sheet to wrap it up. Then he put on his wet shirt and started peering out the door and windows, mumbling to himself.

Rory wanted to sleep, but she understood the urgency of leaving the hacienda as soon as possible. To know what Garza had done made her sick to her stomach. Marcello wasn't his son. He was another man's son, a brother, a kidnapped child. For all the times she'd seen the quiet boy, it never occurred to her he was anything but Pablo's family.

It hurt her heart to think of all the boy could have gone through. She didn't know the details, didn't want to know them to be truthful. But she knew enough. If she didn't have a wound in her side, she would find her rifle and shoot Garza, or possibly kick him in the balls if she couldn't find a weapon.

Benjamin sat next to her, watching his big brother with wide eyes. He hadn't spoken a word, and as far as she knew, never did. Not that she blamed him. If she had endured what the boy had, she might not want to speak to anyone either.

Caleb came back into the room and shut the door. His face was tight with worry. "I can't find a single point of exit that we won't be seen. Dammit."

"What does that mean?" Rory swallowed a yawn.

"It means we can't leave together. Someone will spot us. Garza has guards all over the damn place. Even some out in the dark." Caleb cursed under his breath.

"How do you know they're out there if it's dark?" Rory knew her neighbor was careful but the guards went beyond standard safety. He was hiding something. Perhaps Benjamin.

"Because at least three of them like to smoke. The tips glow orange in the blackness." Caleb tucked his shirt into his pants, even though it was still quite damp.

"Then what do we do?" Rory wanted to leave as much as he did, even if she was weak and healing. That particular fact annoyed her.

"I don't know. Yet." Caleb sat on the floor with his back to the door, looking as though he was ready for a fight. Fists clenched, jaw tight and brows lowered.

Benjamin got to his feet and walked over to the ranger. The boy sat beside his brother, mimicking his pose. Rory hid a smile behind her hand. It was the first time she'd seen Benjamin make an effort to be close to anyone.

Watching him gave her an idea. "Benjamin, do you know of a secret way to leave the house? I'm guessing you have explored every nook and cranny in this house."

The boy looked startled and then his gaze swung to Caleb's. His big brother eyed him with a frown.

"Do you know of a secret way out?"

To her delight, Benjamin nodded.

"Can we all fit?"

The boy nodded again.

"Is it close?"

This time he shook his head.

"Can you show us?" Caleb's tone had dropped low as he leaned toward the smaller Graham. "We need you, Benjy."

Benjy.

The name fit him more than the more formal Benjamin. She waited while he seemed to consider Caleb's question. The boy looked up and met Rory's gaze. His greenish blue eyes so much like Caleb's were full of sorrow and a little bit of hope. She gave him a slight nod.

Benjy got to his feet and held out his hand. Caleb smiled and it lit up his entire face. Rory couldn't believe the change in the hard ranger. He was incredibly handsome without the addition of a geniune smile. With it, he was devastating. Her stomach did a funny flip and her lower belly throbbed. She had shared the marriage bed with Horatio and found pleasure, however, she had a feeling she didn't know what real pleasure was. Caleb was the kind of man to teach her.

He accepted his little brother's hand and got to his feet. "We should be gentlemen and help Rory now. She's hurt and I'm gonna need you to watch out for her."

The ten-year-old almost snapped to attention and swung around to face her. Gone was the sorrow, and in its place was an intensity he must have gotten from his big brother. He approached the bed and held out both hands. Rory swung her legs over and waited until the wooziness passed before she scooted to the edge.

Benjy waited with far more patience than his brother had shown. She finally put her hands into the boy's and allowed him to pull her to her feet. She glanced down and noted her boots were missing, as was her hat.

"I need my boots."

Caleb glanced around. "Shit. I didn't even see who took them. It was either the doctor or Bernadette."

"Why would they take my boots?" A coldness settled over Rory. She already knew the answer.

"They don't want us to leave. There is no other reason. Hell, they haven't even cleaned up the bloody bandages we used." Caleb gestured to the pile in the corner. "I don't care what kind of smiles or how friendly people seem, no one here is to be trusted."

"He must have recognized you." Rory frowned. "You look enough alike. And your eyes are identical color. A shade most folks don't have."

"You think he plans on killing us? Why would he heal you?"

She shrugged. "Maybe he wants us to be hale and hearty when he shoots us."

Caleb swore under his breath. Their situation was worse than she thought. Garza likely wouldn't let any of them leave alive.

"We've got to get out of here. Now."

"I can walk in my socks, but not over rough ground." She wiggled her toes. "Those were a good pair of boots and I don't have money to replace them."

"I'll buy you a new pair. Let's get going. Every minute we stay here is another minute we could get caught." Caleb opened the door and peered out. "Ready?"

Benjy took her arm, like a little gentleman, and waited. Rory shuffled forward, her gut already complaining about moving. It didn't matter. She knew they had to leave. The boy led her to the door and then ran back to the bed. He fluffed up the pillow and blankets, making it appear as though a body still lay beneath the covers.

"He's a Graham through and through," Caleb whispered. "We're all sneaky as hell. Smart too."

"And annoying." She ignored his snort. True was true.

Benjy returned and took hold of Rory's arm again. Caleb leaned in toward them and spoke low enough she could barely hear him.

"Benjy, you lead the way until we get outside, then I'll hand over her care to you again. Right now I need you walk was quiet as a mouse down the hallway." Caleb waited until Benjy nodded. "Don't go any further if you see any guards. Understand?"

Another head bob.

"Right then." Caleb's gaze flicked to hers. "Do you need me to carry you?"

Surprisingly, he didn't ask the question with sarcasm or rancor. He was serious and she appreciated his concern. He might have carried her in but he sure as hell wasn't going to carry her out. She wanted to leave this place of darkness and shadows. The blood money would never take the taste of evil out of her mouth.

"No. I'll walk out of here." She probably looked like death but she would make it on her own two feet.

Caleb took her arm and waited until Benjy slipped out of the room before they followed. Rory's heart pounded as they crept down the hallway as silently as possible. Her ears started to hurt from the thumping going on in her chest. Her side burned and she could hardly put one foot in front of the other. She gritted her teeth and thought about how strong Benjy was. How could she not be just as strong?

They made it around two corners and down one hallway before Benjy stopped in front of a large urn beside a cupboard. He reached into the urn, nearly falling in head first. The two adults watched while the boy located what was apparently a hidden switch. The cupboard made a ticking sound and then shifted left an inch.

It was loud in the quiet hallway. They all stopped, frozen in place. Rory looked behind them at the shadowy passageway, fully expected running feet. Her mouth was cotton dry and she didn't even have enough spit to swallow.

After what seemed like an hour, she sucked in a much-needed breath. Caleb gestured to the cupboard and Benjy swung it open. Fortunately it was well oiled and smooth. Behind it was an opening about four feet tall by three feet wide. The perfect size for a ten-year-old boy. Benjy disappeared through the opening. It was going to hurt like hell to crawl through the hole in her side.

"Can you do it?" Caleb whispered in her ear.

"I can do anything I set my mind to." She hissed the words out through her teeth.

"I'll bet you can." He crouched down and held her hand as she got to her knees.

Pain roared through her but she began to crawl into the dark tunnel. She focused on Benjy's shoes and moved. One knee, one hand, the other knee, the other hand. Over and over without any thought other than escape. She could feel Caleb behind her, his large presence nearly filling the tunnel. Strangely enough, she felt safe sandwiched between to the two Graham brothers. They had little chance of success but even a small chance was enough to motivate her. Rory didn't give up easily. Ever.

When he reached a T in the tunnel, Benjy turned left and kept going. Rory managed the turn a bit more slowly. Sweat poured down her back and face but she dared not stop to wipe it. She didn't know if she could start moving if she stopped. Her stomach threatened to reacquaint her with the milk she'd drunk. She had never been more miserable than she was at that moment, but she kept moving. Nothing but unconsciousness would stop her.

Although the thought of passing out in this tunnel scared her more than getting caught. It would take a miracle to haul her big carcass out of there and although a good helper, Benjy couldn't move her. That left the ranger, who was strong enough, but it would be the end of their escape if she wasn't able to keep going.

Rory dug deep and crawled. She let her mind drift to the image of the ranger's bare chest. It was such a nice chest, whorls of brown hair and muscles surrounding flat copper nipples. He was a magnificent specimen of man. If they made it out of the tunnel, she might be foolish enough to tell him so. Or possibly put her hands on that chest she wouldn't ever forget.

The injury, blood loss and danger had scrambled her brains. She had the absurd urge to laugh and had to bite her tongue from doing so. The tunnel seemed endless and each foot she crawled seemed to add two feet to the length. She was sliding into a place where she might lose control. They had to get out of the tunnel as fast as possible. Somehow she found a well of strength she didn't know she had and picked up speed.

"Damn, woman." Caleb's harsh whisper made her bare her teeth. She enjoyed making that man guess what she would do next. It was a power she could lay claim to.

Benjy stopped and squatted on his haunches, waiting. His pale face glowed in the darkness of the tunnel. She made it to him, breathing shallow, but she made it. If God was merciful, she wouldn't ever have to repeat the last ten minutes.

Caleb tapped her foot. "What's happening?"

"Benjy stopped."

"Ask him what the hell he's doing." Caleb spoke slowly as though he had to enunciate for a child.

Rory inched forward until she could whisper to the boy. "What's wrong?"

Benjy pointed to a spot three feet from him with a sliver of silvery light shining near the floor. The exit! Then he put his finger to his lips and cupped his ear. That's when she heard it.

Voices.

People were right outside the exit. From the look of the light creeping in, the door led outside and moonlight lit their path. How long the people would be outside the exit was anybody's guess. Rory, however, couldn't stay in the tunnel much longer. Not only did she want to puke but she might truly pass out. That would not be the occurrence she was hoping for.

Caleb tapped her foot again. She hissed at him but he did it again. Although she wanted to smack him, she couldn't turn around to reach him and she simply didn't have enough in her to crawl backwards. Sweat stung her eyes and she shook from head to toe. Rory was near to collapsing. Something had to happen, and soon, or she would embarrass herself.

EMMA LANG

CHAPTER FIVE

Caleb was ready to strangle Rory. She blocked his view and he couldn't see what Benjy was doing. She was also puffing like a locomotive, making it difficult to hear. While many things, Rory was not a stealthy escape artist in a tunnel. She could be heard by anyone passing by. He was about to tell her to slow her breathing when Benjy popped up beside her. He put his finger to his lips and then moved his hand to mimic talking.

"We're trapped?" Caleb mouthed.

Benjy nodded.

"Shit." Caleb knew the escape wasn't easy on Rory, especially judging by how much noise she made. He had to give her credit though. She had been wounded and had lost enough blood to make her weak. How the hell she made it through the tunnel at that speed was beyond him. The woman had grit.

"How many?"

Benjy held up three fingers. Three men between them and their escape. He also had no idea where this tunnel led but his horse was secured at the front of the house. Getting Justice was phase two of the plan. First they had to make it out of the house alive and undetected. That would be difficult with three men blocking their path.

Caleb knew they couldn't wait in the tunnel for long. Judging by the way Rory was breathing, they had only a few minutes. He had to calm her down somehow or none of them would make it undetected.

He put his hand on her back. "You need to slow your breathing, Aurora. One breath at a time, in then out."

"I think I remember how to breathe." Her speech was slurred. Oh hell, she was about to hit the floor.

69

Caleb tried to remember what to do. "You have to put your head between your knees."

She snorted, the sound loud in the quiet tunnel. "And how would you suggest I do that? Bang a hole in the wall or the ceiling so I can straighten up?"

Her sarcasm made her stop hyperventilating for a few moments. Perhaps he needed to keep annoying her.

He whispered to Benjy. "Stay by the door and listen for the men to leave."

The boy scrambled back down the tunnel like a little mouse. Caleb had a feeling he knew exactly how to hide and it angered him to know it wasn't because the boy had been playing with others. He had to push that aside and focus on Rory. She had to stay with him or they were done for. It had probably been hard as hell for her to crawl that far in a tunnel. Later he would tell her she did a good job. Now he needed her to find that spine of iron again.

"I thought you were a blacksmith, Aurora." His needling had the desired effect. She growled in her throat. "Blacksmiths are strong and tough. Seems you ain't a smithy."

"And you are an obnoxious jackass." She kicked him in the arm and damn, it hurt even if she wasn't wearing her boots.

"I know that, but you don't seem to know how tough you're not." He patted her leg in sympathy. "That's what happens when a woman tries to do a man's job."

Caleb actually heard her teeth grinding together. The good news was, her breathing had slowed. Maybe she wouldn't lose consciousness. Of course she might punch a few teeth out of his head when they got out of the tunnel. Her temper was as bad as his. No wonder she got his back up. Like two flaming embers slamming into each other after someone threw a bottle of whiskey for fuel.

If he were honest with himself, it was passion. She was brimming with it, more so than any woman he'd ever met. She sunk her teeth into life, and everything she did, never letting go until every last morsel was enjoyed. He envied her in that respect. He'd spent the last four years finding ways to avoid exactly what Rory was fighting to keep hold of.

Then why was he drawn to her? They were opposites, yet like those burning embers, seemingly helpless to stay apart. He had gotten both of them into a dangerous situation by taking his brother from his fake father. Now Rory was his responsibility and not because she was injured but because they now had a bond that couldn't be broken.

Benjy clicked his tongue and Caleb's attention was diverted from the woman, and her shapely ass, in front of him.

"Open the door slow. Like an inch, no more than two. Look out there and if you don't see anyone, or a glow from a smoke, then open it more. You understand?"

Benjy nodded.

"Go." Caleb was proud of his brother. As a small child he had been through more than most adults had. Although he didn't speak, the boy had a lot to say by what he did.

Benjy nearly disappeared in the tunnel, then the silvery moonlight crept in from the exit as the boy opened it just a smidge. Caleb held his breath and he knew Rory watched too, as eager as he was to get out of the fucking tunnel and into fresh air. He didn't think he had a problem with small spaces, but this experience may have given him one.

The light grew a few seconds later, then even more. A breeze brushed past Caleb's face and he sucked in the smell of the dew. Almost outside.

Before Caleb knew what was happening, Benjy disappeared through the opening.

Shit.

Benjamin Graham hadn't been outside in a month and he wanted to roll around in the dew-covered ground until he was damp with life. The dirt, the air, the stars, even the sound of the crickets were beautiful to him. If it was one thing he learned, it was to savor moments like this. He knew Caleb would be mad but it was worth it.

Five years had passed since he had seen his family. He thought he barely remembered his life with them but when he saw his brother, he almost wet his drawers. The second he caught sight of Caleb's face, everything came back at him like a great big thump on his head.

His parents were dead. He remembered their brutal deaths. More than that, he remembered the happiness of his life before the darkness. His four sisters and three brothers. The Circle Eight and his pony, Kickers. All of it raced through his mind until he couldn't catch his breath.

Now he was leaving, no, escaping from Pablo Garza. If Benjy

71

talked he would have used one of the cuss words he'd stored up. More than four years had passed since he came through the gates and he was inches away from walking back through them.

His stomach tingled in anticipation as he lay there and stared up at the stars. He needed that brief respite for himself. Only for him. He allowed himself thirty seconds of freedom before he remembered Rory. She was hurt bad and had crawled through that tunnel behind him. He crawled back to the door to find his brother's angry face waiting for him.

"What the hell are you doing?"

Benjy shrugged and tried to look innocent.

"Don't play stupid with me. I remember how you would beat everyone at jacks and marbles. Your act isn't fooling me. I had to fold myself in two to get around her because you disappeared." Caleb's jaw ticked. "I assume everyone is gone."

Benjy nodded and scooted back to let his brother crawl through. Caleb turned right around to help Rory out of the tunnel, which made guilt creep across Benjy's conscience. She looked horrible. Pale, with sweat running down her face and her hair plastered to her skull. Her eyes were sunken into her face and shone brightly in the moonlight. She held her hand to her side as Caleb practically picked her up to pull her from the tunnel.

Rory had always been kind to him when she was there. Most times he only saw her when she came into the house to talk to Pap— Mr. Garza. Benjy had to stop thinking of that man as his father. His real father was dead, shot four times right in front of him. *Bang, bang, bang, bang.* Those four shots still echoed in his dreams. Stuart Graham had been a hero, a good father and husband, a smart rancher. His death had shattered Benjy's world into tiny pieces. And when he would have turned to his mother for comfort, she too was gunned down. That time three shots sufficed. *Bang, bang, bang.*

Benjy shook off the darkness that crept over him. He wouldn't give in to the shadows today. He couldn't. Rory and Caleb needed him. It was time to act like a man, not the wild creature that slunk around inside him waiting for its opportunity to emerge.

Caleb had wrapped his hand around Rory's arm and Benjy remembered his brother had asked him to be Rory's helper after they made it out of the tunnel. He ran to Rory's other side, the injured side, and gently put his arm around her, tugging until she leaned toward him. He was only about four inches shorter than her but he knew he was scrawny. No one knew how strong he was. Benjy took great pains to hide his strength. No one need know that he lifted iron pots in the kitchen in the middle of the night until his muscles screamed. If Caleb hadn't been in the kitchen, he would have done it tonight.

Now the world had been turned inside out and Benjy had escaped the prison others called a palace. He had the chance to show what he could do as a man, as a Graham.

Caleb let go of Rory's arm and nodded his approval. "There are sentries every fifty feet on the fence. There has to be a man-sized gate somewhere. A man like Garza always has an escape route."

Benjy frowned as he thought. He wasn't allowed outside often but he watched out every window he could. Garza often visited the flower garden, disappearing for hours amongst the blossoms his old gardener tended. The vibrant colors always blew gently in the breeze, calling to Benjy, who was not allowed to smell their fragrance or touch their petals. Prisoners were not given that privilege.

Perhaps what Garza was doing was escaping through a gate in the garden to do evil deeds outside his palace. The man was capable of so many things, why not a secret gate? He already had a secret tunnel. Benjy pointed to the north side of the property, to the garden. Caleb gestured for him to lead the way.

The three of them crept along the side of the house, in the shadows, with Rory's shaky breath echoing in his ear.

Caleb followed the small shadow through the night. He kept Rory in sight as she moved slower than he would have liked, but he couldn't push her any more. She was mobile and that's all he could ask for right now.

Benjy led them into a garden. Its fragrant blooms perfumed the air around them, almost too much. The *patron* obviously liked flowers for whatever reason. The abundance of plants and bushes made for good cover as they wound their way through the garden.

The boy slowed down at the northeast corner and scuttled his way along the wall. He acted as if he'd never been in the garden and was feeling his way along. Things looked different in the dark, though, and perhaps Benjy was trying to match what he knew to what he could now barely see.

It took another ten minutes of slow progress before he stopped and got to his feet. Then he disappeared into the wall. Caleb stared at the place where his brother had vanished for a few moments before he sprang into action. He reached through the vines clinging to the three-foot-thick stone wall until he found something he didn't expect. Wood.

It was a door. A small door hidden in the garden behind copious amounts of greenery. Garza was incredibly smart and knew exactly what he needed for an escape route. Why he needed secret tunnels and secret entrances was another story. Caleb would investigate that after he had Benjy and Rory in a safe place.

His little brother had crouched down at the handle and was busy fiddling with the lock. No doubt it required a key and Caleb had no skills at picking locks. Usually he shot them off. Couldn't do that here of course.

He leaned down and whispered in Benjy's ear. "Can you get it open?" He felt the boy's head nod in agreement. It bothered Caleb that the boy didn't speak and he would find out why eventually. It wasn't natural, but then again, nothing the boy had gone through the last five years was natural.

Caleb went back to Rory. She sat cross-legged on the cushiony grass with her head back. He put his hand on her forehead, hoping like hell it was cool. Other than being covered in sweat, it was lukewarm. Thank God. If they were lucky, she wouldn't catch a fever.

"Are you my nurse now?" she whispered harshly, pulling away from his touch. Her face shone in the moonlight, beautiful and carved from ivory. Rory hid behind her rough ways and her hammer. Being wounded allowed him to see the woman behind the smithy. She was extraordinary, much as he didn't want to admit that.

He was piqued by her rejection, although he shouldn't be. "I'm checking for fever. Doc said it could set in."

"I don't have a fever but I am sweaty as a pig and I stink. Does that help?" Her sarcasm rivaled his. It made him chuckle. "You find that funny."

"No, I am amused by fate and whatever else conspired to throw you in my path." Caleb got to his knees beside her and he lost track of what he was doing. He cupped her face and damned if he didn't kiss her.

Rory's lips were soft as the petals that surrounded him, plump and warm beneath his. At first she didn't react—and then she returned the kiss. His entire body hardened in an instant, a throbbing mass of man and need. He wanted to lay her down in the flowers and taste her, pleasure her, plunge into her until neither of them could see straight.

On and on the kiss went until their tongues met, rasping and dancing against each other, mouths open and lips fused. A groan built up inside his throat and he spiraled out of control. He wanted to possess her. Her hands grabbed at his shoulders, pulling him closer. Caleb lost all sense of time and place. He only knew the woman he was currently kissing until he didn't know where he ended and she began. Kissing her was one of the most sensual moments of his life.

A tap on his shoulder broke the spell and he fell back onto his ass, gasping for breath.

"Holy shit." Her husky cursing summed up what he was thinking. "What just happened?"

"Damned if I know." Caleb could still taste her on his lips and tongue. Her scent filled his nostrils, its appeal stronger than the thousands of blossoms around him. His body pulsed in tune with his throbbing dick, which strained the buttons on his trousers. What had he been thinking? Nothing, of course. His brain hadn't been functioning at all.

He turned to find Benjy beside him, the silent boy who had witnessed their indiscretion. What must he think of Caleb? His reaction to simply kissing Rory had knocked the wind out of him. What would it be like to do more than kiss? His dick jumped at the thought and Caleb decided he needed to stop thinking about fucking and start thinking about escaping.

"Did you get the lock open?" His voice shook right along with the rest of him.

Benjy nodded and pointed to the door. Damn the boy was good. Caleb scrambled to his feet and went to check. Sure enough the four foot high door was open, moonlight streaming through to the night beyond.

He pulled Benjy over to Rory and leaned in close. "Go through the door and then walk along the wall until you reach the south corner of the gate. That's twenty feet from the woods. You two then run for them as best you can. Wait for me there."

"Wait, what?" Rory bumped her head into his. "Wait for you?"

"I have to get my horse. I'm not leaving Justice here. Besides, if I leave out the front gate, it's less suspicious." He knew it was risky but he owed it to the gelding to retrieve him.

"It's dumb is what it is. I know horses are expensive and important, but more so than your life?" She pinched his arm. "I knew you were stupid, Ranger, but they could kill you."

"I didn't know you cared." He was irked she called him stupid and that she resorted to pinching.

"I don't, but now that we're all in this together, I need to make sure no one gets left behind." She blew out a breath. "You going back is more dangerous than running into the woods together."

"I'm a Texas Ranger, honey. I know danger and I do what I need to." He helped her to her feet. "Now I need you to take care of my brother until I get back to you."

"You're still a jackass. And don't call me honey." She stuck up her chin and her expression was thunderous in the meager light.

Something possessed him and he leaned down and kissed her again. He ignored her gasp and pulled her toward the door.

"Benjy, I'm only leaving for ten minutes, no longer. Stay with Rory and keep her safe, okay?" He handed him the supplies they'd taken.

The boy took the bundle, but his expression was unreadable in the semi-darkness. He was disappointed though, Caleb could feel it.

"I promise I'll be there." He pulled the boy in for another stiff hug and then kissed the top of his head. "You are very brave, Benjy, more than most men. I know you can do this."

A reluctant nod and Caleb blew out a breath of relief. He watched his brother disappear through the door and then held out his hand to Rory. She slapped it away and stepped closer on her own.

"Don't call me honey. And you need to stop kissing me," she whispered harshly.

"Stop kissing me back."

"I didn't."

"Oh yes you did."

"You're an infuriating man."

"You're an infuriating woman."

"If I had my hammer, I'd pound you."

"I guess it's too bad you don't then."

To his utter surprise, this time she grabbed his face and planted a hard kiss on his lips. Before he could react, she scooted through the door and was gone. A stupid grin spread across his face and he had to remind himself he was in an enemy's stronghold and to stop acting like a fool. Later on he would find out why she kissed him. For now, he would tuck it aside and focus on getting out of the Garza fortress.

However, he couldn't help licking his lips and tasting essence of Aurora. The woman tasted like passion. It was going to be a long journey.

He shut the door and hoped no one noticed the lock was picked. As he made his way back through the garden, he picked up speed. Without the boy and a wounded woman to worry about he made it back to the tunnel in less than ten minutes. No one spotted him and he was able to get back inside and close the tunnel door behind him.

As he crept along, he kept touching patches of wetness and thought they were sweat. Whose he had no idea nor did he want to know. A bath in a creek would be in order for all of them eventually. For now he would wipe his hands on his trousers and move on.

He made it to the beginning of the tunnel and stopped moving. The night was silent around him, a loud silence buzzed in his ears. He eased the door open and stepped into the hallway. As he made his way back down to the room Rory had been in, he knew he needed to make himself a bit more presentable. Otherwise he would likely have dirt, grass and who knew what else all over him. Things that wouldn't be in the house.

The door opened easily and he let out a breath of relief to find it empty. He reached for the pitcher to pour out fresh water when he saw his hands in the glow of the lamp. They were sticky with blood, not sweat. He stared at the crimson stains. Rory was bleeding, enough to leave patches of it in the tunnel. Panic and worry raced through him. She hadn't said anything the entire time.

The woman had more than grit. She had courage many men would envy. He admired her for that at the same time he wanted to spank her for not mentioning her wound had opened up. Dammit.

He washed up quickly and made sure his shirt was tucked. Now for the performance of his life.

Caleb walked out of the room and made his way back to the front door. He kept his pace steady and unrushed, although inside he wanted to run out of there, guns blazing and shouting the Graham battle cry. Outside he was cool as a Texas Ranger.

A guard stood beside the door. He was a big man, taller than Caleb and broad as a barn door. He held a rifle across his chest and had a pistol riding his though. Caleb nodded at him and held up a pouch of tobacco. The guard opened the door and let him pass.

One down.

Caleb took a deep breath of the night air and opened the tobacco pouch. The last thing he wanted was a cigarette but he rolled one anyway and lit it with a match from his pocket. He walked over to Justice, who stood there waiting. His ears perked up when he caught a whiff of Caleb and he neighed in greeting.

"Hey there, boy." Caleb scratched him behind his left ear, a favorite spot.

The gelding pushed his nose into Caleb's side and if horses could sigh in pleasure, he would have. After a few more scratches, Caleb untied the reins from the hitching post and led the horse toward the gate.

"Where are you going, Ranger?" A man appeared from the shadows, this one well-dressed and wearing two pistols low on his hips.

"Miss Foster needs fresh clothes and asked me to check on the forge, make sure it's burned out so it doesn't burn down her smithy." Caleb kept his voice casual, then yawned for effect. "I won't be long. She's sleeping with the laudanum the doc gave her."

The man stared at him while Caleb puffed on the cigarette.

"Is there a problem with me leaving?" Caleb narrowed his gaze, the star on his belt clearly visible in the moonlight.

"Not at all. I can provide you with an escort." The man whistled and two other men appeared out of the darkness.

"No need. I know my way back. Rangers are good trackers." He vaulted up into the saddle. "Tell Mr. Garza I said thank you for all he's done. I'll be back in a while."

As Caleb led Justice toward the gate, the men's' gazes nearly burned a hole in his back. Thirty feet. Twenty feet. Ten feet. Five feet. The gate was in front of him along with another two men.

"Evenin', fellas. I'm off to Mrs. Foster's smithy." He puffed on the cigarette and waited.

The men looked behind him at someone, perhaps the well-dressed man, before they opened the gate. The squeal of the iron was music to his ears. He tipped his hat at the men before he trotted out into the night.

Rory was ready to hit something or someone. The tension around her and Benjamin was thicker than summer air in Texas. Neither one spoke but they were both thinking about Caleb, the man who had helped them escape and then walked right back in to get his horse. Damn him. A horse was not worth his life. If he had been there, she would have punched him. It sure as hell would have made her feel better.

She crouched in the bushes with her side throbbing and sticky with blood. To make it worse, her head was pounding. Her stomach had decided to roll around and throw bile up her throat every five minutes. The wonderful milk she'd had threatened to come back with a less sweet taste.

Benjy stared a hole at the house, his expression more intense than a ten-year-old should wear. She didn't know exactly what he'd been through but it had been harsh enough to steal his voice. Sometimes people choose not to speak rather than an ailment taking their words. She expected Benjy was one of those who'd made a choice. Perhaps one day he would change his mind and put sound to his thoughts. For now, he stared and gestured, making himself understood well enough.

"He'll make it out one way or another." Rory was surprised to hear how ragged her voice was. Sounded like she was gargling rocks instead of hiding in the woods. "Texas Rangers can fight their way out of anything. I sure couldn't shake him off my land. Stubborn cuss."

The boy didn't even blink.

"You did real good getting to the woods. You're quiet as a mouse with socks. I didn't even hear anything and I was two feet from you." She smiled at him, resisting the urge to ruffle his hair or show any kind of affection. He'd always kept his distance from her each time she was at the ranch. Even though he was now reunited with his brother, it didn't mean he would welcome her touch.

If Caleb didn't come back soon, she had to come up with a strategy and quick. They had little time before her absence, and more importantly, Benjy's absence, was noticed. On foot, her house and smithy were hours away. In her condition, definitely more. Eloise and Sven were closer. They might be able to help her get Benjy to his family. She was sure that was what Caleb would want if he was unable to be there to guide them.

The problem was, she had no idea where the Graham family was.

"Benjy, if necessary, could you remember where your family

lives?"

At the question, he turned his head to look at her. His scowl was very much like his brother's.

"If we get separated from Caleb, I want to make sure we can get you back to your family. Without him, I need to rely on you to guide us."

His expression changed to one of panic, the face of a little boy who was lost.

"You're tough, Benjy. I know you are. If necessary, you could find your way home. I'm sure of it. I know it's northeast of here but that's all I know. From there, I might need you to try to remember. Can you try?"

If he shook his head, she had no idea what she would do. More than likely head in the general direction and keep asking until she found someone who knew the Grahams. There wasn't much else to pick from. She could only hope Benjy could remember some landmarks or something familiar to help them.

To her surprise, he nodded, a little, but it was an affirmative answer.

"Good. I always like to have a plan just in case I need it. It's saved me more than once." She looked behind them but saw nothing but shadows and fireflies. "If he doesn't come in the next ten minutes, we're going to start moving. He'll catch up."

Benjy shook his head vigorously and crossed his arms across his chest. A stubborn ten-year-old was not what she needed.

"Did Caleb ask you to look after me?"

A hesitant nod.

"Then you need to carry through with that promise and get me to my friend Eloise. She can help me. I'm bleeding, Benjy." She held up one bloody palm. "I started bleeding when we were crawling through the tunnel. I'm a little woozy too."

His eyes widened and he nodded slowly. Good. He would go with her even without Caleb. It was a bit of a dirty trick to play the wounded damsel, but she had to do it. Truth was, she *was* bleeding and woozy. Normally she would press on and ignore it. Today was different, the situation was different. She had stepped into a role she wasn't used to—the weaker female.

A soft whoosh of air was her only warning before a pair of hands grabbed her shoulders, then one clamped across her mouth.

"Shh, it's me," Caleb's welcome, but annoying, voice sounded in her ear.

She did not sag in relief. Absolutely not.

"Sorry about the hand on your mouth but I had to make sure you wouldn't scream."

She snorted. "I've never screamed in my life."

"I don't doubt you believe that." He helped her to her feet. "Why didn't you tell me the wound had started bleeding again?"

His accusatory tone made her bristle. "I am a grown woman, a widow and a blacksmith. I do not answer to you or any man."

"I don't care if you keep your own counsel, Aurora, but we are in this as a troop. All three of us. If something happens to one of us, our entire troop is affected." He leaned in close enough their noses touched. "You kissed me."

Surprised, Rory stared at him for a few beats before she managed a grin. "And you kissed me."

Their breaths mingled in the cool, humid night air. She breathed in him and he breathed in her. For a moment the earth stopped spinning and there were only two. This close, Caleb's blue-green eyes almost glowed in the moonlight. She could see a small scar that bisected his right eyebrow, the day's worth of dark whiskers on his cheeks, and the full outline of his lips. Those she knew personally were soft and talented.

She wanted to kiss him again.

The thought shocked her and excited her. What was it about this man that made her act so far out of herself? She barely kissed Horatio once a week and she'd been married to him. With Caleb, she wanted to kiss him again and again until their bodies did more than touch lips. A shock rippled through her. She wanted him in her bed, in her body.

Now wasn't the ideal time to realize she had cravings for the man. He was a fine specimen of manliness and she had no doubt there would be great pleasure had by both of them. Yet they were in the woods, hiding from Pablo Garza, she was wounded, and they had a ten-year-old mute boy who had been kidnapped five years ago, only to be taken by force again, this time by his brother.

The situation could not be any stranger.

Caleb cleared his throat and moved back, breaking the spell. "We need to get moving."

"Yep and head straight for my smithy." She allowed him to help her to stand. When had she gotten so stupidly weak? Damn tree and its damn branches.

"You and Benjy ride on Justice and I'll lead him through the woods. Any way to get back to your place without crossing the bridge with Garza's men?" Caleb kept his hand on her elbow as they picked their way through the forest, whispering their words.

"Yes, but it takes us two miles out of the way." She saw the horse secured to a tree up ahead. "Follow the tree line due south. They're thick enough to hide us at night, but come daylight, we will be spotted."

"Got it. Now let's get you up in the saddle."

As if she were light as a feather, he scooped her up and lifted her onto the enormous horse, placing her gently in the saddle. Shock kept her quiet as he did the same with Benjy. The boy nestled in the saddle in front of her, stiff as a board.

Caleb took hold of the gelding's bit and led the horse through the trees, keeping the sound to a minimum. She swayed with the animal's gait, her side protesting each time she moved to the left. Her wound throbbed harder with each passing moment. Normally a ride on horseback to her place would only take an hour and a half. At this slow walk, it would take twice that long, or more. She wished for some of that laudanum now but she had to settle for sending her mind elsewhere.

Caleb found the shallow portion of the creek and led them across safely. Then he doubled back to find the trail that led to her property. Or in his opinion, the Republic of Texas property she squatted on. When they got back, she would send the ranger and his brother on their way, never to see them again.

The advantage of helping him kidnap his brother meant he wouldn't be concerned about kicking her off her land. In the end, she would win and he would forget he even met her. Some other faceless ranger might appear on her doorstep but it would be some time, and perhaps she could earn enough money to buy the land herself. Although without Pablo Garza, she had little chance of making enough to survive, much less pay Texas. She would never give up and never give in. The Republic had no idea who they were going up against and neither did Ranger Caleb Graham.

Benjy remained stiff in front of her, his shoulders straight as an arrow and his body as far from hers as possible without climbing over the pommel. The boy obviously didn't want to be touched, by anyone. She tried to keep her back as straight as his, but exhaustion had her sagging. There was no help for it, he would have to endure it for as long as it took.

Her mind wandered in and out of focus, and she would swear on a Bible she saw Horatio sitting on a tree branch ten yards ahead. She knew the wound, the loss of blood, and the stress of the entire day wore on her. She could barely keep her eyes open. Several times she nodded off and Benjy's sharp reflexes stopped her from falling on her head.

The darkness was absolute, all encompassing. She listened to the night creatures singing their nocturnal song, taunting her with the knowledge they were safe and sound in their hiding places. Her simple but sturdy bed awaited her. At some point they would make it to her house and she could lie on the straw mattress and close her eyes for much-needed sleep.

"If you fall off that horse, you're going to need a few more bandages and I don't feel like being your nurse anymore." Caleb's voice cut through her dazed state.

"You're still an ass."

"I never denied that, but I need you to sit up on that saddle or I'll make you walk so I can sit up there."

His reminder that he was walking while they rode brought a pinch of guilt. She pushed it away. He chose to take the boy and she chose to think of her own needs. However, he was right to remind her to be alert. They had snuck away from Garza's hacienda, taking a boy who was claimed as his son. There wasn't a chance the rich man wouldn't follow.

"How close are we? I reckon we're maybe five miles out, but this is your place. I've only seen it the one time." Caleb looked ahead, squinting in the darkness as though her smithy would stand up and wave at him.

Rory forced herself to focus. She glanced to her right and left, then spotted the large mesquite tree she knew well. Damned if the ranger wasn't right. This was the halfway mark between her tiny place and Garza's.

"Five miles is about right." Her voice was like sandpaper rubbing on her throat. It hurt to even swallow.

"Stay strong up there, Aurora. I can't worry about both of you."

Worried? He was worried about her? She was momentarily nonplussed, unable to even form a response that didn't make her sound like a silly girl. Most of her life she'd been tough, unflappable and independent. She barely allowed anyone to help her, much less save her life as the ranger had done. Rory had fallen victim to her own arrogance in climbing the tree, then fate had taken over from there. Her thoughts about the ranger had taken a strange turn, one she was unfamiliar with. It made her jittery and out of control, two emotions she did not welcome.

"You worry about your own ass, Ranger. I'll worry about mine."

To her surprise, he chuckled. "Damn but you are a constant surprise. I'm used to outspoken females, but you?" He snorted. "You put them to shame."

She didn't know whether to be flattered or insulted so she chose to ignore him instead. The silence between them was invaded again by the sounds of the night. They pushed on, each minute more uncomfortable than the last. She gritted her teeth and held her stomach as tight as she dared.

When they passed the pin oak at the edge of her property, she let loose a noise that was a cross between a sob and a hoot. They were almost there. Almost.

"Five minutes," she managed to say through clenched teeth.

"Good. I don't think you're going to last much longer."

It was her turn to laugh, more of a squeak. "I gave up an hour ago. It's sheer stubbornness keeping me up here."

Caleb led the horse up to the tiny house and secured him to the hitching post. He plucked Benjy off and set him on the ground. He bent down and whispered to the boy, who scampered into the dark house like a rabbit. Soon a warm glow emanated from the windows. Home.

The ranger turned back to her and held up his arms. "Do you trust me?"

She didn't know how to answer or if she were honest with herself, whether she wanted to answer. "Why?"

"Let me get you down and into the house. You need to get cleaned up before we leave. I'll give you some time to pack a few things too. Do you have a horse?" His words came at her like bullets.

She managed to sort through them all. "Leave? What do you mean leave?"

He didn't respond but he did pull her off the saddle. She couldn't help the moan that crept up her throat. Her body screamed with discomfort and soreness.

"You'd best answer me, Ranger, before I make you regret picking me off that horse." She sounded weak as a kitten and it annoyed her.

"You can't stay here, Rory." His tone was gentle as was his touch. "Garza will know you helped me, will blame you for Benjy leaving. He doesn't seem like the type to forgive or forget."

"This is my home. I'm not leaving." She could hardly focus on the door as he walked through sideways with her in his arms.

"You can't even piss by yourself right now." He didn't sound mean but his words hurt just the same. "Let me take care of you. Trust me."

"I don't need a man." She saw her bed, the sight she had been praying for through their night escape. Within moments, he laid her on the mattress and she sighed in relief. Her eyes stung with unshed tears as she remembered the last time she'd been in the bed and her life had been so very different.

"What you need is a short nap. Go to sleep, Aurora. Trust me." His face hovered above hers.

She lifted up her hand and touched his whiskered cheek. "Your eyes are too pretty for a man."

He grinned and kissed her palm. "Sleep."

She wanted to tell him that she didn't take orders but she couldn't fight sleep. It swept over her in seconds, taking her into darkness where there were no dangers to avoid. She gave herself over and hoped when she woke it would have all been a nightmare.

CHAPTER SIX

Caleb did not want to undress Rory for a second time. Well, he did, but not because she was unconscious and bleeding again. What a strange twenty-four hours he'd spent in this woman's company. His life had been turned upside down in that time, all because of a blacksmith named Aurora Foster.

She lay there, pale as milk, yet still strong as steel. He'd meant it when he told her she had grit. Many men wouldn't have been able to survive, much less put forth the physical effort she had. Now she was exhausted and in need of some care. He could only let her rest for an hour at most and even that was pushing their luck. If Garza wasn't on their trail already, he would be very soon.

Yet he had to tend to her wound and let her body heal for a short time. Benjy stood in the corner watching them, still silent but not missing a thing. Caleb walked over to him and spoke softly into his ear.

"I need you to get some water boiling. I'll have to clean Rory's wound before we dress it up again." He nodded to the stove. "I'll get the fire going, you get the water."

To his surprise, Benjy saluted him. A rusty chuckle burst from Caleb's throat. The boy was a bit of a pain in the ass like his older siblings. That was good. Caleb was afraid he would be a ghost of his former self, the smiling, laughing little scamp who loved caterpillars and lizards.

Caleb watched his brother grab the bucket sitting by the door and head outside into the dark, more than likely with no idea where the well was or what direction to head. The boy had heart and courage.

The fire wouldn't light itself and there was no time to sit and contemplate stupid shit. He got a blaze going in no time, thankful she had dry wood in the basket in the corner. Although he felt strange doing it, he looked through her meager possessions. There were a few shirts and another pair of trousers.

A careful search of the small house yielded matches, a few cans each of peaches and beans, a hairbrush with a tarnished silver back, a bar of soap and three washrags. Setting aside a washrag and a shirt, he put everything else in a traveling bag and set it by the door. Benjy stepped back in with a full bucket of water.

"Good job." Caleb took the bucket from him before it broke his arm. The boy was skinny as a rail but that was common for Graham boys. Once they hit fourteen, they all filled out and grew tall and wide. It would happen for Benjy too.

While the water heated, he walked over to the simple cot and sat on the edge. Dark smudges marked the skin beneath her eyes. Her short hair was in disarray, sticking every which way. He took her hand, clammy and warm. Not hot yet, but he was afraid a fever might follow given the rough night she'd had.

He unbuttoned the borrowed shirt enough to reveal the bandages, which were an angry dark red. She'd bled more than he expected. Damn. He'd need fresh bandages and the sheet would have to be the sacrifice. She could yell at him later.

Caleb didn't have supplies for new stitches so he hoped bandages would be enough. As he unwound the bandage, her eyes fluttered open. Those amber orbs regarded him with confusion and then she smiled.

"I love it when you wake me with a kiss."

Caleb felt like he'd been kicked in the balls. "Pardon?"

"You are such a good husband. Mother was wrong. There are men just as wonderful as Papa." She closed her eyes again, leaving him gaping like a fish.

She'd mistaken him for her husband. Apparently she'd loved him a great deal, and still did even after death. Caleb told himself he didn't care. She was out of her head and wouldn't even remember what she said. It didn't bother him a bit. Not at all.

The water began to boil and he jumped up to get the supplies he needed to clean her up. He sure as hell was not running away from an unconscious woman because she thought he was her husband.

He used the bucket dipper to put hot water into the wash basin and put the clean washrag in the water, carrying the soap and basin back to the bed. After setting it carefully on the floor, he used his gentlest touch to clean the blood from her skin, stopping frequently to rinse the washrag. Benjy sat cross-legged on the floor, watching with wide eyes.

"Toss this out the door and get me fresh water." Caleb waited while Benjy did as he bade. His hands cramped from keeping them steady so he tried to flex the discomfort away, but only ended up making it worse.

Benjy set the basin on the floor as carefully as if it were made of eggshells. He stepped back and wiped his hands on his trousers, then plopped back down on the floor.

"Did you see another horse?"

Benjy shook his head then stuck two fingers above his head and pushed out his teeth.

"A mule? Is there a saddle and tack for it?"

This time a nod from the boy.

"Well hell. Beggars can't be choosers, eh?"

At least they would have two beasts to ride, even if one of them wasn't going to be particularly fast. It was better than walking, but not by much.

He focused on getting her cleaned up and not on the fact the lady blacksmith owned a mule that she apparently rode. Just another odd thing about an odd female.

By the time he had finished the chore of ridding her of the blood, he was pleased to note there was no fresh blood from the wound. The crawling, running and riding must have been the culprit. A fresh bandage, a nap and the mule might be enough to keep it from opening up again.

He took the sheet and tore it in to bandages that would fit her small frame, leaving a few thick pieces to fold over the actual wound. The doctor's stitches were impeccable, tight and even. There might hardly be a scar. Too bad the healer lived in the pocket of a man who would buy a kidnapped child. Bastard.

Caleb bandaged her as best he could and thankfully, she stayed out the entire time. He, on the other hand, was sweating and shaking when he finished. Too bad he didn't have a clean shirt of his own. He did spy a few men's shirts on hooks in the corner. They were too large for Rory so they must've been her dead husband's. He wouldn't miss them and she wouldn't begrudge Caleb a shirt, considering her blood had ruined both of his.

Mind made up, he dumped the dirty water and rinsed out the basin and washrag. He stripped off his shirt and washed up, glad to have the dried sweat and remnants of blood off his body too. A strange sound like a squeak sounded from behind him. He swung around to find both Benjy and Rory watching him.

His brother looked wary, perhaps because of Caleb's size. Rory's expression was hungry. Both surprised him. He stared at them, the water dripping down his chest onto his trousers. He'd never been modest or embarrassed but he sure as hell was now.

"We've got to leave." He slipped on the tattered but clean shirt from the nail. Her husband was about the same size, but the shoulders were a bit tight. Although he expected argument from her about the garment, instead she narrowed her gaze and stuck up her chin.

"I'm not leaving."

He should have expected it but it irked him just the same. "We can't stay here."

"The hell I can't. This is my home. You and Benjy can go." She closed her eyes and turned her face away.

Caleb took his time buttoning the shirt, tamping his temper down. She was wounded and the day had not turned out like anyone planned. He had to give her a few minutes to adjust to what would happen.

He sat on the edge of the bed and breathed in deep before he spoke. "I know this is hard to accept, but Garza will be here within the next hour or two."

"That's not my problem." She spoke from behind closed eyes.

"Yes, it is. You left with me, and in Garza's eyes, both of us took Benjy. We kidnapped him." He touched her arm and her eyes flew open. "Think about him, Rory. He has armed guards around him and out a mile from his house. If he catches us here, he will kill us and take Benjy back. If he finds you here alone, he'll do worse to find out where Benjy is. I can't leave you here to be raped and tortured, or worse."

He'd seen the evil that men do up close and personal. The last thing he wanted was for Rory to find out firsthand. She might be a stubborn cuss, but she was a good person. He had a clue to her integrity as soon as he met her and she fought so hard for a scrap of land. Helping him take Benjy back solidified that opinion.

"He wouldn't. Mr. Garza might be demanding but he isn't a murderer." Her tone had lost its strength.

"You know that's not true. He might not pull the trigger, but he kills people who get in his way. He's dirty and I'm not going to let him hurt you." He hadn't meant to say that last part but it was out of his mouth before he could stop it.

"I, uh, thank you." She blinked.

He needed to change the subject. "I packed supplies you'll need."

"My tools. The hammer and tongs with the notch on the handle were my father's. I can't and I won't leave those behind."

His brows went up. "You want to carry a hundred pounds of tools. You're riding a mule, right?"

"Cora is a sturdy mule. Don't doubt she has as much heart as that big quarter horse of yours."

"Heart or not, those tools are damn heavy for any animal to carry." He had a feeling she would not give in on the tools. They were a piece of her family and although he did all he could to avoid his for the last four years, he knew how important family was.

Finding Benjy reminded him of that fact with startling clarity. While Caleb had been out with guns on his hips and a hunger for adventure, his little brother had lived as a prisoner two hundred miles from his family's ranch. Nothing was more important than family.

"Fine. I'll get the tools. You can get changed." He got to his feet when she grabbed his arm, stopping him.

"Thank you." Her eyes were too bright, but perhaps it was the lantern's glow and not the first signs of a fever.

"Don't thank me. You'll be hating me after we ride hard for my family's ranch. It's going to be hell." He handed her the clean shirt he'd found and turned around while she changed. He saw his brother do the same.

"I didn't know. About Garza I mean. Or about your brother." She sounded guilty.

"How could you? Benjy doesn't speak and Garza sure as hell wasn't going to tell you." He stared down at his dusty boots, noting a few speckles of dried blood on them.

"Still, I should have realized, perhaps from Bernadette. Do you think she knows?"

"She might. Somebody has to. He couldn't just bring a five-year-old into his house and announce he had a son without help from inside

91

his household." It was something Caleb would investigate after he had the two of them safe at his family's ranch. He would investigate the hell out of Garza and his dirty dealings.

"That's true. I still feel stupid for not realizing something was wrong."

At this Caleb whirled around, her modesty be damned. She struggled to pull the shirt onto her left arm while keeping her right over her breasts. He took hold of the shirt and closed his eyes. She slipped it on, the fabric rustling and igniting all sorts of naughty thoughts in his head.

"Don't blame yourself, Rory. Garza is dirty and everything he touches is tarnished. I'm glad he never did anything to harm you." The moment the words were out of his mouth, he wanted to snatch them back. He had no idea if Garza had ever done anything to her or even if they'd had a romantic relationship. That thought made him a little queasy.

"Oh he tried, but my hammer was in my hand at the time and I convinced him we had business together and nothing more."

That made Caleb grin. "I'm beginning to like your hammer."

She snorted. "Not if I use it against you."

"Are you finished yet? I need to get the animals ready." Impatience nibbled at his back along with a healthy dose of urgency.

"I'm buttoning. You can open your eyes." She stared up at him, with those amber eyes and that face he would see in his dreams for years. How could he have ever thought her manly? She was pure feminine, without all the gewgaws and frippery that other women surrounded themselves with. Rory was genuine.

"Your bag is by the door. I'll get the hammer and tongs for you and meet you outside. Do you think you can walk?" He frowned at the possibility she was too weak.

"I can do what I have to do. Don't worry about me."

His frown deepened. "I'm not worried about you. I'm worried you'll slow us down."

"You are still a jackass."

He nodded. "I have to be." He turned to leave when she spoke.

"Thank you, Ranger." She cleared her throat. "I don't like owing folks anything, but in this case, I owe you my thanks and my life."

Caleb headed for the door, unwilling to accept gratitude from her. Because he had taken Benjy, he was forcing her to leave her property while she recovered from a wound. He had been obligated to evict her, but now his actions had caused her to be in danger. That rankled him and he sure as hell didn't want her to thank him for that.

He pointed at Benjy. "Can you saddle the mule?"

Benjy shook his head. Of course not. Why would Garza teach his pretend son a real skill like saddling a horse, or in this case, a mule?

Caleb went out the door alone, in need of air and a moment to gather his thoughts. Rory tangled him up in his own feet. He had to find a way to stop thinking about that kiss, or rather, the kisses they shared. Damned if he couldn't still taste her on his tongue hours later. How did everything get like this? On the run, a wounded woman, a mute boy, and a ranger who needed to get his head out of his ass and think.

Their lives depended on it.

Rory managed to stay in a vertical position without falling on her face. This was a feat considering her head buzzed louder than a hive of bees and her stomach rolled back and forth, threatening her with more than queasiness. She was a wreck but she also knew Caleb was right. They had to leave.

The very real threat of what Pablo Garza would do frightened her. She didn't tell him that of course. He kept telling her how tough a blacksmith was and she wasn't about to disabuse him of that notion. She could be tough, hell she *was* tough. Most women would have fallen to pieces the moment the ranger stepped on their property and said git.

She glanced at Benjy. He stood at her side, his solemn eyes that odd blue-green color like his brother's.

"We need to douse the fire. Probably should take that lamp with us. It gets awful pitch black out there. We could use a light." She shuffled toward the door, which seemed to be a hundred feet away instead of six feet. Benjy walked beside her, never touching but making sure she made it to the other side of the small cottage.

After she stopped moving, he shifted the bucket on the stove and then opened the door. She ought to stop him since he was a child and could get burned. However he sure looked like he knew what he was doing. Besides she couldn't lift the handle of the bucket much less move the damn thing. He took a dipper full of water and dripped it onto the fire to limit the smoke. The fire slowly went out with each pass off the dipper until it was completely extinguished.

Benjy picked up the lantern and her bag and waited. She smiled weakly and opened the door. He managed to put the lantern and bag outside and then take her elbow to help her outside before she could even protest. Truth was, she leaned too much on the thin boy and she was no lightweight.

The cool night air bathed her overheated face. She was itchy and anxious and the fresh air was marvelous. Her mule, Cora, stood beside the overly large quarter horse. Her sweet brown eyes regarded the horse with unease. Rory didn't blame her. Everything about the ranger, from his shoulders to his gun to his equine, were larger than life.

As if she'd conjured him, the ranger appeared out of the darkness with a burlap sack and two bedrolls. Judging by the weight, it held her hammer and tongs. She let out a breath of relief. There was no way she could leave that piece of her father behind. Since she couldn't take the forge or the anvil, the tools would have to be it.

He tied the sack to Cora's saddle along with one bedroll and then looked at his brother. "Set the lantern down and then tie the bag to the other side of the mule."

"What about me? Do I get tied to her too?" Rory didn't even know what she was saying but the words tumbled out of her mouth anyway.

The ranger pushed his hat back. "Are you funning with me?"

She shook her head. "I don't think I've ever felt less like funning."

"Let's get you up on your mule."

"Her name is Cora."

"Of course it is. Now shut up and let me help you."

She managed not to squeak when he picked her up and deposited her on the saddle. Cora shifted and shied away from Caleb.

"Easy girl." Rory patted her furry neck. "We're going for a ride and I need you to help me."

Caleb checked his horse's saddle, then he secured the second bedroll to his. At least they would all have a blanket and some food. He spoke softly to his brother, then blew out the lantern. She was glad of the darkness. It embraced her, kept her from looking at the ashy remains of the house and smithy she had called home most of her life. A lump formed in her throat and she had difficulty swallowing the emotion behind it. Her father would understand why she was leaving and would approve of keeping safe. Yet it hurt to leave. A lot.

The two Grahams walked to the big quarter horse and within seconds, were both seated and ready to ride. The boy had the same grace as his brother. It was obviously a family trait. Rory didn't have much grace. Instead she had a healthy dose of stubborn, muscle and sass. It was all she had and she clung to it.

She looked up at them from her perch on the mule. "Where are we going?"

"We're going to the Circle Eight."

Rory vaguely remembered the name but didn't bother to ask any more questions. They started moving southeast with the moon guiding their path. Minutes blurred together and hours passed where she could only focus on staying on Cora. Her side throbbed right along with her head. At least when her hands started itching, she had something else to think about.

The night grew darker and deeper as they rode together. Cora was a good mule and she followed the horse's path without hesitation. Rory had ridden her and used her for transporting heavier items to clients. Sturdy and strong, just like her owner. They were a match for sure.

Sweat trickled down her back and although the temperature had dropped, she was hot. Really hot. She wiped her forehead with her sleeve but it made little difference.

"Ranger." Her voice was weak as a kitten and he didn't hear her. "Ranger." This time she managed to bark his name loud enough.

He pulled the horse to a stop. "What?"

"Not to interrupt your grand escape plan but I have bad news." Rory started to shiver and knew she had little time before she wouldn't be able to stay upright.

"Do you need to piss?" The ranger certainly had a way with women.

"No, jackass, I have a fever." Her teeth started to chatter and she considered untying the bedroll behind her.

"Shit."

Rory chuckled rustily. "Damn right. I won't last much longer."

"Let's find shelter then. We'll get some water into you and see if we can break that fever." He turned right then left. "If I'm right, we're not too far from some caves. That might be our only choice."

95

A cave sounded great, provided she didn't have to sit on the mule any longer. She couldn't manage to endure any more constant jarring and bumping on her bony backside, along with the pain in her side and head. The day had been one of the hardest of her life, certainly one of the hardest physically. She needed it to be over. Although it was past midnight for sure, it seemed like a never-ending day.

Before she knew what was happening, Caleb had lifted her out of the saddle. Her head lolled and she scrambled for purchase on his shirt. When she'd seen him wearing Horatio's shirt, her body had tightened almost painfully. He filled that shirt out much better than her late husband ever had. She was glad he could use it. Truthfully, she should have given the clothes away before now, but she hadn't. Perhaps something told her another man would come into her life and need them. Or her fever was boiling her brain.

He walked up a small hill, followed by Benjy, who lit the lantern and led the horses behind them.

"Did you find the caves?" She slurred her words, worse than she expected. "Oh, no. I'm slurry."

"Yep, I reckon you are. Hang on, Rory. We're almost there." He held onto her, heavyweight and all, keeping her safe as he climbed the hill.

The mouth of the cave yawned open, an inky blackness even darker than the night around them. Benjy scrambled ahead with the lantern, tying the horse and mule to the bushes. He took the bedrolls and disappeared inside. Caleb ducked down a foot to walk in with Rory still in his arms.

"You know it's very strange that you've carried me twice when I don't even know anything about you." Rory was glad the cave was dry and didn't smell of bat shit. Anything but bats.

"Yes, you do. You know I have seven brothers and sisters. You also know I am a ranger and my horse's name is Justice."

Her head started to spin and she hung onto him. "Those are just facts. I mean I don't know what's in your heart."

He stumbled a bit then righted himself before they both fell. "Nobody does."

She didn't have time to respond to his cryptic remark before he laid her down on a bedroll. Finally still, she huffed out a sigh. Her eyes stung and she told herself it wasn't tears. She was tired, that was all. There was no way Rory Foster would be crying.

"Go check the other caves to see if there's room for the animals." Caleb spoke softly to Benjy.

She heard the boy's feet slapping the cave floor as he ran out, leaving her alone with his brother. Caleb's hand stroked her face.

"You're hot."

"Mmm, knew it was coming." She leaned into his touch, now strangely familiar and comforting.

"It's not good news." He blew out a breath. "We're going to have to hole up here until it passes."

The talons of the fever bit into her, tightening until she had trouble pulling in a breath. Rory didn't want to die in a cave with the ranger and his brother for company. Hell, she didn't want to die at all.

"Don't let me die." The words fell out of her mouth, small and weak. She wanted to shout them.

"I promise I won't. You're too stubborn to die anyway." His thumb caressed her cheek. "It's gonna be a bumpy few days, Aurora."

He was the only person who called her by her given name. She liked the way it rolled off his tongue. It made her feel like Aurora, and not the Rory she'd been for so many years. Like a girl, like a woman. When he leaned over and kissed her forehead, a feeling of being safe washed over her. She had no reason to trust him but she did. Perhaps the fever was affecting her brain.

She found herself sinking down into blackness, unable to fight the sleep that threatened. Her body needed to heal, to gain strength to overcome the fever.

"Fight like I know you can." He kissed her forehead one more time and she surrendered to sleep.

Elizabeth Graham was finishing a few dishes when heard the horses riding hard into the yard. Eva was helping Rebecca with her hair and no one else was about mid-morning. No Texan worth her salt would be unable to take care of her property or herself. She dried her hands and walked to the door. She might be only sixteen but she knew how to use a gun, and the Grahams didn't answer the door to strangers without one.

The shotgun hung above the door, loaded of course, but high enough the younger siblings couldn't hurt themselves. She took it down and opened the door, the gun a welcome weight in her hands. With the muzzle pointed at the ground she walked out onto the front porch.

Six men on horseback waited. Her stomach clenched but she kept her expression cool. At the center of the group was a well-dressed man with a dark brown flat-brimmed hat. He took it off and nodded to her. Although the men around him were dark-haired and browned by the sun, this man had pale skin and dark blond hair. He obviously did no work outside.

"Good morning, miss. My apologies for interrupting your day but I'm looking for someone."

Elizabeth tightened her grip on the gun. "State your business."

His smile made her skin crawl. "I'm looking for Ranger Caleb Graham. I understand this is the family ranch."

She had a feeling whatever this man wanted, it couldn't be good for her brother. Although she wished Matt was there to speak to him, she was capable and strong.

"He doesn't live here. Now be on your way, mister."

The man laughed. "A woman who speaks her mind. I like that. You have the same eyes as Ranger Graham. I think I'm in the right place. Now as soon as you tell me where he is, I can be on my way."

"He doesn't live here. Hasn't for four years. I don't know where he is." She lifted the gun a bit higher. "I told you to be on your way. You're trespassing."

"Do you mind if I look around?" The men started to move, spreading out.

She pulled the shotgun up in an instant, cocked and pointed straight at the stranger. "I do mind. I'm not going to tell you again, mister, get moving."

The man held up his hands, hat dangling from one of them. "She knows how to use the weapon too. You're not married are you?"

Elizabeth didn't answer. She kept her arms and hands as steady as possible. Her aim was pretty damn good. Every one of the Grahams were taught to use weapons. Their Pa and now Matt made sure of that.

"We will leave for now. Your brother took something that belongs to me and I will get it back." He smiled again. "Tell him Pablo Garza is looking for him."

She noted the name didn't quite match the man who looked more like a Tom Johnson than one with a Mexican name. Another unsettling piece of whatever puzzle he was crafting. Whatever Caleb had done, it was big trouble.

"Get moving then. Don't stop until you pass the big banyan tree." She didn't lower the weapon or even blink, although she wanted to puke up breakfast. After they left, she might do that anyway.

Garza put his hat back on his head, keeping his gaze locked with hers. It was unsettling and she wanted to shout at him to stop, but she held her tongue. Silence was a weapon Elizabeth knew how to wield.

"You have beautiful eyes, *niña*. Such a unique color." With that he signaled his men and they rode off, leaving a cloud of dust behind them.

She waved her hands in front of her face to clear the air. Whatever Garza wanted with Caleb, it was bad, really bad. That was a man who took what he wanted, no matter who or what stood in his way.

Elizabeth stood there, gun still at the ready, and watched them ride away until she could only see a puff of dust. Only then did she lower the weapon and go in search of Matt. Caleb was in trouble and they had to help him.

Caleb wiped Rory's body down for the dozenth time in twenty-four hours. Her temperature had finally started to come down, but she'd sweated and burned as the fever ravaged her body. She scratched and bit, fighting him every time he tried to cool her down. The woman would have made a hell of a soldier if she'd been a man. Her arms were muscled and lean, not overly so. He found himself touching her simply to touch her. Not good for a Texas Ranger who needed to be in control, certainly not acceptable, but he couldn't help himself.

He was fascinated by this woman. She was different from any woman he'd ever met, and that was saying a lot. Caleb wasn't one to have ladies in his bed one after the other, but he'd had his fair share of encounters. Never met a woman to make him want to stop for more than a day or two. Now he'd spent the last three days taking care of Rory. Unfortunately she'd been unconscious the entire time.

How could he have developed such an affection for her in four days? Only one of which she actually spoke. Truthfully, he was embarrassed by how much he had come to know her by taking care of her. It was odd and he couldn't have explained it if asked.

He wrung the rag in the makeshift basin made from a concave rock Benjy had found. They had some food left, but not much. He did his best to pour the peach juice down her throat when she would let him. Her cheeks were sunken and he could almost count her ribs. If the fever didn't let loose soon, she wouldn't survive.

It was that thought alone that kept him up all night and all day. He napped when he could. Benjy didn't want to touch her, but he was good at finding what they needed. He was the one who found the rock for the basin, and dry kindling to keep a small fire going. The boy also took care of the animals, cleaning their shit from the cave and foraging for food for them after the feed ran out the day before.

Benjy was a smart one, resourceful as hell, but still silent. It bothered Caleb quite a lot. He hoped his brother would start talking after he was out of Garza's grasp, but it didn't happen. They were lucky to have stayed undiscovered for so long. Caleb fully expected Garza and his men to find them any minute.

Yet three days had passed and still they remained hidden. Garza must've assumed they had kept moving. Caleb had gone back and erased their tracks for at least a mile, leaving nothing for the patron to follow. The ruse had worked well enough to give him time to nurse Rory, or at least try to nurse her. He wasn't sure how good his work was since she hadn't gained consciousness yet.

Benjy crept back into the cave with the canteen. He'd gone to get fresh water from the creek nearby. Caleb took the canteen from him and handed him the rock.

"Go dump this and bring it back quick."

The boy took the makeshift basin without hesitation and left the cave again. Caleb opened the canteen and held Rory's neck, dribbling the water into her mouth. She swallowed, which was a good sign. He stared down at her face and wished she would open her eyes. He missed her amber gaze, full of spark and fire.

"Don't give up on me, Aurora. You're stronger than that. Hell, woman, you tried to kill me with your forge. You can't give up because a tree decided to poke a hole in you." Her eyes flew open and he almost dropped her head in surprise. "Rory?"

"Ranger." Her voice was a raspy whisper.

He was ridiculously pleased to see her awake and aware. "You done lying around and being lazy?"

She blinked. "Just about."

He grinned. "Good because I was hoping someone else might cook."

"I don't cook." She shifted beneath the blanket and grimaced. "Have you been kicking me?"

"You caught me. I thought it would be fun to kick you while you were unconscious." He held the canteen up to her lips. "Now drink. You've barely had enough to wet your lips."

She obeyed, probably because she was too tired to fight with him. After she'd had enough, he pulled it away. Her eyes drooped as she looked at him.

"I have trouble showing appreciation." Her confession surprised him.

"I noticed."

"You would mention it too." She closed her eyes. "Thank you."

"You're welcome." He smoothed her limp hair off her forehead. "Now first thing we're going to do is get you clean, because woman, you stink."

"Jackass."

"I aim to please."

The corner of her mouth twitched. "I think I'd like to get clean. I can smell myself."

Caleb barked a laugh. "I guess that's when you know you need to find soap." He missed sparring with her. It was good, better than good, to have her back. Damn he might even say something stupid to her. Thankfully, his brother saved him from making a fool of himself.

Benjy came back in with the empty basin and set it down. Caleb reached over to pat his shoulder but his brother pulled away. He fisted his hand and held back the curse that bubbled up his throat.

"She's awake."

Benjy's brows went up. He peered at her and jumped when her eyes popped open. She gifted him with a small smile. Caleb told himself he wasn't jealous.

"Thank you. I know you helped." Her face had softened.

Benjy nodded and sat beside her. He seemed to need to be near her, to make sure she was okay. He had lost his mother so long ago, perhaps he saw Rory as the maternal figure he needed. That housekeeper Bernadette certainly wasn't it—she'd been too stiff and bossy. The lady blacksmith wasn't a typical mother figure but she was a good person. Perhaps her influence would pull Benjy out of his silence.

"We'll need to leave as soon as possible. Tonight if you're up for it."

She frowned. "How long have we been here?"

"Three days."

Rory's eyes widened. "And Garza hasn't found us."

It wasn't a question. "No, we've been lucky but that's gonna run out sooner or later." He looked at Benjy. "Gather up as many of those berries you found and whatever else you scrounged. Let's get everything ready to leave as soon as we can. Rory is going to want to get cleaned up so wait until I come get you before you come back in."

The boy nodded and took a rag and the empty saddlebags, then disappeared back out the entrance to the cave. Caleb turned to find Rory staring at him, her expression dark.

"You took a big chance stopping for so long. Why?"

How could he explain when he didn't understand? "We need to stay together to survive."

"I don't understand." Her brows deepened.

Caleb leaned down and kissed her lips. She gasped in surprise, then returned the kiss. When he straightened up, she touched her lips, now moist with their kisses. What the hell was he doing? She didn't say anything and neither did he. An uncomfortable silence pulsed between them.

"Can you help me wash up?" Her soft question knocked him sideways.

"Are you sure?" Foolish man that he was, he actually asked.

Her lashes swept down and he was struck again by how feminine she was when she wasn't swinging a hammer or shouting at him. Aurora wasn't classically beautiful, but all her parts came together to form a perfect harmony. One that sang to him.

"I'm sure. I need to get clean and you don't seem to have anything else to do." Her silly smirk made him chuckle. "I'd like some coffee too while you're at it."

He had to move away before he kissed her again. Damn, even his dick had woken up, straining at his trousers like it hadn't ever seen a woman before. Rory was quiet as he stoked up the small fire and put the last of his coffee into the pot. Doing a mundane chore helped him get a bit of control back. Lack of sleep was affecting him. That was the explanation.

While the coffee heated, he took the rock bowl and set it on the other edge of the fire and poured water into it. It might not be the prettiest way to heat water but it might work. He couldn't think about the fact he would soon be washing a very awake Rory. If he did, he might forget what he was doing and act even more foolish. Perhaps blurt words he shouldn't be thinking or feeling.

He used one of the shirts to carry the rock bowl over to her and set it down. Her eyes were closed but he didn't think she was sleeping. The coffee bubbled and he poured some into the tin cup he carried with him. He picked up the sliver of soap and the rag, then sat down beside her again.

"You're staring at me." She opened one eye and speared him with her gaze.

"I'm waiting for you to drink your coffee, your majesty." He held up the cup and she looked surprised to see it.

"I didn't think you had any coffee."

"I always have some staples with me. I'm on the trail most days. What kind of ranger would I be if I wasn't prepared?" He peered at her, looking for signs of the fever. "Can you sit up?"

She pushed with her hands slowly, and painfully if he were any judge, until she was half-sitting against the saddle behind her. This time the sweat on her brow was from the effort, not from a fever.

"I could have helped." He handed her the cup.

She accepted it with shaking hands. "I wouldn't have asked."

He clucked his tongue in annoyance. The woman was stubborn as the damn mule. Perhaps that was why she kept the beast.

"Drink up so I can get you clean. We need to leave in a few hours." He dipped the rag in the water, pleased to find it was still hot. The rock bowl kept it warmer than a regular basin. Too bad there wasn't a smidge of room in his saddlebags or he'd take it with him.

She slurped down the coffee noisily then handed him the cup. "That was better than sex." Caleb almost choked on his own spit. She shook her head at him. "What? I was being honest."

Rory was a widow and she obviously had been with her husband. The fact she talked about sex was shocking. What other women did that? None that he knew of. Not even his outspoken sister did.

"Don't you like sex?"

This time his mouth actually dropped open.

She smiled widely. "I didn't think I would ever shock you, Ranger."

Caleb shook his head. "I don't think I've ever met a woman like you."

"I'll take that as a compliment." She yawned widely.

"I, uh, guess we should get you washed up then." He didn't know what he'd do once he actually touched her. Not after the mention of sex and enjoying it. "Can you unbutton your shirt?"

She did as he asked, revealing her alabaster skin, large breasts and light pink nipples. He managed to swallow while she waited, her expression unreadable. He wrung the rag out and swiped the soap across it.

Caleb lifted her arm and began to wash her, telling himself it was like washing up his little sisters ten years ago. It was a far cry from brotherly duty though. He felt every stroke as though it was his hand touching her and not a rag. His body pulsed with need yet he continued on, washing her entire upper body, then rinsing her.

"You're sweating, Ranger. You might need to wash up yourself." Her voice had dropped into a husky whisper. He told himself it was the water, the cool air, or the rag that made her nipples hard. There was no way she was aroused.

"I'm not a saint, Aurora. I have needs like any man." He met her gaze and let her see the hunger that prowled beneath the surface. She would either accept it or turn away.

"Take my drawers off and finish the job."

Sweet Jesus. He dropped the rag into the bowl, his dick painfully hard.

"Are you sure?"

"You keep asking me that, I'm going to think you're not interested." She cupped her breasts and held them up.

It took sincere willpower not to pluck those dark pink nipples, hard and tight, a mere foot from his salivating tongue. He reached for her drawers, knowing he was about to cross a line with Rory and was helpless to stop.

She lifted her hips as he slid the plain cotton fabric down, revealing her pussy, covered with dark brown curls. He swallowed the need to taste her and focused on getting her clean first. Now his strokes were more sure, long sweeping ones designed to torture both of them. By the time he reached her feet, he had almost given up seven times.

Her skin had heated beneath his touch, the small hairs rising to meet him. He put the rag in the bowl and then finally touched her.

Really touched her with his hands. He slid his fingers up her legs, reveling in the softness of her skin. She was softer than flower petals, exquisitely so. Her muscles were sculpted from the finest artisan.

When he finally reached her core, he dipped his fingers into her wetness and groaned. He circled her clit with his thumb and thrust two fingers into her warm core.

"Oh, that's better than a bath." She hissed out a breath.

Caleb kissed her stomach all the way up her sweet smelling skin until he reached her breasts. The two things that had haunted him since the second he'd seen them days ago. They were perfect, round and large. The puckered nipples begged for his mouth so he obliged them.

He lapped at the right, nibbling and sucking while his hand continued to pleasure her. She growled her approval, arching up into his mouth. His mouth closed around her nipple and he sucked hard, pulling her deep.

She made a gasping sound and her pussy closed around his fingers. A keening cry, barely a whisper, greeted his ears. She scratched at his shoulders, her body shuddering and clenching as she found her pleasure. He gentled his movements, bringing her down from the heights.

Caleb finally kissed her and she wrapped her arms around him. This time there was no surprise, no fumbling kisses. It was hard and deep, tongues clashing and rasping against each other in tune with his pulse. He wanted to plunge into her, lose himself in the depths of the hot pussy he'd just brought to orgasm.

When he came up for air, she made a mewling sound of protest, but let him loose. He looked down into her face, never more pretty than she was at that moment, sated and full of bliss. Her eyes were at half-mast and she couldn't quite stifle a yawn.

He would hate himself for this but he released her and sat up. She frowned.

"What are you doing?"

"If we do this, Aurora, I want you completely awake when we do."

"I am awake." Another yawn.

"Barely. Take the next few hours to sleep. When we ride it'll be hard. I don't want to contribute to your, ah, discomfort in that area." He danced around the words, trying to maintain his status as a gentleman, or something like that.

She smiled wanly. "There is a good thought underneath that ranger jackass."

"Sometimes I surprise myself." He kissed her forehead then helped pull her drawers up, brushing her fingers away when she tried to button her shirt. "Now sleep."

She took his hand and kissed the palm. "Thank you, Caleb."

It was the first time she'd said his name. He found he liked the sound of it on her tongue. Foolish man that he was, he held her hand until she slept, then sat there a few minutes longer watching her sleep.

Caleb finally got up and went in search of Benjy, knowing he left a piece of himself behind in that cave, tucked into the hands of a lady blacksmith.

CHAPTER SEVEN

Although she still dreamed of Caleb's touch, his callused hands and talented tongue, she still wanted to punch him. He drove them relentlessly, barely allowing time for necessities. He had warned her it would be a hard ride, but her body was still weakened by the wound and the subsequent fever. She was no weakling and could endure quite a lot.

What she couldn't endure was the ranger ignoring her requests one more time. She had to stop and take care of business or she would piss herself right there on Cora. Benjy had long since fallen asleep, drooping in front of his brother on the saddle. The sun painted the sky pink and orange as it rose in the east.

"If you don't let me stop, I'm going to hit you with my hammer," she said through clenched teeth. "I mean it."

He didn't even turn his head. "This area is too open. There is a line shack up ahead about two hours. Belonged to a rancher who lost everything about five years ago. Land has gone to hell but the shack is still there."

"Two hours? I will not mess my drawers because you don't want the world to see my bare ass." She pulled Cora to a stop and managed to slide off the saddle although her legs quaked. A couple bushes nearby were all she needed. She managed to pull her trousers down and squat when the ranger appeared in front of her. "You want to watch me piss?"

His cheeks flushed, which she found amusing as hell. "No, I want to spank your ass for being so stubborn."

"Get in line. My father did it, so did my husband. Nobody is going to smack the stubborn outta me." She held her own, never giving into any man. Sooner or later they accepted her the way she was and stopped trying to change her. The ranger was a slow learner.

"Dammit, woman. You try my patience. Do you know that Garza could have a sharp shooter ready to take your pretty head off your shoulders at any moment?" His face was tight with anger and what she would only assume was worry.

His words sank in and she had to take a minute to finish her business before she spoke. No one had ever accused her of being pretty nor shown such concern for her. It was another piece of the puzzle that made up Caleb Graham.

She used a few leaves to finish and then stood up. After she buttoned her trousers, she walked back to Cora with the ranger hot on her tail. His hot breath nearly set her neck on fire. When she reached the mule, she whirled around to face him.

"You called me pretty."

He blinked quickly, then opened his mouth and closed it. He cleared his throat before he spoke. "Nobody ever call you pretty before?"

She gestured to her trousers and her shorn hair. "Not hardly. I am plain as dirt, Ranger. If you think any different, then you might need spectacles."

He shook his head. "I don't think so. You might be the one who needs to see better." With that cryptic remark he took her arm and scooped her into his arms to deposit her onto Cora's back.

She bent down to whisper as he took his hands away. "We're not done talking about this."

The ranger, of course, didn't respond. She wanted to kick him but he was already vaulting back onto his horse with more grace than she had in her little finger. They started riding again until the sun was bright in the sky. By then Rory's ass was numb. Her entire lower half was numb and she wasn't sure if it was a good thing or not. If she couldn't feel then she didn't feel pain but she also wouldn't feel a snake sliding up her trouser leg either.

True enough, a small shack appeared in the distance. Half taken over by the trees that surrounded it, it was about the same size as her house. A lump formed in her throat at the thought she might not ever see her own small shack again. However, she had made the choice to help him because it was the right thing to do. Benjy didn't deserve what had happened to him but if her actions helped right a wrong, then she couldn't regret it.

Caleb dismounted and snatched his brother off the saddle

quickly. He knocked on his forehead. "You awake in there?"

The boy pushed his hand away and stumbled. To his credit, the ranger didn't reach to help him. He appeared to be giving Benjy time to wake up and find his feet, just as a big brother would.

"I'll take care of the animals. You take your bedroll and go on inside. Make sure there's no critters before you lay down to get some sleep."

Benjy took the proffered blanket and opened the door to the shack. He waved his hand in front of his face before he stepped inside. While he was busy checking for unwanted houseguests, Rory was going to have trouble dismounting. It stuck in her craw to ask for help but she was going to have to swallow her pride.

"Ranger."

Caleb glanced up from unsaddling his gelding. "What?"

"I, uh, don't seem to be able to get down. I need help." The words were like castor oil on her tongue, slippery with a bad taste. "Please."

He took off his hat and grinned at her. She was torn between appreciating how handsome the man was and being annoyed with his cocky attitude. He set the saddle down on a rock hidden by some bushes, then secured the horse to a tree nearby.

"I'll be right back, boy. I've got to rescue the damsel."

"I'm not a damsel." She scowled at him. The man spent far too much time enjoying her discomfort. "And this isn't a rescue."

"Oh that's entirely not true." He sauntered up and put his hand on her thigh. She stared at the strong fingers, the callused appendage that had brought her to the heights of pleasure. Her body jumped to attention, and blood started flowing to her nether region. "You are most definitely a damsel."

He put his hands around her waist and picked her up off the saddle as though she weighed no more than a bedroll. She knew he was strong, of course, but this time his strength echoed through her body. Damned if she didn't want to feel all of him without the encumbrance of clothes. His hands stayed at her waist as feeling flooded back into her legs, the pins and needles making her wince.

The door to the shack banged open and Benjy stepped out. He had a few critters in his hand, none of which Rory wanted to see, that he tossed into the woods. With his bedroll tucked under one arm, he clomped back into the cabin no doubt to lay down to sleep.

"I'm a woman."

"I definitely remember that." He didn't move away and she found herself leaning toward him. His blue-green eyes were full of heat and she ached to feel that burn.

"And I don't appreciate being compared to a simpering idiot like a damsel."

Up close and in the dappled sunshine, Caleb Graham was beautiful. A few scars here and there on his face just added to the natural handsomeness. She could hardly believe he found her pretty. Rory decided he was funning with her about that. Nobody had ever accused her of being pretty and she damn sure would have a hard time believing it. She had seen her reflection before, and she'd also seen pretty girls. They didn't match.

His hand trailed down her shoulder and arm until he found her hand. Then he raised it to his lips and kissed the back. "Oh I don't think being a damsel is a bad thing. They're not all simpering idiots. Some of them are strong and capable." His lips traveled to her palm and then up her wrist. Fluttering commenced in her stomach as a throb beat low in her belly.

"What are you doing?" She sounded breathless, dammit.

His gaze flickered to hers. "Seducing you. Is it working?"

Yes.

"Depends on what you want." She hedged away from the truth, unable to admit she wanted to drop her drawers and invite him to plunder.

"I want to finish what we started last night." He leaned into her, his hard body trapping her against the mule. Her hands itched to touch him but she held back. She didn't want to appear too anxious.

"What about Benjy?" She glanced at the shack, unable to do anything with him if there was any danger of the boy seeing them. He'd already been traumatized enough.

"He's sound asleep by now." Caleb nodded to the woods. "I'm sure I can find a shady spot to, ah, relax."

She almost grabbed his hand and dragged him. Truth was, she hadn't been anxious to have sex with Horatio. It was mediocre at best, and she was left feeling restless and unsated. She had used her own hand to find pleasure until now. Until Caleb had used his to bring her the most pleasure she'd ever experienced. She wanted more.

"We should bring the bedrolls." She turned to get hers when he stopped her.

"Trust me."

This time, she didn't deny it but she didn't confirm it either. Somehow in the last four days, this ranger who had come to her land to throw her off it had become her friend of sorts, a man she trusted with her life. Rory raised her brows and smiled instead.

He smiled back and took her hand. His thumb swept back and forth across her hand, leaving a trail of tingles in its wake. They traveled straight up her wrist to her arm to her entire body. Her nipples peaked beneath her shirt, rubbing against the cotton with each step she took. It was erotic in the most mundane setting imaginable. Excitement raced through her and she could only wait impatiently for the pleasure she knew was forthcoming.

Around the back of the shack were three trees whose trunks were wrapped around each other, forming a natural seat. Vines grew around them, giving the seat a cushion of green. It almost looked like a small bed.

"That's the most amazing thing I've ever seen." She approached the trees, enchanted by the unusual sight.

"I spotted this a few years ago when I was first working as a ranger. Shame that no one lives nearby to use it." He raised one brow. "Then again, we've got privacy because no one is around."

Her heart thumped but she kept her expression neutral. However she couldn't stop the urge to crawl up onto the tree bed. It wasn't as soft as a feather bed but it wasn't too far from a straw mattress. She laid back, her hands behind her head, and stared up into the tops of the trees. It was so peaceful, with birds chirping, squirrels chattering and bees droning nearby.

Caleb crawled up beside her and lay back, mimicking her pose. "It's nice, isn't it?"

"Mmmm, it's perfect." She closed her eyes and breathed in fresh air. It was wonderful to not be riding Cora. Her body had barely recovered from the injury and fever. She was exhausted from the ride, but the promise of Caleb's touch kept her body on edge.

He leaned up on one elbow and looked down at her. "I'm going to agree with you on that."

Her eyes flew open and she tried to read his expression. What did he mean? He was staring at her when he said it. Did that mean he thought she was perfect? Ridiculous thought.

"Are we going to do anything other than admire the trees?"

Caleb barked a laugh. "You are one of a kind, Aurora." He bent down and kissed her, his lips hot and smooth against hers. He kissed and nibbled his way across her mouth then back. His tongue lapped at the seam of her lips until she opened her mouth, then she was lost.

His mouth fused with hers, the heat from their kisses alone enough to singe her eyebrows. Then his hands start moving, sliding up and down her body, sneaking beneath her shirt and trousers, caressing skin and leaving goosebumps behind.

Oh yes, Caleb was going to give her the most she'd ever received from a man. She laid there, enjoying every second of his touch, her body happy to be off the mule and pleased to be finding pleasure with a man.

His nimble fingers unbuttoned her shirt, spreading it wide for his mouth to feast on her aching breasts. His tongue laved and nibbled, then he pulled the nipple into his mouth and sucked hard. She closed her eyes and let herself give up any pretenses. This was what she wanted.

When he lifted his hot mouth, the breeze made her nipple pucker more. He removed her trousers with little effort, then she heard the sound of him shucking his own clothes. She opened her eyes and looked.

Oh my.

Caleb Graham was blessed with a classically beautiful body. Honey touched skin stretched over muscle and bone in a perfect balance. His chest was covered in whorls of light brown hair, circling flat nipples and leading down his belly to that which stood at attention between his thighs. His cock rose from the nest of curls cupping the staff. Oh yes, he had been granted more than his share of gorgeous maleness.

She swallowed hard, knowing she probably looked foolish with wide eyes and quite possibly drooling.

"Like what you see?" He grinned, unrepentant and full of pride.

"As a matter of fact, yes." Her response knocked a bit of the cocky out of his expression. "I'd like to experience it up close though."

He shook his head. "You will continue to surprise me, right?"

"I hope so, otherwise my plan is foiled." She crooked her finger at him. "I don't want to be lying out here buck naked all day, Ranger.

Let's get busy."

"Never let it be said I didn't do what you told me to." He climbed up onto the bed of tree trunks.

As soon as his body made contact with hers, she gasped at the sensation. Pure heat, hard and intense, washed over her. He nudged her legs apart and his staff tapped against the side of her thigh. She was wetter than she'd ever been, eager to feel him within her, rubbing and thrusting.

Up close, his beautiful eyes were like the Gulf of Mexico after a storm. Now they were dilated with arousal. She cupped his cheeks and pulled him down for a kiss. As his mouth plundered hers again, she wiggled her hips a bit. He crept closer, the head of his cock teasing her entrance.

She groaned and yanked at his shoulders although it was more like a scratch given her strength at the moment. He slid in an inch then back out, once, twice, three times. Her body clenched, trying to hold onto him but he slipped out each time. It was an incredible tease and she loved every second of it.

Soon he was going deeper, lingering longer, thrusting harder. She met him stroke for stroke, her body tingling. He let her mouth loose and kissed his way down her neck to her breasts. The man certainly liked her nipples. Yet when his teeth closed around the right one, she was surprised to find an orgasm building inside her.

She tugged at his hair, needing more, harder, faster. He picked up the pace, pounding into her as he continued to make her nipple sing with his teeth and tongue. Then she fell off a precipice, her body alive with a million points of light at once. She scratched at his back, her voice stolen by the waves of ecstasy crashing through her.

He grunted, then buried himself deep within, pulling her along for another round of pulses of pleasure. She could hardly breathe, much less think, floating in a sea of what she could only identify as bliss mixed with a bit of joy. His weight pressed down on her and she pinched his arm.

"You're crushing me, Ranger."

He rolled off her, landing on his side. "I think you can call me Caleb."

She ignored him and focused on the floating sensation she had found. It was incredible, more than she ever imagined it could be like between a man and a woman. Horatio had been a bumbling fool with a good heart, but Caleb had brought her to a place she never knew existed.

Her heart fluttered and thumped once, hard. She was afraid the ranger had come to mean much more than a man. Now that she'd had a taste of his passion, knew what lurked beneath the hard exterior, she found he was a man she could fall in love with. Something she never, ever expected.

When the breeze caressed her skin again, she shivered, but this time it wasn't from pleasure or from cold. She was scared.

Caleb slipped his clothes back on and then helped Rory do the same. She could barely keep her eyes open by the time he finished buttoning her shirt. Although she protested, he picked her up from their leaf-lined bed in the trunks of the trees and carried her to the shack. Benjy was a lump in the corner, snoring softly.

He laid Rory beside the boy, tucking the bedroll around her. She looked up at him with her amber eyes half-open. He saw shadows of something in her expression but the gloom of the shack didn't give him a clear view. Then she rolled over and pillowed her head on her arm. Within seconds, she slept.

The ride had been hard on the two of them, but especially Rory. She was weak from the fever and wound, and what had he done? Fucked her in the woods without regard for her exhaustion or her healing body. He was a rutting fool, driven by his base instincts to own the woman.

He shouldn't have touched her but hell, she invited him to. Nearly insisted he take her. Now he regretted it. At least part of him did. The other part, well, it was running wild and doing stupid things like craving Rory's company and falling in love with her.

If asked, he would deny it, but if he were brutally honest with himself, he had fallen for the gruff lady blacksmith. The unusual, strong, amber-eyed vixen had completely bewitched him. Now he was helpless to stop the downward slide he found himself in.

He walked out to the animals and led them to the same spot behind the shack. The beasts immediately started feasting on the sweet, succulent grasses growing in the shade of the trees. He unsaddled them and rubbed them down. They had served their humans well and deserved a rest too. Caleb found a bucket without a handle half-buried in the dirt. He wiggled it out and followed the sound to a small creek nearby. After rinsing the bucket, he filled it and carried it back to the animals.

The bucket leaked like a sieve, but it was enough to satisfy Justice and then Cora. Satisfied with their comfort, Caleb made sure nothing was visible from the trail, including the saddles before he headed back into the shack. His body was used to being in the saddle for days but he was unaccountably tired. Perhaps it was the worry over his brother and Rory, combined with several days without sleep catching up to him.

He crept into the shack, his bedroll hanging from his hands. When he closed the door, the gloom of the cabin closed around him. Dust motes danced in the sunlight coming through the warped boards, giving him enough light to see the two people sleeping in the corner. Right now they were the most important things in his life, perhaps forever.

After spreading out the bedroll beside Rory, he laid down and closed his eyes. The last thing he remembered was the look on her face when she found pleasure in his arms. It had been the most beautiful sight he'd ever seen. He hoped to see it again soon.

Caleb woke in an instant. He was momentarily disoriented until he remembered the little shack. It was pure dark outside, which meant they'd slept a long time, more than the four hours he wanted to. He got to his feet and rolled up the blanket, then opened the door to let in some fresh air. The stale dust in the shack had invaded his mouth and nose.

He squatted down beside Benjy and shook his shoulder until the boy opened his eyes. To Caleb's dismay, he shrank away, fear in his gaze.

"It's okay. It's me, Caleb." He forced himself to smile and keep a safe distance. "Do you remember?"

After a few painful moments, Benjy relaxed his grip on the blanket and nodded. Caleb got to his feet and moved to Rory. He had to give the boy a moment to get his bearings. Fury warred within his heart, as a brother and as a ranger, for whoever had done dark deeds to make a ten-year-old boy afraid of his brother. It made him sick to swallow the rage.

He gently touched her face, her warm, soft skin still surprising him. She was a mixture of brash strength and feminine wiles.

"Rory, it's time to wake up."

No movement.

"Rory."

Nothing.

He didn't want to shout and gain attention from anyone or anything outside, but he had to get her up. Whatever Justice was doing, he also had to check on the animals. There was no time to fuss around with her delicate woman sensibilities.

Caleb frowned at her and then decided to do whatever he had to do. So he kissed her.

Her eyes flew open and her fist followed, slamming into his jaw with more force than he expected. He fell back on his ass, his face throbbing from the blow. She sat up, clenching the blanket, her eyes wild. When she saw him, a laugh burst from her throat.

"It's not funny." He got to his knees then to his feet. Damned if he didn't feel a bit lightheaded from the punch. The woman had fists like her hammer.

She pulled the blanket up to her mouth to muffle the sound, but he heard it anyway. In a grumpy mood, he left the shack. At least Justice wouldn't belt him for waking him up, not that he would kiss the damn horse.

He found a raccoon sniffing around the animals, scratching at the bucket and being a nuisance. The gelding tried to stop it but the critter kept scooting out of the way. Caleb growled at the masked animal and it turned tail and ran. Obviously some critters were rightfully afraid of him, unlike a certain female who had punched him.

After a few minutes of saddling the horse and mule, he had calmed down some. It was no use getting upset at her, even if she was amused by his reaction. She had swung on instinct, not at him. He had woken her abruptly and she defended herself. That was all of it. He had no reason to be upset but he was. It scratched at his pride that she'd gotten the better of him. It had been quite some time since Caleb had ended up at the losing end of a fist. He'd had plenty of chances to throw punches in his career as a ranger and as a Graham brother.

Yet she'd knocked him down with one blow.

He led the animals to the front of the shack and took a few minutes to listen to the sounds of the night. Nothing unusual to alert him to anyone else around except the usual night creatures. It was good to hear their song since they wouldn't sing if danger came in the form of a two-legged kind.

Benjy and Rory stood side by side, the bedrolls in their arms. Both silent and wide eyed, waiting for him. It was the first time he noted the boots she wore. They were enormous, likely had belonged to her husband. Caleb had forgotten hers had been taken at the Garza hacienda. He should have thought to get her new footwear. Instead she took care of herself, which didn't surprise him in the least. He took the bedrolls and secured them to the back of the saddles.

"We stayed here too long but I reckon we all needed sleep." He gestured to the horse and mule. "I know you're probably hungry but we'll eat as we ride."

Rory nodded then whispered to Benjy. He hopped into the saddle and waited. Rory walked a bit more slowly to Cora. She got herself into the saddle, albeit with less grace than the boy. No doubt she was sore from more than just the injury.

Caleb told himself she was a grown woman and knew what she was doing when she initiated sex with him. As a gentleman, he should have said no. But as a man, he had said, "Hell yes!" and taken what she offered.

"Is it safe for the animals to keep riding at night?" Rory asked in a husky voice that made the small hairs on his arm stand up. Damn he was a fool.

"They did fine last night. Besides, Justice is used to it and can pick his way across any terrain. The mule followed him and I expect she'll do the same tonight." They hadn't made very good time at the pace they had to keep to ride in the dark but people were unlikely to spot them. Staying unseen was worth the loss of speed.

"Not all females are as docile."

Her quip made him smile but he didn't respond. He kneed Justice into motion and they set off into the night.

"How far have we come and how far until we get where we're going?" Her voice carried to him on a breeze.

"We've come maybe fifty miles. Three times that many to go."

He heard her groan above the sound of the crickets singing. Two hundred miles was a long distance for anyone to travel, especially a woman not used to riding. The trousers helped and they framed her ass so well he had trouble keeping his hands off it. Now he knew why women didn't wear trousers. Men would never get any work done for thinking about a female's ass. It would be chaos.

They traveled in silence for some time, much to Caleb's delight. He was used to being alone and having a woman's chatter changed things. Hell, he'd left the Circle Eight to escape the constant chatter and bickering amongst his siblings, and the girls were the worst. Now Matt had to go and add two more females to the mix. The twins were cute as buttons but they did talk faster than a hummingbird's wings.

Much as he tried to deny it, he did miss them. Growing up in a house with eight children was an adventure in itself. Being away from them for four years had been lonely. He definitely enjoyed the silence but at the same time, he was isolated and had no one to talk to or laugh with. To his shame, he hadn't been home more than a handful of times until he hardly recognized the younger girls. Elizabeth in particular looked just like Ma and had the quiet strength their mother had carried.

Meeting Rory had started a chain of events he couldn't stop. He'd found his brother, nearly fallen in love, broken the law and was now on the run from a crazy blond *patron* who called himself Pablo Garza. Where did he head when all this happened? The Circle Eight.

Home.

Family.

Caleb hadn't known how much he had grown a shell around himself until that moment. He'd blocked out friendships with other rangers, refused any kind of long-term female relationship, and spent time patting himself on the back for escaping from the drudgery at the ranch.

He really was a fool of the highest caliber. Family was what mattered and he'd been a selfish young buck with something to prove. Now he was a man who recognized the most important thing in the world was what he pushed aside for his own benefit.

When his brother-in-law Brody quit the rangers, Caleb thought he had lost his mind. Nothing was more exciting or appealing than carrying a gun in the name of Texas. After all this time, Caleb understood why he'd done it. And he also recognized he wanted to quit himself.

The assignment to evict a squatter named Foster had been his last one. He would travel to headquarters and turn in his badge as soon as he had Rory and Benjy safely tucked away at the Circle Eight. And, of course, after he had taken care of Pablo Garza. The man would be relentless in his pursuit, of that Caleb had no doubt. However, the *patron* didn't know what Caleb was capable of, or the Graham family.

They didn't know the meaning of surrender.

That left the future wide open for Caleb. He wanted to live at the Circle Eight again, to wake up in the morning and shovel horse shit before taking care of the herd. He wanted to battle Mother Nature and his sisters on a regular basis. He wanted to see his sisters and brothers grow up, to know his nieces and future nephews, and most of all, he wanted to do it with Rory by his side.

The thought startled him so much the horse felt it and tossed his head in protest. Caleb couldn't believe he had decided to make Rory a permanent part of his life. He had found a partner and his heart had made up his mind to keep her.

Well, hell. She'd probably kick him in the balls and tell him to go scratch. However if he didn't ask, he would regret it for the rest of his life. Now probably wasn't the best time, however, since they were running for their lives and all. He would have to pick the right moment to ask her, one that didn't involve furtive flights into the night, healing wounds, fevers or sex in a tree.

He couldn't shake the notion, though, that she was the right one. He'd heard stories about falling in love and love at first sight. Of course, he had dismissed it all as foolishness concocted by females. Now he understood it and although it scared the piss out of him, he was man enough to admit it. At least to himself.

The moon shone bright in the sky, illuminating a good deal of the trail. He needed to stop his mind from meandering off to Rory. Again. The danger around them hadn't decreased. If anything, it had increased with each passing hour they traveled. He could protect them but not if Garza had a posse chasing them. The unknown threat of what the *patron* would do and when hung over them like the moon in the sky.

Benjy adjusted his position on the saddle behind him and tentatively put his hands on Caleb's waist. That brought a smile to the big brother's face. It was the first time the boy had voluntarily touched him. Thank God he was starting to accept him.

While smiling into the night, Caleb glanced to his right and what he saw stopped him cold. He pulled Justice to a halt and hopped from the saddle. To their credit, Benjy and Rory didn't say a word, although he expected questions. He knelt on the ground and examined the tracks. At least half a dozen horses, possibly eight, had passed this way at a hard speed heading in the same direction as his family's ranch. It could be a coincidence, but these tracks were not there when he rode through a week ago. Not too many folks passed through this way and very few of them were riding like the hounds of hell were chasing them.

If he were to make a bet, he would put his money on Garza and whoever he'd brought with him. Damn. There was a posse and they had already headed to the Circle Eight. His family could take care of themselves but he had brought this trouble on them.

He stood up and looked at Rory. Before he could speak, she seemed to read his thoughts.

"He's already been through here, hasn't he?"

"I reckon he has and headed straight for my family's place." He cursed under his breath. "We've got to pick up the pace and ride hard."

"I thought we had been riding hard already." She frowned.

"No, we've been sauntering. We need to ride like our lives depend on it because they do, and possibly my family's." He ran his hand down his face, the rasp of whiskers loud in the silence that had fallen.

"I can ride just as hard and long as you can." Rory didn't sound like she was boasting. The woman had balls of steel.

"What about the mule?" He had doubts the little beast would last as long as his horse.

"Cora has heart. She will do whatever I ask her."

"It might kill her." He had to be honest and let her make the choice.

"She would give her life for me." Rory's voice cracked. "Your family is worth more than a mule even if I love her."

He wanted to tell her it would be okay. They would triumph in the end and everyone would live. She wasn't a fool and he wasn't a liar. The risks were clear as the moonlight that shone down on them. Garza was rich and had his own small army. They had a woman, a boy who wouldn't speak, a horse and a mule, plus Caleb's guns and Rory's hammers. Pitiful against half a dozen guns, but their little band of misfits also had smarts. And heart. Rory was right on that count, having heart made even a mule into something stronger than normal.

The decision was made and they had to go. Now.

"Then let's get moving." He vaulted back into the saddle then leaned back to speak to Benjy. "You're gonna have to hang on to me as much as you can. If you don't, you might fall off and might get trampled by that mule."

Benjy nodded and carefully placed his arms around Caleb's waist, locking his hands. Satisfied the boy wouldn't fall off, he kneed Justice into motion, waiting for Rory to start moving. When he heard the mule's hooves behind him, he leaned down low and whistled in the gelding's ear.

Soon they were flying through the night, moving as fast as they could to the Circle Eight. He could only hope they would be on time to stop whatever Garza had planned. If anything happened to his family, Caleb would tear the world apart until he hunted down that blond bastard.

They rode hard for two days, only stopping to water the animals or take care of personal needs. When Cora went down, Rory was nearly asleep in the saddle. The sun crept over the horizon, bathing the world around them in orange. She was nodding off, even as they tore across the countryside, the wind whipping around her.

Then the mule with the heart of gold was suddenly gone and Rory flew through the air, too surprised to do anything but tuck into a ball and roll when she landed. She had the wind knocked out of her, but she didn't suffer any injuries other than some scrapes and bruises. Perhaps being half-asleep had saved her life.

She scrambled to her feet and tried to shake off the shock of the fall. Caleb hadn't noticed what happened. He was a hundred yards away and nearly out of sight before she called to him. He immediately pulled his horse to a stop, almost unseating both of them.

Rory turned to Cora and found the mule lying on her side, her chest heaving, mouth frothing. She had given everything to her mistress, riding herself into the ground. Rory dropped to her knees and petted her neck. The mule's brown eye looked up at her, full of pain.

"I'm sorry, girl." She took the canteen off the saddle and dribbled some into the animal's mouth. The froth covered her muzzle, giving her the appearance she'd been eating bubbles instead of dying on her feet.

Caleb's hand landed on her shoulder. He didn't speak platitudes or yell at her for letting the mule get to this desperate point. She appreciated that since her throat was tight with emotion. It was just an animal, but her impending death hit Rory like a fist to her gut. When she'd left her home, she had been half-awake and frightened. Now she was healing and very much conscious of what she'd lost.

Now she was about to lose another connection to her life, a thread broken. She had her father's hammer and tongs, but everything else was gone. Perhaps never to come back into her life again.

"Fucking hell." She pressed her forehead into Cora's neck.

"I like a woman who knows how to cuss." Caleb rubbed her back. "That way I don't have to do it all."

She appreciated his attempt at humor but it didn't make a dent in her grief. Her throat worked to clear the tears she swallowed. She grieved for not only the mule, but for everything she'd lost in her life, which by her count, was a long list.

Benjy knelt beside her, petting Cora's snout. The mule closed her eyes at his touch, and Rory could have kissed the boy for his sympathy. She wasn't surprised to see him comfort the animal; the Graham family obviously cared a great deal about each other and that translated to those around them. She envied their closeness and the abundance of family.

"What do you want to do, Rory?" Caleb rubbed the center of her back.

It was cruel to let Cora suffer, knowing she would never recover from the injuries and damage to her body. The mule was already fifteen years old. She'd been her father's purchase, much to her mother's dismay. Rory had ridden the animal since then and she'd been a companion of sorts.

She would have to say good-bye.

With one last pet for Cora, Rory got to her feet, trembling with regret and sadness. She uncinched the saddle and started pulling things off the mule's body. Benjy helped and she was glad of it. After she made a pile of everything she owned, which was a small pile, she turned to Caleb.

"Put her out of her misery."

His expression was grim as he nodded and pulled his pistol from the holster. She turned away, unable to watch. The shot was muffled but loud enough to make her body jerk in response. It was done. She wrapped her arms around herself and stared down at the remnants of her life sitting in the dirt in the shadows of a Texas night.

Caleb stepped up beside her. "We're about ten miles from my

family's property line. If we stick to the trees, you and Benjy can ride and I'll lead you through." He looked up at the sky. "Sun will rise in about three hours. We can make it."

She nodded, unable to speak.

"We can come back for the saddle and blanket. I'll tuck it over by that big oak. The rest of it we can bring with us."

She appreciated his consideration for her things. Keeping at least most of it with her would help a little. Benjy crept up beside her and leaned against her. She put her arm around him and stood there with the two new men in her life, two Grahams, with a pitiful excuse for a woman and blacksmith between them. Her world couldn't possibly get any worse.

An hour later, she knew she'd been wrong. The sounds of dozens of galloping hooves echoed through the night. Caleb stopped and looked up at her, his face grim.

Garza.

Matt Graham sat on the front porch in a rocking chair, staring off into the night. Ever since Elizabeth had raced up to him the day before talking of a blond man and a posse chasing Caleb, he'd been worried. More than that, he wanted to protect his younger brother but he didn't know how.

He paced the house, then the front porch and the barn, until everyone, including the horses, kicked him out. Now he sat and waited. It stuck in his craw that he did nothing to help. His wife had lectured him on his responsibilities and his children, the ranch and his other siblings. He knew she was right but that didn't make it any easier.

Matt was the oldest, the leader of the Circle Eight and when one of his family was in danger, he couldn't sit idly by and do nothing. He needed to figure out what his brother was doing and how to help him.

The front door creaked and a figure stepped out onto the porch. Elizabeth was the tallest of the girls and easily recognizable even in the gloom of the night.

"Why are you up?"

"Same reason as you I reckon." She sat in the chair beside him and rocked gently. "I don't like doing nothing. You didn't see those men, Matt. They meant to kill him for whatever he did."

She sounded so damn grown up, it made him pause to soak it in.

She'd turned sixteen and that didn't mean she was a woman, but her actions and attitude told him she was.

"I sure as hell don't like it either but I don't even know where to start." He stretched out his legs and crossed his arms. "If I could figure out where he was maybe I could help him."

She was quiet for a few minutes and the sounds of the night echoed around them. "I've been thinking about all the facts and I think we have a place to start."

Matt was immediately on alert. "I'm listening."

"Caleb's assignment to kick the squatter off the land? It was a blacksmith named Foster, about two hundred miles north of here near Marks Creek." Elizabeth sounded quite sure of herself.

"How do you know all that?"

"I went through his saddlebags and found his orders." She didn't sound the least bit apologetic about going through her brother's private things.

"You little sneak." He was both surprised and impressed by what she'd done.

"I didn't want to tell you because I figured you'd be mad but now it's been a whole day and we still haven't seen him." She sighed but it didn't appear to be with remorse. "I want to do something but a woman alone is no match for seven armed riders."

"A woman is no match for one armed rider." Matt wasn't expecting the knuckle punch to his arm. "Ow!"

"Don't ever think a woman can't do something. We are strong, smart and capable, same as any man." She bared her teeth, shining white in the moonlight. Damned if she didn't look as fierce as any soldier he'd met. Where had sweet little Elizabeth gone?

Matt held up his hands. "I promise I won't. Don't punch me again. You only get one free pass in this family."

"Fair enough. But you did deserve it." She crossed her arms. "I figure something happened with the smithy, something that involved this rich blond man. Caleb does what he thinks is right no matter if he puts himself in danger. He always has."

"Truer words were never spoken. He always knew how to find the mischief." Matt had tried to rein in his brother, but there was no stopping a force that strong. "He could be anywhere between there and here. Two hundred miles is a long distance."

"It's a big hunting ground too." Elizabeth's reminder of the posse made Matt's gut clench. "If we ride out with you, me, Nicholas, Javier and Lorenzo, we can fan out and head north. Ride close enough to hear a gunshot if we find something. We look until we find him or he finds us."

It was a damn good plan. He didn't want to show her too much enthusiasm yet. She was a girl and only sixteen. Obviously she'd gotten a bigger share of brains than most folks though. Smarter than most of them put together. He ran through what she said and stopped on the one suggestion he couldn't abide.

"You're not going with us."

"Oh yes I am, and you can't stop me. I can saddle my own horse, load my own rifle and ride faster than everyone except Catherine. You won't keep me from this, Matt. I will go whether or not you like it." This time she not only looked like Mama, she sounded like her.

Matt still missed his parents, but the reminder of just how much the younger siblings had lost was painful. Elizabeth had been eleven, a tender age before womanhood changed her. Losing their mother had forced her into growing up faster. Now she was a woman, hell, she could be married by now. It might kill him if she decided to do that, but he would accept it. However, letting her risk her life against a pack of angry, armed men? Not a chance.

"I don't like it and I won't let you go." He ignored her sharp intake of breath, knowing the conversation wasn't over with. She would probably wake up Hannah and Eva who would browbeat him until he gave in and let his little sister take up arms.

Matt knew he had little time to act before that happened. He left the porch and headed for the bunkhouse in the barn to wake up Javier and Lorenzo. It was time to do something to help his brother and fight for the Grahams.

CHAPTER EIGHT

Caleb heard the horses coming and knew there was little time to lose. It could be his family but he doubted it. They didn't know where he was or what he was doing. Besides whoever rode those horses had no regard for their safety. In the deep recesses of the woods, there were plenty of dangers ready to snap a horse's leg. That likely meant the horses were led by Garza, hunting them. Probably found the mule's carcass and picked up their trail.

Damn.

They had at least five miles before hitting the property line for the Circle Eight. The only advantage he saw was his knowledge of the land and terrain. Garza was a stranger, one who was driven by dark thoughts without regard for anything but what he wanted. Caleb had spent most of his childhood here. He knew it better than anyone.

"Ride hard due south, follow the tree line until you see a big banyan tree. That's the Circle Eight." He didn't expect Rory's response.

"And leave you here without a horse and only one gun against however many men he has?" She scowled at him. "Not in a million years."

"Jesus, Aurora, would you stop fighting me for once? I need to get you and Benjy to safety. You want to put him in danger because of your own stubbornness?" He held the reins so tightly, Justice tossed his head in protest.

"It's not stubbornness. Together we can do better than apart. To hell with your manly stupidity."

To Caleb's consternation, Benjy speared him with the same expression Rory did. He told himself to hang onto his anger and not

127

let it loose. They didn't know they were acting like fools, either that or they didn't care.

"Let's keep moving. Together." She kneed Justice and the damn gelding started moving. Caleb growled at them.

"You're going to get yourself killed."

"Then we go down fighting. I won't run like a coward to leave you to fight my battles. I made the choice to leave with you and help Benjy escape. I won't turn yellow now." She pointed south. "Run alongside and we'll all get there together."

Caleb wanted to argue with her but there was no time. He started running to keep with the horse. They wouldn't get far at this pace, but he needed time to figure out what to do. At least moving meant they were getting closer to his family's ranch and safety. He wouldn't let Garza get his hands on Benjy again. No matter what he had to do.

He led the way, sprinting through the woods until he thought he might burst from breathing so hard. His discomfort didn't matter though. All that mattered was getting to the ranch.

Justice stayed behind him, keeping his big body between Caleb and whoever was chasing them. The first bullet strike on a tree nearby startled him and he tripped on a tree root. Justice reared up, avoiding stomping his master to death, but unseating Rory and Benjy. The two of them hit the ground and rolled.

Caleb scrambled to his feet and rushed over to them. Justice pranced around, throwing his head and making that strange screaming noise he always did when he was agitated. Another bullet whizzed past his head and he dropped to his knees to crawl. Rory was already huddled with Benjy behind a fallen tree. Her short hair was sticking up every which way.

"Are you okay?" he whispered.

"Fine. We need to get back on the horse and get the hell out of here though." A bullet slammed into the fallen tree startling a squeak out of her.

Caleb agreed wholeheartedly and knew they only had moments before Garza closed in. Right now they were just pumping rounds into the trees hoping to hit something. He reached for the horse's reins to calm him when the bullet slammed into his back.

As he headed for the ground, he cursed long and hard. Rory was beside him in seconds, her amber eyes full of worry. He glanced up at her, leaves partially blocking his view.

"You got yourself shot, Ranger. That wasn't very smart."

"It wasn't my plan." He sucked in a breath as the pain sliced through him. It was a good hit, deep inside his body and it hadn't exited the premises either. Fuck.

She dragged him over behind the tree and propped him up on his side. "Put your hand here, Benjy. Hold it hard, okay?" She guided the boys hands to the wound, which was a few inches above his lower back.

The boy pressed down on his wound, sending shards of pain through Caleb's body but he didn't let even a peep escape his lips. There was no need to remind the boy he was hurting his brother. He already knew.

"I'm going to get the horse. Stay put." She disappeared from view leaving Caleb alone with Benjy.

"It's okay, Ben. We'll find a way to get out of this."

The boy shook his head but Caleb wasn't going to give up hope. They had to survive. He wouldn't accept any other outcome.

Rory returned, her face taut with tension and worry. "Benjy, I know you're not going to like this but you're going to have to go by yourself."

Caleb tried to protest, but she slapped a hand over his mouth. He thought about biting her.

"If I don't help your brother he's going to bleed to death alone in the woods. If you ride for your family's ranch, you can fly like the wind. With only your weight, Justice can run faster." She cupped his small face in her hands. "You have to save your brother and me. I know you can do it."

Benjy blanched, his eyes wide. Caleb understood Rory's plan and agreed with her. It was their only option and the one chance to get Benjy back to the Grahams. It was also dangerous as hell and could put all of them six feet under.

She set the saddlebags beside Caleb and took out one of her shirts, pressing it to his wound. "You have to go now, Benjy."

The boy got to his feet and stared down at Caleb. With his heart aching, Caleb nodded his approval, knowing he could be sending his brother to his death at the hands of a madman. One who had already done damage to the boy's young life.

With an agility that didn't surprise his big brother, Benjy flung himself up into the saddle. Rory pointed in the right direction.

"You heard him. Follow the tree line, stay low in the saddle, until you pass the banyan tree. Then ride as hard as you can toward your family." She sounded as desperate as he felt. They had no idea if they'd see the boy again. "Go. Now."

The horse raced off, leaving the two of them alone in the forest. A woman, barely recovered from a wound and fever, and a man, bleeding into the leaves beneath him. The world was a cruel place but if God was kind, he would save Benjamin Graham.

Elizabeth knew they'd left without her, but she didn't let that stop her. As if the sounds of four horses leaving the yard could be muffled. Did they think her a fool or deaf? She pulled on her leather riding skirt and buttoned up her blouse as fast as she could.

When she ran through the kitchen, she ignored Eva's protest. The housekeeper could yell at her when they got back with Caleb. For now, Elizabeth would do what she knew was right. She snatched the familiar rifle from above the door and burst out into the early morning light.

She hadn't told Matt everything she knew, like the fact that Caleb's gelding had a nicked right shoe, or that Caleb favored riding through the woods rather than out in the open. Matt wasn't ready to believe she was capable but that was about to change.

Her horse, Bella, greeted her at the stall, seemingly eager to go on an adventure. She saddled the mare quickly, taking the time to be sure the cinch was tight although she wanted to simply race out of there bareback. After stowing her rifle, she led her out of the barn and found her sister-in-law, Hannah, waiting, arms crossed and expression grim. Her long brown hair was still in a braid and she wore her nightclothes. "You know Matt wouldn't approve."

"I don't care what Matt thinks. This was my idea and he ran off like a shadow without me." Elizabeth held onto her control, although a scream threatened to burst forth at any second.

"I know you can do anything, Ellie." The nickname, long since forgotten, buried with her mother, came out of Hannah's mouth so easily. It stopped Elizabeth in her tracks, emotion swamping her.

"Where did you hear that?"

Hannah frowned. "Ellie? I don't know. I've wanted to call you that since we met and I guess it just came out. If you don't like it—"

"No, it's okay." Elizabeth found she missed it. The world had been a softer place when she had her mother's arms to hide in. Now she had a different kind of life, one that would have been very different if her mother hadn't been murdered.

Hannah pulled her into a hug and Elizabeth took a moment to enjoy the embrace. She didn't allow much physical affection but found this morning, she needed it. Hannah pulled back and put her hands on Elizabeth's shoulders.

"Be careful, Ellie."

Elizabeth nodded, her throat tight. It was time to catch up with her brothers and the ranch hands. Time to save Caleb and keep the circle as complete as it could be. There was no way she would lose another brother. She hadn't gotten over losing the last one.

She rode out of the yard, following their trail with ease. With her weight and her mare's strength, they would catch up to the men. It was time to go to war.

Benjy rode hard, his breath caught in his throat from the speed of the animal beneath him. It was as if the gelding's hooves didn't touch the ground. Rory had been right. He was flying.

He didn't want to leave Caleb or Rory but he knew they would all die if he stayed. Benjy was only ten but he knew how to survive, one way or another. He leaned over the horse's neck and closed his eyes for a moment, letting the wind buffet his face.

The sounds of guns faded and he found himself at the edge of the forest. They burst into a clearing and he saw the banyan tree. It had been so long since he'd seen it, but he recognized it. A bubble of memory rose up inside him. Riding on his father's shoulders so he could touch the lowest branch of the tree. He swallowed the lump in his throat and did what Rory told him to.

He rode even harder, letting the gelding have his head, galloping over the terrain with ease. It seemed the horse knew where he was going and was as eager as Benjy to get there. Fear burbled in his stomach as he heard horses. He wasn't sure where they were so he kept riding, hoping he wouldn't feel a bullet in his back.

"Hey!" A shout sounded from his left and he ignored it. Home. He had to get home. He had to save Caleb.

"Benjy?" The voice, the sound of his name, echoed through him, making his heart thump harder.

He turned his head and saw a lone rider coming toward him, a big man with a blue shirt and a brown hat. Then he took the hat off and he recognized his big brother Matt.

A wall of relief and exhaustion rolled over him and he yanked on the reins, heedless of the horse's protest. Tears sprang to his eyes. Matt. It was really Matt.

"Holy shit. Benjy?" His big brother rode closer until he pulled up beside him. "Oh my God."

Benjy flung himself off the horse and into his brother's arms. Tears streamed from his eyes and he sobbed so hard, his stomach hurt. Matt mumbled his name, his hands running up and down his back. There weren't enough words to express the relief and joy coursing through him.

"How did you get here and where is Caleb? This is his horse, right?" Matt pulled back and looked at him. Benjy was surprised to see his brother crying too. He thought men didn't ever cry. "Can you talk? Are you okay?"

A thousand thoughts crowded his brain and he finally wanted to voice them out loud. It had been so long, he almost forgot how to form words with his mouth.

"Caleb's shot. In the woods with Rory. He needs help. There are bad men out there." His voice was rusty from disuse, crackly and deeper than Benjy expected. It would have been funny but it was only sad that he hadn't spoken in more than four years.

"How did he—? Oh never mind that. We can figure that out later." Matt kissed his forehead. "I can't believe you're here."

Neither could Benjy. He spotted another rider coming toward them, a streak of brown on a paint he recognized as Elizabeth's. She rode up in a cloud of dust, her mouth open in surprise.

"Benjy?"

He smiled, realizing he was finally here. His family. His home. After five years of darkness, he had found the light.

"Hi, Ellie."

She smiled back at him. "I missed you." Her voice shook and she bit her lip as though holding back more words. He appreciated that.

"Me too." Elizabeth had been the middle child, the sister who had taken the time to play with him when Rebecca and Catherine wouldn't, and the boys ignored him. She had grown into a pretty lady while he'd been away.

"We'll have to save the stories for later." Matt plopped him back on Justice. "Elizabeth, I will tan your hide later for disobeying me. For now, take Benjy back to the house and don't argue with me.

"I won't." She frowned at Matt and Benjy knew their family was still the same. Liked to bicker and argue, but always loved each other. He picked up the reins and waited. "Where's Caleb and why is Benjy riding his horse?"

"All I know is he's shot in the woods. I'm going to get the boys and go after him." He fired his pistol in the air and shouted, "To the Graham!"

Elizabeth wheeled her horse around and gestured to Benjy to head toward the house. "Race me?"

Benjy leaned low in the saddle and raced toward home. For the first time in five years, he was back at the Circle Eight, his family around him.

Rory took Caleb's pistol and kept her other hand against his wound. She straddled his thigh, doubly glad she wore trousers. It was awkward and it made her back hurt but there was no other choice. Her hammer sat beside her, ready to swing if necessary. Her hand itched to do just that.

Caleb's breathing was even but slow. She assumed he was trying to keep himself calm and slow the blood flow. It had already soaked through the shirt she held to the wound. How strange that less than a week ago, she was wounded in her side and needed his assistance to save her life. The situation was now reversed and she was saving his.

Or at least she hoped she was. The bullets had slowed down but not stopped. She prayed that Benjy would be okay. He was stronger than he looked, gangly with long limbs and big feet, but he was a Graham. If she learned anything from Caleb, it was that his family did not give up. Ever. She could appreciate that and in fact, had the same core of stubborn strength.

"What do you see?" He barely whispered but she heard him anyway.

"Nothing but the breeze." She peered around, the thick canopy of leaves blocking much of her view. They were hidden but so were the men chasing them. It was a blessing and a curse to be in a dense forest.

"Did Benjy get away?"

"I'm sure he did. He was riding like the wind when he

disappeared from sight. He's a natural horseman." Rory was surprised by how well he reacted and rode off, alone and unprotected. He would be a hell of a man when he grew up.

"That's from Pa. He was born riding a horse." Caleb coughed and a moan followed. She hadn't seen the tough ranger so vulnerable before. The fact he was letting her see it said a lot about their relationship, or whatever it was.

"What happens after all this is over?" She didn't know what her future held, but knew she wasn't the same person she'd been the day before she met Caleb Graham.

"I'm hoping we win."

She clucked her tongue at him. "That's not what I meant and you know it. You took me off my land, and apparently Texas thinks it owns it. I have nothing but a few possessions and my father's tools."

He was quiet for a few moments before he spoke. "I'm sorry for that but if it wasn't me, it would have been another ranger who came for you. The land belonged to your father and when he died, it belonged to the Republic of Texas. The fact is, women can't own property."

It was a lance to her heart. She didn't own the property because she had tits. How frustrating. Maddening. Infuriating.

"You mean because I don't have a swinging dick, I lose my home?"

He barked out something like a laugh but it was too odd to be one. "Something like that. Damn, woman, how do you keep surprising me?"

"I'm going to fight you or Texas or whoever I need to." She tightened the grip on the gun. "I might just keep this weapon so I can shoot them."

"Don't shoot me, Aurora. I won't kick you out of your home." He sounded so sincere. She wanted to believe him.

"You already did."

He frowned at her. "No, I saved your life when you fell out of a tree."

"Same result. I lost my home and now I'm alone hundreds of miles away." Her fear of the men chasing them got mixed up with her feelings for Caleb.

"You're not alone." He put his hand over hers, the weight no doubt making the pain worse, but he hung on. "I'm right beside you."

She stared into his blue-green eyes and her heart twisted. "For how long?" That was the question she wanted to ask, the one she needed the answer to. Yes, they had kissed and even been intimate, but what did it mean? Did he want something more with her? She needed to ask herself that question too.

His expression changed, becoming more guarded. "I don't think either one of us knows that."

At least he didn't lie to her. "You're the first man I've met to treat me like a woman."

"You are a woman. A beautiful, strong one with a big hammer." He managed a small smile.

She shook her head. "I'm not beautiful but I am strong and I can swing my hammer. You are crazy if you think I'm anything but plain."

"No, you tried to hide yourself as plain. You cut your hair, wear trousers and that ugly leather apron. And you put your heart and soul into that forge." He squeezed her fingers. "There are other things to put them toward."

"Like you?" Her heart leapt at the idea. He was a hell of a man and she was already falling in love with him.

"Like me. Aurora, would you—" He stopped in mid-question, his jaw clenching tight and his gaze beyond her shoulder. The butt of a gun pressed against the back of her head.

"Look at what I found."

She recognized Garza's voice and her stomach dropped to her feet. She'd been so involved in talking about their future, she ignored everything else. Her own foolishness had put them both in danger. They wouldn't survive if she failed to protect them.

"Drop the gun, bitch. Now."

She had no choice but to let the pistol drop into the leaves. Another man picked it up. She wanted to kick him in the balls.

"Where is my son?" Garza's hot breath burst across her neck.

She slid her hand toward the hammer, its wooden grip familiar. The *patron* pushed the gun harder against her head, scraping an inch of skin from her scalp. She hissed and tightened her grip on the hammer.

"Get that thing off me, you son of a bitch." Her snarl startled Caleb. "I'll kill you where you stand."

"Brave words, *chica*. You come to my house, my doctor saves your life and how do you repay me? For all the iron I bought from you

135

and kept you fed?" He humphed his disapproval. "I should use the same bullet to kill you and your ranger."

"He ain't my ranger." A lie, oh yes, a big fat lie.

"Then I can kill him first." Garza moved the gun until the muzzle was next to her cheek and pointed straight at Caleb.

She had seconds to say good-bye to him or to save them both. His gaze snapped to hers and she saw a wealth of emotion in his eyes. She saw what she needed to see, enough to give her the courage to do what had to be done.

"I'd like to stay with you, Caleb. Call me a fool but I love you."

Rory swung her hammer.

Matt rode like the hounds of hell were chasing him. Nicholas, Lorenzo and Javier rode behind him, their presence a comfort. He had no idea what he was up against, just that Caleb was shot and in danger. It had to be the same men who had been looking for him.

Now he knew whatever decision Caleb had made involved Benjy. He'd put his own life in danger to rescue their brother. Matt was proud of both of his brothers and he'd give anything to make sure Caleb survived. He didn't know where he'd found their missing brother or what he'd done, but Matt would back him up no matter what.

A shot echoed ahead and he leaned down low over Winston, his gelding, and whispered in the horse's ears. "C'mon, boy. Give me everything you got. Don't let my brother die."

He saw a group of three men on horses, with two additional mounts without riders. They turned to him in surprise, but he was already clearing leather. He picked off two before the third shot back. One of his own men got off a shot and the last man went down.

That left two more but where were they?

"Bitch!" A scream, and another shot echoed through the forest.

Matt turned toward the sound, praying he was on time.

Caleb stared at the body of Pablo Garza, his arm broken in an L-shape and a bullet hole square in his forehead. His warrior goddess, Rory, wrestled with the second man. She was stronger than the stranger expected and they were evenly matched.

He wanted to help her, but he could barely move, weakened from blood loss and pain. He'd managed to get the gun and end Garza's reign of terror, but he couldn't get to the other man unless he could flip over. Frustration roared through him and he forced himself to slide forward.

"Bitch!" The stranger swung his fist, connecting with Rory's cheek.

She stumbled backward but didn't fall. It brought her closer to the hammer and damned if she didn't pick it up and swing it again. The man screeched and backed away from her, his gaze never leaving the hammer.

Caleb slid again, making stars of pain exploded behind his eyes. He clenched his teeth to keep from losing consciousness. If he did, Rory still had more men to handle without any help. He wouldn't let that happen. Hell the woman told him she loved him. *She loved him!*

His heart had closed around her, and she was now permanently in there, never to leave again. Damned if he would give up what he could have with her. There wasn't another woman for him, and he was damn lucky he'd found her. Now he had to help her or die trying.

He rolled on his belly, his heart in his throat, pulse pounding so hard his ears hurt. Almost there, another roll onto his wounded side and he could shoot. The gun was slippery in his hand, slick with sweat and blood.

"Come closer, you coward," she growled at the stranger. "You afraid of a woman?"

"You are *loca, puta.*" The man jumped away, trying to circle back around behind her.

She followed, not letting him get the upper hand. She was an avenging angel of old, like a Norse goddess swinging a hammer and snarling, blood on her clothes and skin, sporting trousers and a stained shirt.

He had never seen such a beautiful thing in his life. Caleb rolled one more time and he gasped from the pain as he rolled onto the gunshot wound. The grunts and curses continued from the stand-off above him while he tried to catch his breath. The hardest part would be aiming his gun and not hitting the woman he wanted to marry.

Hell and damnation. Stupid time to suddenly realize she was his future wife, but there it was. Strangely enough, it helped calm him, to push away the pain and lift the gun. He closed one eye and aimed.

Rory swung the hammer as he pulled the trigger and the stranger went down with her on top of him. Caleb screamed in terror and he wondered if his bullet had hit his woman instead of his enemy.

He tried to crawl but he had no strength to move an inch. Growling, he scrabbled at the ground, dirt and twigs digging into his fingernails. He had to get to her.

"Aurora." His voice was barely a whisper.

The sound of horses echoed through his body from the ground and he knew he had only moments to get to her. God, he couldn't lose her now. When would he ever find a woman like her? No one and nowhere.

"Caleb!" His brother's voice was like music to his ears. He didn't know how Benjy had gotten back to the ranch to send Matt so fast, but he didn't care at that point.

"Help her, Matt. Help her." Caleb's raw command ripped from his throat as he continued to crawl around the fallen log.

Matt's boots came into view and his hand touched Caleb's back. "You're bleeding."

"You're so observant. Fuck my injury. Check Aurora, please. She went down when I fired." Caleb's voice cracked as he imagined the worse.

Then suddenly she was there beside him, her hands grabbing his. "I'm right here, Ranger. Right beside you."

Something wet slid down his cheeks as relief coursed through him. She kissed his cheek and he surrendered to the blackness. It swallowed him whole and he knew no more.

Elizabeth let the wind take her tears. She wanted to stop and ask Benjy a thousand questions but it was more important to get back to the safety of the ranch. Matt could yell at her later for following them, but if she hadn't been there, they would have had to be one man down to fight whatever danger Caleb was in.

Bringing her brother back to the house wasn't what she had in mind when she left the ranch this morning. However, it was an important task, one she would gladly give anything to do. She didn't know how Caleb found him, but her heart was whole for the first time in five years.

When the first bullet whizzed past her face, she was surprised but she didn't hesitate to act.

"Make yourself as small as possible and ride like hell, Benjy." She pulled the rifle from the scabbard and pulled her horse around to face whoever threatened them.

A lone rider was coming toward them, a rifle aimed straight at her head. She pulled her own up and lined up her sight. She took a few seconds to make sure her aim was true even as a bullet slammed into her thigh. It burned like a hot poker but she steadied her arm and fired.

The stranger flew backwards off the horse, leaving it riderless. She sucked in a breath and scanned the horizon for more. After a few minutes, she lowered the rifle and tucked it back into the scabbard. She tore off her sleeve and tied it off on her leg. It would slow the bleeding enough to get back to Eva for doctoring.

Her stomach heaved and she threw up what little she'd eaten that day. Her horse danced around a bit, disturbed by the smell. Elizabeth didn't blame the mare at all. She didn't like the smell or the fact she had puked after killing a man. She couldn't be a tough defender of the Circle Eight if she got sick every time she shot someone.

She used water from the canteen to rinse her mouth before chasing after her brother. It wouldn't be fair to leave him to explain everything when he arrived back at the ranch alone. She leaned down and whispered in her horse's ear.

"Get him, girl."

The mare jumped into motion, flying across the terrain with more speed than most horses could dream of. She was part-Pegasus, her hooves barely touching the ground. Within a few minutes, she saw Benjy ahead, still riding Justice fast. The quarter horse was fast but her mare was faster.

"Benjy!" she called without much hope that he would hear her. Yet he reacted, glancing behind him. She waved and he slowed the gelding down.

By the time she caught up to him, she was feeling a smidge lightheaded. Fortunately they would make it back to the house in ten minutes' time. His eyes widened at the blood on her leg.

"It's a flesh wound. I'll be okay after Eva fixes me up." Elizabeth hoped her smile was stronger than her voice. Her stomach roiled again and she swallowed back the bile that threatened.

"Eva?" Her brother's voice crackled.

Elizabeth smiled. "Yes, Eva. She's been waiting for you as long as the rest of us."

Benjy nodded, his actions jerky and unsteady. She wanted to hug him and tell him everything would be all right. But she had a feeling it wouldn't be that way for a while for him. He'd been lost to them for five years. She knew he had been sold, eavesdropping had been a useful pastime, but other than that, she didn't know what he'd been through. Judging by the shadows in his eyes, it had been a dark place.

She gestured toward the house, barely a dot in the distance. "Come on, little brother, let's go home."

Rory didn't know Caleb's family but she knew that's who these men were. One older, one younger, plus two Mexican men who seemed as concerned as the brothers. Her body vibrated with anger and fear, mixed with a little battle lust. She had enjoyed swinging that hammer, making her mark on the men who wanted to hurt her and who had already hurt both Caleb and Benjy.

It left a taste of sweet revenge mixed with regret in her mouth. She wasn't a killer by nature but those men deserved it. Her hammer had never been used to cause harm and now she'd used it to defend herself and her man. Caleb was her man no matter what happened.

The older brother glanced around, taking it all in. His gaze landed on her and surprise spread across his face. He also spotted the hammer still in her clenched hand.

"You Foster, the smithy?"

She nodded. "You a Graham?"

"Matt Graham." He gestured to the other three standing behind him. "That's Nicholas, Javier and Lorenzo."

"Caleb needs a doctor. He's been shot." She dropped the hammer. He was unconscious, pale and covered with blood. Her stomach picked that moment to flip. It was only through sheer force of will that she didn't puke.

Matt's jaw tightened. "We've got a lot to talk about."

"Later. Now Caleb is important." She ignored the big man's scowl and held out her hand. "I need some help so we can staunch the bleeding."

"I can see how you and Caleb ended up together. You sound just like him." Despite his complaint, Matt turned to his men. "Javier, you and Lorenzo go get the horses so we can take care of these bodies. Get one ready to carry Caleb. Now."

The two Mexican men took off running. The younger Graham squatted down and stared at Caleb, his eyes wide. This one was probably the same age as her, but she felt so much older. Ancient.

"Can you find some ash? I saw remnants of a fire a few yards east. I'm going to make a paste." She had little time to work and no time to explain.

The young Graham went off to do as she asked, leaving her alone with Matt and the unconscious Caleb. The older brother remained standing, perhaps to let her know he still held the power. She could care less what he was doing.

Rory brushed back the hair from Caleb's brow, daring to show her vulnerability for the ranger in front of his brother. He looked lifeless and it pinched at her heart.

"You care for him."

"I've got the ash!" Nicholas came rushing back with his hands full of ash.

"Put it down here." Rory gestured to a spot a few feet from Caleb. After Nicholas dropped the ash, she dropped her trousers.

"What the hell?" Matt stepped back as if she was going to hurt him.

"I need to make a paste with the ash and piss. It's a good way to stop the blood. My father taught me when I was a girl." She forced herself to piss enough to make the paste the right consistency. After she'd yanked up her trousers, she mixed the ingredients together until it was ready.

The two Grahams stared at her while the other two men stood behind with the horses. All of them were silent and motionless.

"Someone peel back the shirt so I can smear this on him."

Nobody moved.

"He's going to bleed to death."

Matt moved closer and put his hand on his pistol. Rory's fury knew no bounds. She growled at him and removed the blood-soaked shirt herself. The sound of the pistol clearing leather was loud in the forest.

"I won't let you smear piss on my bleeding brother. Move away."

"I don't really care what you say or do right now, Matt Graham. The only thing that matters is Caleb. I won't let you stop me from saving him." She got to her feet and shook the bloody shirt. "He's dying and you're letting it happen." She threw the shirt at him. "Now are you going to help me or stand there showing me your dick is bigger than mine?"

Someone whistled but she ignored them. Matt put the gun back in its holster, apparently convinced.

"You and me will talk later. Tell me what we need to do."

Relief mixed with annoyance at his man pride. "Clean the wound with fresh water as best you can."

Matt grabbed the canteen from his saddle and squatted beside Caleb. She joined him and waited while he washed away the blood. Fresh bubbles appeared from the angry wound, but it was enough to allow her to do what she needed. She pressed the paste onto the hole, making a plug of sorts.

"Now give me your shirt."

His brows went up.

"I can take off mine if you prefer. You've already seen my ass."

Matt's cheeks colored at her bald reference, but he took off his shirt and handed it to her. She grunted her thanks and used the sleeves to tie it around him as best she could. Caleb moaned and she had to grit her teeth to ignore it. She knew this hurt him but she had to do what she had to do, no matter what.

"He's ready." She stood up and clenched her hands so the men wouldn't see them shaking. "Which horse?"

One of the men brought forth a beautiful black stallion. Garza's horse, Diablo. She knew him on sight and better yet, he knew her. She had shoed him a number of times. Forcing herself to keep calm, she reached out to pet his neck.

"Hey there, boy, you ready to take a ride."

The horse snuffled her belly and she breathed a sigh of relief. Stallions were notoriously unruly and this black beauty was no exception. She'd seen him kick a hole in a two-inch thick-stall door. The smell of blood didn't seem to bother him and neither did the sight of his master dead on the ground.

She threw herself up into the saddle and held out her hands. "Lift him up to sit in front of me. I'll follow you back to your ranch."

The men were silent again. She wanted to shake them all until their brains rattled.

"Diablo has a smooth gait but he's not going to let any of you ride him. Your horses won't take the weight of two grown men without jarring him too much. And Caleb can't ride belly down." She bared her teeth at them. "Now hand him up here so we can get a real doctor to dig that bullet out of his gut."

Matt nodded and finally they listened to her. All four of them lifted him up, his body limp and lifeless. She bit her lip and forced the tears back. Later when she was alone, she might let herself cry. For now she had to help him survive.

Be strong, Aurora. Don't show weakness. Hold your head high. You are a blacksmith.

Her father's words echoed through her head and she straightened her back. They slid Caleb into the saddle in front of her and she wound her arms around him.

"Take the leather strap out of the saddlebag and tie his waist to mine, then to the saddle horn."

"You are bossier than my wife, Olivia and Eva combined." Matt scowled but he did as she asked.

"I'm going to take that as a compliment since you seem to know what a bossy woman is like." She held tight to the man who she willed to survive and waited for his brother to secure the leather.

He looked up at her, his gaze icy cold. "I'm going to trust you with my brother but I'm also giving you a warning. If he dies, I'm going to lay the blame on you and your foolish notion to put piss on him."

She flinched from the sharp words. If Caleb died, there wouldn't be anyone who blamed her more than herself.

"Let's ride, Graham."

After giving orders to Javier and Lorenzo to bring the dead men to the ranch for the sheriff to deal with, Matt swung up into the saddle, as did Nicholas. Rory set off for the Circle Eight with a Graham in her lap, flanked by his serious brothers.

They moved at a canter, as much as she thought Caleb could handle in his condition. She hung onto him until her arms shook from the effort. The sight of another dead body and a riderless horse didn't stop her. She rode right past, knowing it was another of Garza's men taken down by the Grahams.

The house appeared in the distance and she focused on it and the feel of Caleb's strong heart beating against hers. They were almost there. She wanted to urge Diablo into a faster speed but held back, exhaustion and emotion washing over her. She had to be strong, to help Caleb survive or she might not possibly survive herself.

Benjy stared at the faces around him, their familiarity overshadowed by the changes in them. Eva, Rebecca and Catherine, along with two women he didn't know watched him as he dismounted.

Elizabeth got down more slowly, her breath hissing through her teeth. Eva didn't move, however, her gaze locked on Benjy.

"*¿Hijo?*" Tears ran down the housekeeper's face. "Benjamin, *mi hijo.*" She held up her arms and Benjy froze in place.

He wasn't her son. He wasn't anyone's son. Yet he wanted nothing more than to slide into Eva's welcoming embrace, to feel the affection he had buried in his memory from so long ago.

"Don't push him." Elizabeth hobbled over to them. "Let him come in when he's ready. I need you to stitch up my leg."

Eva finally turned to look at Elizabeth. Her eyes widened. "*¡Dios mio!* You've been shot!"

A stream of Spanish exploded from the housekeeper's mouth so fast he could hardly distinguish between the words. She led Elizabeth into the house, followed by the two women he didn't know, one old and one young.

Rebecca and Catherine stood there watching him, their eyes wide. When he'd left they'd been gangly girls. Now they were tall and curvy. Heck, Catherine looked like a fairy creature and she wore trousers. He didn't know them anymore, much as his heart ached for it to be untrue.

Catherine stepped forward and offered him a small smile. "Welcome home, Benjy."

He dismounted with care, not used to riding a horse, much less one sixteen hands high. Caleb's horse was a good one, though, and stood still as Benjy awkwardly made his way to the ground.

"Are you thirsty?" Catherine hooked her hands in her trouser pockets. "We can go to the well and rinse off the travel dust too."

He nodded and let his childhood best friend, his sister, lead him around the side of the house. The sight was a ghostly memory that scratched at his brain. The garden grew thick with vegetables and flowers and he had a flash of his mother working in it. The well pump was still red but faded and chipped, thousands of hand touches had worn it down.

Catherine pumped the handle a few times until water gushed from the spout. She leaned down and sucked in a mouthful, spraying it all over her shirt. Her grin made the knot in his gut loosen a little.

He stepped up and leaned into the water, letting it rush into his mouth. He closed his eyes and wished it could wash away the last five years of his life. If only the well were magic. Benjy was not the same boy he'd been when last he'd drunk from this well.

His family was a group of familiar strangers and his life had been turned upside down for the third time in his ten years. Catherine watched him, her blue eyes different than anyone else in the Graham clan. She had obviously chosen her own path, dressing and acting different than their sisters.

"You want to go into the house and watch Eva sew up Elizabeth?" She leaned on the pump, bracing her chin on her wrists. "Or we could stay out here until you're ready to go inside."

He raised his face to the sun and let the heat penetrate the coldness that lived within him. Catherine sat down in the grass, then lay back, pillowing her head with her hands. He had been closest to her and she seemed to know what he wanted before he did. With gratitude, he lay beside her on the grass and closed his eyes.

Benjamin Graham was home.

Elizabeth peered out the kitchen window and saw Benjy and Catherine lying on the grass. It was good for him to take his time before he was subjected to the women fussing over him. She had never seen such an ancient look in a young person's eyes before. Her heart ached for him but she would give him the room he needed.

"What happened, *hija*? You followed your brother, didn't you?" Eva tsked at her. "He told you no and you disobey? Why do you girls never listen?"

"I listen just fine." Rebecca had to announce her ridiculous record of following the rules.

"Shut up, Becky." Elizabeth hobbled over to the table. "Yes, I went after Matt and the rest of them. It was my idea and I wanted to help."

"Who shot you?" Eva helped her onto the table and pulled up her riding skirt to expose the wound. "Ah, you are lucky it went straight through."

"Nothing to dig out." Elizabeth had never been shot but it burned and pained something fierce. "I need you to stitch me up quick, Eva. Matt is bringing Caleb in and he's been shot."

The cacophony of noise that followed was enough to make her ears hurt. Even Granny Dolan, Hannah's outspoken grandmother, threw in a few curses to the noise pile.

"I don't know anything more than that. He sent me back with

Benjy, to keep him safe." She closed her eyes against the pain as Eva started cleaning the wound.

Benjy's name shut everyone up. They went back to looking outside at the boy who had left the Circle so long ago. She wasn't the only one who never expected to find him again. No matter how many lost souls Olivia and Brody had found. Perhaps her pessimism came from exactly what was happening now. He was a stranger in his family's home, preferring to sit in the sun than with them.

She assumed he hadn't been living in the lap of luxury and had endured much in those five years. It changed someone, especially a child who knew nothing but the love of his family. Her heart ached for him and for the Grahams. Although they'd found him, things were far from whole again.

CHAPTER NINE

Rory focused on the house, counting to ten over and over in her head, anything not to focus on the man in her arms. She wanted to scream, cry and punch something. Yet she hung on and did what she had to do. She remained strong for him and for herself.

"Nick, ride ahead and let Eva know Caleb's in a bad way. Then ride into town and get the doc. Tell him Caleb's got a bullet to get dug out and he's lost a lot of blood." Matt sounded so calm. She wanted to smack him. How could he be calm when his brother's life slipped away with each passing second?

The younger Graham took off at a gallop, racing toward the house until he arrived in a cloud of dust they could see half a mile away. Within seconds, the young man was back in the saddle, a streak of brown horse against the sky, riding hell for leather toward wherever the doctor was.

She was relieved there was a doctor to be fetched. Where she lived, most times the midwife doctored folks or they begged at the Garza hacienda for his personal doc. Rory had been lucky to receive his services. Most folks were turned away.

"How's he doing?"

"Breathing." She didn't feel much like talking.

"Is there bleeding?" He was persistent, just like his brother.

"Not that I can see or feel. He's mighty hard to keep upright and keep the horse in a straight line. So if you don't mind, I'd appreciate it if you could shut up until we get there."

Silence met her clipped words and she waited for him to curse or yell at her. Rory wasn't a soft-spoken miss but she didn't normally tell a big man like Matt Graham to shut up. Her own emotions were overwhelming her, making her act like a bitch protecting her cub. It was madness.

"I'm guessing my wife would say you're just anxious about Caleb. If I listened to my own counsel, I'd take care of him myself." Matt's voice was low and tight. "I'm gonna give you a chance, Miss Foster."

"Mrs. Foster."

He whistled through his teeth. "Are you telling me that my brother is keeping time with a married woman?"

"We are not keeping time, and I'm a widow." She could see the flowers in a garden behind the house. It all looked so normal, so homey. She wanted something like this for herself, had it when her parents had been alive. Until the fire destroyed their house and death took them.

"If you're not keeping time then Caleb is an idiot because I can see you have feelings for him. What I don't understand is how you could be with my brother and be the blacksmith he was sent to kick off Texas land." Matt pulled up close, his blue-green eyes so much like Caleb's, it made her heart ache.

"I'm done talking about this, Graham. We can wait to pull out our fists until Caleb wakes up." Her voice vibrated with anger.

"It's hard to sleep with you two yammering at each other." Caleb's voice scared her bad enough she let loose a cry of surprise.

"Caleb? Damn, boy, you still alive?" Matt sounded relieved and shaken.

"For now, but you two are making my ears bleed."

Rory kissed the center of his back and closed her eyes. Thank God he'd woken up. She didn't know what she was going to do if he hadn't.

"We're almost home, Caleb. Eva should be ready to fix you up. I sent Nicholas for the doc." Matt reached over and touched his brother's arm.

Caleb cracked one eye open and looked at his brother. "Why are you half-naked? Are you telling me you were stepping out on Hannah with my woman?"

Rory barked a laugh at the same time Matt did.

"You don't need to worry about that. He'd probably rather shoot me than kiss me." She touched his makeshift bandage. "That shirt is keeping your wound clean until we get you a real doctor."

"Hannah is gonna be mad you ruined your shirt." Caleb's words slurred.

"I'm sure she'll forgive me." Matt turned toward the house. "Here come the women."

True enough, a tribe of women emerged from the back of the house and stood in a crowd waiting for them. Rory counted six of them, some young and some old. Every one of them were wringing their hands and looking as worried as she was. Caleb did have a big family. He said four sisters and three brothers, but there were older women there too, along with a pair of twin girls with crooked braids. Whoever they were, she was glad they cared for him.

When they arrived at the front of the house at last, the women were waiting. Matt dismounted and rushed over to Diablo. The stallion tried to bite him and he jumped back.

"Damn." He speared Rory with a glare. "That horse is dangerous."

"I warned you he was difficult." She reached for the leather strap. "Help me get this undone."

Matt grunted at her, sounding like his brother, and together they managed to get Caleb untied. Without his brother and friends to help him, it was now up to Matt and Rory to get Caleb down off the big horse.

She hopped down, keeping her hands on Caleb to steady him. He wasn't unconscious but he wasn't in any condition to dismount. Matt took the bulk of his brother's weight while Rory grabbed his legs. The women hovered around, none of them of any size or strength to contribute. One of them looked like she wanted to help more as she held the door open.

Caleb was a big man and Rory had little strength left after the last week, but she dug deep and found a well to tap. A huge table dominated the big room and Matt headed for it. Rory set Caleb's feet down and then dropped to her knees. She sucked in huge breaths, willing herself not to puke or pass out in front of his family.

One of the twins came over and put her tiny hand on Rory's shoulder. "You need water, lady?"

Rory glanced up and saw the Graham look, but didn't know which one the little one belonged to. "Water would be good."

She took off running, her chubby legs pumping until she slid into the wood sink, making the Mexican woman screech.

"Meredith, *hija*, slow down. We do not need any more injuries today." The woman helped her pump water into the sink, then put some into a tin cup.

The little one, Meredith, carefully walked it back over to Rory and held it out to her. "I didn't spill none."

"Thank you." Rory sipped at the cool water until she was more in control, then she threw back the rest of it, letting it slide down her throat.

They had already removed the makeshift bandage and his shirt. Water was currently heating on the stove and they all stood there, watching Caleb breathe. Rory got to her feet and their gazes turned to her.

"Who is she, Mama?" The other twin, the one in a blue dress, peered at her from beside the brown-haired woman. She wasn't a Graham by birth, so she must be Matt's wife.

"Hello, I'm Hannah Graham and these two are Meredith and Margaret. Elizabeth, Rebecca and Catherine Graham." The young woman all nodded as their names were offered. "My grandmother Martha, and Eva, who runs the house." The woman smiled at her, although lines of worry creased her face.

Eva. She'd heard of this woman but didn't remember much about her other than she had been their housekeeper and cook. The others were Caleb's sisters and nieces. So much love, so much family. A pinch of envy coated her tongue.

"I'm Ror—Aurora Foster." She glanced at Caleb, whose glassy eyes were focused on her. "I'm a friend of Caleb's."

Matt snorted. "Friend? She's more like a bodyguard. Thought she'd take my head off with that hammer of hers."

"Hammer?" Eva looked between Caleb and Rory. "I think there is more than a hammer at work here."

Rory wasn't ready for that conversation. Hell she was barely upright. "If you folks don't mind, I'm gonna go outside and tend to the horse, get some air." She had the irresistible urge kiss Caleb but didn't think it wise considering the company. Instead she took his hand and squeezed it tight. "Don't die on me, Ranger."

"I'll do my best." Caleb's shaky smile made her lips twitch.

Their gazes followed her as she stepped back outside. The morning heat shimmered in the air, but it was better than sucking in the thick atmosphere in the house. She sat on the porch steps and put her head in her hands. Her entire life had changed since Ranger Graham had stepped onto her property. Now she had to make sense of it.

The door opened and closed behind her and she wanted to run like hell away from whoever had followed her. She didn't look up while whoever it was sat beside her.

"The Grahams can be a little overwhelming." It was Hannah, the woman who had married into the family. Her soft voice was welcome after all the noise and violence Rory had been through. "I see that you care for Caleb and so do I. He's a good man, one who is so wrapped up in trying to prove himself, he forgets how much he is worth to his family."

"I can believe that." Rory rested her arms on her knees and stared down at the ground.

"I'd like to be your friend if you'll let me."

Rory's laugh was more like a sob. "I could use one right now."

"Don't let Matt intimidate you. He's all manly bluster but inside, he's only concerned about his brother." Hannah snorted. "Now that I'm increasing again, I can make any demands I want and he'll follow through. I've had to put him in his place more than once."

Rory would have liked to have seen that. "I think Caleb and I have had a few of those moments too."

Hannah chuckled. "I knew there was something special there. I was hoping you would be able to tell me what happened, how Benjy came home with Caleb and most of all—" Hannah put her hand on Rory's, "—how you came to be in love with my brother-in-law."

Rory looked up at her new friend. The urge to tell somebody everything raced through her. "It started on Friday when a neighbor, Eloise, told me a ranger was looking for me. Then everything changed when he walked into my smithy."

The entire story spilled out, and she found herself telling Hannah things that hid deep in her heart. Her feelings for Caleb sharp and poignant, dug down deep within her lonely existence. She spoke of Horatio, losing her parents and having no family. Hannah sympathized with it all, an orphan with no one but her grandmother until she met Matt Graham.

Their paths had been different but similar enough that by the time Rory had finished the story, she truly was friends with Hannah. It was a relief to unburden herself to someone who cared, although the situation was still grim.

A carriage pulled into the yard with the young Nicholas beside it on his horse.

Hannah's expression tightened. "The doctor's here. You want to be inside for this or find something else to do?"

Rory was no coward and Caleb might need her. "I'm coming in."

Caleb gripped the sides of the table, hanging on as Eva poked and prodded at him. She made all kinds of hmph noises as she peered at him. Her dark gaze moved to his.

"Is this ash?"

"Ash?" He tried to see what she saw. "What are you talking about?"

"It's a mixture of ash and urine." Rory stepped up to his side, her face tight with worry.

"You pissed on me?" He stared at her, not understanding what she was talking about.

"It's an old remedy from my father. Stops the bleeding and keeps a wound clean until it can be doctored." She shrugged. "It worked, didn't it?"

"Yeah, but you pissed on me." He didn't know whether to be insulted or amused.

"No, I pissed on the ash." She peered at his wounds, bringing her tits within inches of his mouth. Now was not the time to be thinking about them but he couldn't help it. He knew what they tasted like and his mouth watered to lap at them once more. Perhaps the blood loss made him stupid.

"Interesting." Eva raised one brow at Rory. "I never heard of this remedy but you are right. It worked."

Doctor Simpson washed his hands at the sink, listening to them. He was an older man, with a balding pate and a protruding belly, who had moved to Texas a year ago to get away from the climate in New York. He was a bit gruff around the edges but had served the people of the area well, delivered plenty of babies and doctoring lots of wounds.

After drying his hands, he pulled his spectacles from the top of his head and gingerly placed them on his nose. "Now, let's see what we have here."

"A bullet in his back." Rory was as blunt as always. "No exit wound, bled plenty, enough that he's paler than milk. Dig it out of him with care, Doc."

The doctor's eyebrows went up. "Didn't know you had a guard

dog, Caleb."

Although a little color graced her cheeks she didn't lose an inch of her sass. Caleb enjoyed her discomfort as much as he enjoyed the way she protected him.

"Get to it, Doc. It's been at least an hour since he was shot." Rory settled on a chair, taking Caleb's hand in hers. It was what he needed, knowing more pain was coming.

"Ah, an ash poultice. Nice work, whoever did it." The doctor scraped away the ash, then used clean water to wash away the rest.

Caleb gritted his teeth, his side on fire. He'd been shot before, but never in the back. Most times wounds like that could fester and kill. Funny how he'd been shot on the left side and Rory had been wounded in the right. Like two halves of one wounded critter.

The doctor worked for a while, Eva at his side, for an hour. Rory didn't leave her perch, her hand the anchor he needed. She flinched when he flinched, groaned when he groaned and tightened her grip when he did. Rory might be a tough, hammer-swinging smithy but she was a hell of a human being too.

Fortunately the rest of his family stayed at a distance. He didn't want an audience, especially if he started crying or something equally as embarrassing like shitting his drawers.

"Ah, there it is." The doc used some kind of torture device to pull the slug out of him.

Caleb saw stars as pain ripped through him. A hot gush of blood slid down his side. Eva murmured and leaned in close, sopping it up with rags. Rory scowled at her and the doctor.

"You about done bleeding him? I think we need to leave some left in his body."

The doctor didn't pause with what he was doing. "I don't know you, young lady, but I would appreciate it if you could keep your opinion to yourself. I'm trying to save this young man's life."

She grunted but didn't say anything further. Rory didn't take her gaze away from what the doctor was doing. Caleb closed his eyes and tried to think about something besides the hot pain ripping through him as the doctor stitched him up.

"There is damage, but it doesn't appear as though any of the organs were injured. You had an angel on your shoulder, young man." The doctor chatted away as though he didn't have his hands stuck in Caleb's innards.

"What am I supposed to do now?" Rory whispered in his ear.

"Sit by my side and weep for my recovery."

"That's not what I meant and you know it." She leaned her forehead against his shoulder. "I don't belong here, Caleb. I'm a stranger in a strange place, with nothing but my tools and a bad attitude."

He found himself smiling at her description of herself. "You have a lot more than that, Aurora."

Instead of asking him what she meant, she asked a different question. "Why do you call me Aurora?"

His mind drifted and he had trouble focusing. "Aurora means the dawn. Did you know Aurora was the Roman goddess of the morning? The first time I saw you, it was the morning and you were hard at work at your forge. I was smitten."

She chuckled. "Smitten? I don't think that's the right word. I tried to smash you with my hammer and smother you with smoke."

His mind drifted back to the day they met. "I've never met a woman who stood toe to toe with me. You impressed me. And then I saw you naked."

She gasped, something he never expected to hear from her. "Are you mad from the pain?"

"When you were naked and I took care of you, I couldn't help but touch you." Caleb forgot where he was and what was going on. He could only picture her smooth skin, taut muscles and beautiful body. "I think I fell in love with you then."

She pulled her hand away and stood up, her face pale and drawn. "I know you're out of your head from the pain but now you're being cruel. I'm leaving before I can't resist the urge to punch you."

He tried to focus on her face but his eyes wouldn't cooperate and her image wavered. "I'm not being cruel. I mean it. Don't be mad."

Rory stepped away and he reached for her. She hesitated and then sat back down. He held out his hand and didn't put it down, although he shook like a leaf in the wind. She finally placed her hand in his and he breathed a sigh of relief.

"Almost done, Caleb." The doctor's voice reminded him they were not alone. That meant someone else had listened to a private conversation. Caleb's eyes flew open.

Ah hell.

Eva's gaze flickered to his and she raised one brow. Caleb

couldn't shrug so he tried to tell her with his eyes that Rory meant a lot to him. No matter how foolish he acted or how blustery she got, there was something between them. Eva would understand.

"Aurora." Eva tried to get the other woman's attention.

"Please call me Rory." Her voice was rough with emotion.

"Rory, could you get a fresh cup of water? I'm going to give him something to sleep."

"That will shut him up for a while, right?" Rory got to her feet and left him for the sink. She obviously was done talking to him for a while and didn't want to hear what he had to say.

He listened to her move around the kitchen, pumping water and filling a cup. She walked back to the table and spoke quietly to Eva. After another few moments, Rory stepped back up to his side. She held his neck and pressed the cup to his lips.

"What is it?" he spoke around the tin cup.

"Drink it, Ranger. It's good for you." She tipped the cup and he had choice but to swallow or choke. She poured it into his mouth, the gritty flavor making him gag a little.

When she pulled the cup away, he made a face at her. "That tasted like shit."

Her lips twisted. "You have eaten shit before?"

He couldn't help the chuckle that escaped his lips. "Nope, but I've smelled it and that stuff you poured down my throat was close enough."

"It was laudanum the doctor brought with him. It will help you sleep." To his surprise, she brushed the hair back from his forehead, a gentle gesture. "You need to heal."

A wave of sleepiness hit him, followed by a roaring sound in his ears. He fought against it, unwilling to fall asleep because Rory wanted him to. She caressed his cheek and he leaned into her touch. Then promptly fell into the black hole that beckoned.

Rory let out a breath and met the housekeeper's gaze. The older woman stood up to wrap the bandage around Caleb's midsection. Rory took the end and together they managed to get the linen secured.

The doctor had risen, moving to the sink to clean his instruments and the basin he had used. Now that Caleb was asleep, things were less tense for Rory. She was still mortified he had talked about her body and being naked, but done was done. The housekeeper didn't seem like the type of person to tell tales.

"Watch him for fever and seepage. If he gets worse, send one of the boys for me." The doctor set his tools into his bag and patted Caleb's shoulder. "He is a strong one. He should be fine."

"*Sí*, he is strong and he has help to heal." Eva's gaze slid to Rory's for a moment before she went to the door to see the doctor out.

"I'll speak to Matthew and settle my bill." The doctor nodded to both women before he disappeared out the open door.

That left Rory alone with an unconscious Caleb and a curious housekeeper. Before she could be interrogated, Caleb's brothers came in with the two men she recognized from the woods. She didn't realize so much time had passed since everyone appeared to be home. Her first thought was where Garza's body was and whether he was on the Circle Eight.

"We've come to put him in bed." Matt gestured to the others and the four of them surrounded the table.

"His bed is still empty. I will put clean linens on there quick." Eva scurried out of the room.

The men waited, sneaking furtive glances at her. Matt apparently felt sorry for her because he stepped over to speak to her.

"You have blood all over you, Mrs. Foster. We'll bring the tub in so you can get washed up."

Rory glanced down, horrified by what she saw. A tub was a logical idea but she didn't think it was worth the effort.

"I'll just wash up at the pump in the back. No need to go to any trouble with the tub." The stickiness of her hands, the coppery stench of blood and the other unnamed stains on her clothes made her stomach heave. It wasn't all Caleb's blood. Remnants of the men she'd fought still clung to her.

Suddenly it was very important to get herself clean. She pushed past Matt and out the door. The Graham women were out on the porch talking. They stopped to stare at her as she flew past. She ran around the corner of the house and focused on the red well pump. She yanked off her shirt and threw it on the ground, then pulled off Horatio's big boots and trousers, putting them all in one pile.

She pumped the handle and squatted in front of the water and let it sluice all over her. A bar of soap sat in a basket next to the pump and she scooped it up. She scrubbed her face and arms, all over her body until her skin stung. Then she scooped up her clothes and did the same.

By the time she was done, her hands were red and raw, and her eyes stung. She didn't realize she'd been crying until her face remained wet. Rory sat on the ground, half-naked and wet, weeping over the men she had killed.

A warm blanket landed on her shoulders and she shivered at the sudden covering. Hannah stood beside her, clean clothes on her arm. She didn't look at Rory with pity, thank God, but with sympathy.

"The men are off doing manly chores. No one can see." Hannah waited patiently while Rory regained her self-control.

"I'm sorry. I don't know what came over me." Rory struggled to her feet and hugged the blanket around her. "I don't normally walk around naked behind folks' houses."

"You've been through a lot the last week. There's nothing to apologize for." Hannah averted her gaze as Rory wiped her face on the blanket. Matt's wife was a wonderful person, sweet and considerate.

Yet Rory felt foolish for what she'd done. "Thank you for bringing me the blanket."

"Why don't you slip on these clothes and the boots Catherine outgrew? You're a bit taller than me but they should fit you. You and I both have ah, large endowments." Hannah was right on that count. Big tits on both of them. "I guessed on the boots since you wore some that seemed too big."

Rory took the clothes and dressed quickly, rinsing off her feet and muddy drawers after she slipped on the dress. The boots fit well. She wasn't one to wear female fripperies but the clean clothes were welcome. It almost took away the darkness of what she'd done earlier. Almost.

"Why don't you come into the house and have some coffee and dinner? Eva is making ham sandwiches and opening up some pickles and peaches." Hannah smiled, her easy manner soothing to Rory, still raw and exposed.

Awkward didn't even describe the feelings Rory experienced walking back into the Graham's house. Not only was she wearing a dress that was too short, but it was a *dress*. Plus, she had been running around naked in their yard. She wondered how many of Caleb's family had seen her ripping through the yard in the altogether and scrubbing herself. It didn't matter, she supposed. The men had already seen her when she pissed on the ash. Eva had overheard Caleb's embarrassing comments as well. Nothing like a good first impression for the Grahams.

When she stepped into the house, the twins ran up to Hannah calling her Mama. They looked up at Rory with curiosity.

"This is Uncle Caleb's lady?" The outspoken one, Rory thought it was Meredith, tugged at her dress.

"Yes, I believe she is."

Just like that Hannah brought her into the house, and into their home. The family all pitched in setting the table, pouring milk, slicing bread. All the while no one stared or whispered at Rory. She watched in amazement as this great big family put a meal on the table together.

How had they created such a jackass like Caleb?

In truth, she saw glimmers of this family in him but he was still heavy-handed and arrogant. He always assumed he was right and everyone else was wrong.

Hannah led her to the table and had her sit on the corner beside her. The twins sat between Hannah and Matt. Everyone else settled into what she assumed was their usual place. The conversation went on around her, no one silent or staring, except for Rory of course. She ate a bit of ham and a slice of bread with one pickle. However she wasn't in the mood to eat.

She glanced around the table and noted two people were missing. Benjy and Caleb. She assumed the older one was sleeping off the potent laudanum she'd put down his throat. But where was Benjy?

Rory leaned over to her new friend. "Where is Benjy?"

Hannah shook her head. "He is sitting with Caleb. Eva tried to convince him to eat but he said he wasn't hungry."

Rory's mouth dropped open. "Benjy told you he wasn't hungry? With words?"

"Yes, with words." Hannah frowned.

"He spoke?"

"Yes, he did." Hannah glanced around. Everyone had stopped to look at Rory. Exactly what she didn't want. "Was he silent before?"

"I've seen Benjy off and on the last year but he never spoke. All the while we were, ah, traveling together, he never spoke." Rory glanced around at the family's faces, expressions of sadness and sympathy met her gaze. "I guess he needed to be with his family to find his voice."

Silence followed her words and she wanted to stuff them back in her mouth. It wasn't her business. Hell, she would only be there for a short time. She had to find a way back to her property, to salvage what she could of her life and figure out what to do.

"Thank you." Matt's words startled Rory. She turned to look at him over the tops of his daughter's heads.

"You don't owe me thanks."

"We do. All of us. I don't know how any of this happened, but if Caleb hadn't met you, he wouldn't have found Benjy and we wouldn't have him back." Matt's voice, previously gruff and cold, was now full of emotion. Enough to make her throat tight. "He's been gone five years and not a day went by that we didn't miss him. Now, thanks to you, we have him back."

"It was a series of accidents, I really—"

"No more." Eva cut off Rory before she could continue. "There are no accidents. God always has a plan and you were part of it. For Benjamin and for Caleb."

She didn't want their gratitude because she didn't feel she deserved it, but she wouldn't argue. It was enough to be accepted and have a meal to eat, clean clothes. As soon as she knew Caleb was healed, she would make whatever decisions she needed to. For now, she would stay with the Grahams and try not to make too much of an ass of herself. Although she already had a head start.

The rest of the meal passed a bit more quietly and then the crew got to work cleaning up. Eva brought coffee to the older family members while the younger four did the dishes. It was efficient and impressive.

Rory sipped the coffee, strangely content in this family's house. They put her at ease without meaning to, or perhaps they had meant to. Either way she experienced a measure of peace, at least for a few precious minutes.

After she finished the coffee, only Eva, Martha and Hannah were left in the kitchen. The rest of the Grahams had disappeared to do chores or whatever they had to do. Hannah smiled at her over the cup in her hands.

"You can go check on him." She gestured with her head. "Second room on the right."

Rory opened her mouth to say no but shut it without speaking. She did want to see him and make sure he was healing well. After all, he'd saved her life, more than once. It was the least she could do to

159

repay him for his services.

If there was another reason, her buried emotions for the man, her hope he meant what he said about loving her, well, she wasn't going to admit it to anyone. Even herself.

Caleb woke up in an instant, as though someone had poked him with something. His eyes flew open to find Benjy sitting beside his bed. The boy was quiet and still, watching him.

"Benjy, how long have you been here?" Caleb didn't expect the answer but the question slipped out.

"A while." Benjy's voice, deeper than a five-year-old's but not as deep as a teenager's, startled Caleb.

He stared at his brother. "Holy shit, did you just answer me?"

Benjy shrugged. "I didn't want to talk before."

Caleb tried to sit up and pain sliced through him. "Oh, fuck, that hurt. I mean, oh pretend you didn't hear me cuss."

Benjy, as expected, was silent. Caleb decided lying down was a better option. He managed to smile at his youngest brother.

"You doing okay? Being back at the Circle Eight?"

"I remember some stuff, but I forgot a lot." Benjy looked at the floor, shuffling his feet. "Everybody's staring."

"They missed you is all. Nobody wants you to feel uncomfortable. Give it time and it'll feel like home and family again." Caleb sure as hell hoped that was true. This boy deserved that and more. It would take time to find out exactly what had happened in those last five years, if ever.

"Cat laid in the sun with me in the back."

Caleb had a flash of a memory of the two youngest Grahams, thick as thieves, always hiding and playing together. They used to lie in the grass while Mama worked in the garden, too small to help, and she'd convinced them the sun would make them grow bigger. He smiled, pleased to know that Catherine had broken through Benjy's shell a little.

"She's tall, isn't she? Pain in the ass too. She can outride any of us, a natural rider on a horse. Gonna break her neck if she's not careful." Caleb noted Benjy's interest in their sister's riding ability. He would tell Matt to pair them up, provided Catherine didn't try to talk Benjy into something stupid.

A soft knock on the door preceded Rory sticking her head

160

through. She smiled at Benjy and the smile faded when she caught sight of Caleb. He didn't know whether to be insulted or pleased she'd come to see him.

"Supper is on the table, Benjy. You need to eat."

Supper? Caleb had arrived in the morning. It was already six o'clock in the evening?

"It's my turn to sit with him." Rory stepped into the room wearing a dress. A pink one he'd seen Hannah wear. A dress!

Caleb tried not to gape but it was damn hard. He didn't even contemplate what she looked like in anything but her trousers and, except maybe her leather apron. Now she was dressed as a female. The soft lines of the dress accentuated her curves. Her short hair just emphasized how feminine she was.

Benjy got to his feet and left the room without a word. He might be talking but it wasn't much. God only knew how long he would be a stranger to his family. Caleb hoped it wasn't very long.

"I've been lying here eight hours?" He groused as she sat down in the chair Benjy had vacated.

"You needed to sleep."

"You made me sleep."

"Six of one, half dozen of the other."

"Hmph. You wouldn't see it that way if the situation were reversed." He dared her to contradict him.

"I wouldn't take laudanum even if someone forced it to my lips."

He clenched his teeth to keep the chuckle inside. She amused the hell out of him at the same time she drove him crazy.

"I'll remember that."

"You do that." She crossed her arms, pushing up those breasts, straining the buttons on the front of the dress.

He tried not to look but hell, he was a man and she was the woman who had taken over his life and his heart. Now they were safe from the threat and he could focus on figuring out what they had and what to do about it. Her tits would be a distraction though.

"Stop staring at them." She dropped her arms and huffed at him. "They aren't a private show for you to ogle."

He tried to look innocent. "I can't see well in here, what am I looking at?"

Her gaze narrowed. "You are full of shit, Caleb Graham."

At this, he couldn't stop the laugh from escaping, then his belly hurt and he gasped in pain rather than amusement. She dropped to her knees beside the bed, concern in her gaze.

"Don't rip out those stitches by acting foolish."

He frowned at her. "Don't make me laugh."

"I assure you that was not my intention." She put her hand on the bandage and peered at it. "I don't see any fresh blood coming through."

He didn't want to talk about his wound but he did want more of her touch. Caleb wanted her to stay and not just for now. How could he tell her? She was tough and valued her independence more than any woman he'd ever met.

"I'm hungry."

She got to her feet. "That's a good sign. Be right back."

When she left the room, he was very much alone. For the first time in a long time, while he was by himself, he was lonely. Is this what she'd done to him? Made it so that he didn't enjoy his own company any longer? It was disconcerting. She had power over him and he was helpless to control her. It would be the height of foolishness to let her know.

She came back with a bowl and a spoon. When she sat in the chair, he caught a whiff of what could only be beef stew. He made a face.

Rory raised one brow. "You said you were hungry."

"That's beef stew."

"I am aware of that." She scooted closer to the bed.

"It has carrots in it." He could almost taste their gritty flavor already and shrank back into the pillow.

"Are you afraid of carrots, Ranger?" Amusement lit her features. "Big, strong you?"

"I'm not afraid of anything. And did you just call me big and strong?" He smiled at her. "I like that."

She leaned in with a spoonful. "You're going to like it less if I force feed you this stew."

He scowled. "I really don't like carrots."

"You need your strength back. Eat."

The spoon hovered an inch from his closed lips. In her eyes he saw she would not give up unless he ate.

"You are a bully."

"You are a jackass so we're even." She pressed the spoon to his lips. "You can either eat the stew or wear it."

At this he laughed and she took the opportunity to shove the spoon in his mouth. The delicious salty flavor was ruined by the orange chunks of demon root, but he dutifully chewed and swallowed.

"That wasn't so bad, was it?" She scooped up another bite.

"It was actually. Nasty." He knew he was acting like a little boy but carrots had always been the one food he couldn't tolerate.

"Then you'd better eat fast so you can avoid the taste." She proceeded to feed him with vigor, quick enough he had barely enough time to chew before the next spoonful entered his mouth.

When she scraped the side of the bowl with the spoon, he was surprised. He'd eaten the entire stew. Her tactics worked. Damn. Now he had carrots rolling around in his stomach.

"More?" She raised her brows.

"No. I'm full." He was, indeed, full. Sleepiness knocked at his door and he slid the blanket up to cover him. A yawn escaped and she got to her feet like a shot.

"I'll leave you to sleep."

He caught her wrist. "No, don't go."

"You expect me to watch you sleep?" Her tone was unusual, and he couldn't put his finger on why.

"No, I want you to climb in here with me." He patted the mattress. "I'm cold."

"I'll find another blanket."

"Please." Caleb was surprised as she was to hear the word pop out of his mouth. "I want you here."

She set the bowl down on the washstand and sat on the edge of the bed. Her expression was vulnerable and his heart skipped a beat.

"Why?" Her soft question made him smile.

"Hell, woman, I can't imagine spending another night without you near me. Preferably next to me." He reached up and cupped her cheek, the skin softer than a flower petal.

"I don't understand why." She looked as though she was about to run so he pulled on her until she tumbled into the bed.

His wound screamed but it was worth it when she stayed in the bed. Although she didn't snuggle up beside him, she did take his hand in hers. It was enough. For now.

When he was healed, he would convince her to stay beside him for good.

Benjy sat on the stump and stared up at the stars. There were so many of them, like someone was up there poking holes in the black velvet of the night to peer down at earth. Fanciful notion but he often wondered who was looking at him.

He was home. Finally. Back at the Circle Eight, a hazy memory from so long ago. The scents, the tastes, were more familiar than the sights. His family had all changed, especially the girls. Olivia was off somewhere having a baby, so he hadn't seen her yet. Liv would be the same, he just knew it.

Their parents' graves were in the shadows of the big tree and he hadn't brought himself to go visit them yet. Perhaps they wouldn't remember him. He had been gone such a long time and he wasn't the same boy.

He didn't belong here. Yet he didn't belong anywhere. Staying here would give him a safe place to be, clothes, food, and a family who tried too hard to make him feel at home. Yet, they knew it the same as he did. Benjy didn't belong. The name didn't either.

For a while he had been "boy" and then Garza decided he needed a name and started calling him Marcello. In truth, he had no name other than what he gave himself. Perhaps one day he could explain that to the Grahams but not today.

Eva would be looking for him if he didn't get back in the house. He was more comfortable outside and didn't want to be under a roof. Maybe he could sleep under those stars and let whoever was looking get their fill of him.

He stretched out on the grass and closed his eyes. Although he didn't know what tomorrow would bring, he was free. Finally free.

Rory hadn't intended to sleep in the same bed with him, but when the sun peeked into the window and tapped at her eyelids, she woke up beside Caleb. Perhaps it was the physical closeness of being on the trail together or something equally as annoying that drove her to act so foolishly. This was the man who had cost her all of her land. What was she thinking having feelings for him? Worse, having sex with him and wanting to do it again.

There was no help for it. She had officially lost her mind.

He lay on his belly, his arm across her middle, heavy and warm. The scent of man and of home surrounded her, made her want so much more than a lonely smithy. She wanted so badly to stay there forever, snuggle into his life and keep the wonderful spot for good. It was too soon though, much too soon, to make that wish or to make it happen. The ranger and she had plenty more knowing to do first.

She tried to climb out from beneath him and out of the bed, but his grip tightened. There was no help for it—she'd have to wake him up. That meant he might try to convince her to stay in the bed, in his life. She couldn't let that happen, not yet.

"Wake up, Ranger." She poked his shoulder.

One blue-green eye opened. "Hm?"

"I need to piss and you're holding me down." She would always be honest with him, that was her way.

He chuckled but he moved his arm. As she climbed out of the bed, his hand slid up her thigh. A shiver of pure arousal raced through her at the feel of his callused palm on her skin.

"I like the skirt. Easy access."

She wanted to smack at the same time she wanted him to put his hand on her again. "You have smutty thoughts."

"All the time." He grinned at her and closed his one open eye. "Now hurry up and do your business then climb back in here with me."

She headed for the door, slipping her boots on. He grumbled from the bed but didn't protest her leaving the room. Rory crept out into the kitchen and found a pot of coffee on the stove but no one about. She went outside to the necessary and did her business. On the way back, she spotted Benjy asleep in the grass, his body damp with dew.

He looked like a little boy for the first time since she'd seen him. His face was relaxed in sleep, his cheeks still round with childishness. She used the outhouse, then returned to the boy. After contemplating what to do, she knelt down and gently touched his ankle, not wanting to startle him.

Benjy was instantly and entirely awake. He jumped to his feet in a crouch, his hands fisted and eyes wide. When he saw her sitting there, still as she could keep herself, he relaxed his hands.

"I heard you've been talking to your family. That's good."

He shrugged.

"If you don't want to talk to me, that's okay. You were very brave yesterday, riding alone and with bad men behind you." She gave him a small smile.

"I was scared." His voice was deeper than she thought, on the verge of changing into a young man.

"Me too." She folded her hands in her lap. "But we all made it back and the bad men are dead."

"Ellie killed one of them." Benjy picked at the grass, not meeting her gaze.

"I wondered who had." She didn't want to scare the boy by telling him she was glad they were all dead and deserved worse.

They fell silent. The dew was soaking her dress. Unused to anything but trousers, her legs were cold and she started to shiver. Although it wasn't cold, it was cool enough she was uncomfortable. How had Benjy slept out here without even a blanket?

"You want to come inside and have breakfast? I think Eva is awake." She got to her feet, hoping the boy would follow her.

"Not hungry."

"You need to eat sometime and Eva is a good cook." She walked toward the house and wrapped her arms around her. That coffee was sounding pretty good right about then.

To her surprise, Benjy fell into step beside her. He didn't say anything but he said a lot without speaking. When they walked into the house, Eva was in the kitchen. She glanced up at them and a wide smile spread across her face.

"*Hijo*, there you are. You need some hot breakfast I think." She gestured to the table. "I make eggs and ham and biscuits."

Rory's stomach growled and Eva winked at her. Now that she had convinced the boy to come back into the house, she couldn't leave to return to Caleb. Much as her body urged her to, she needed to show good manners to her hostess.

"Coffee, Mrs. Foster?" Eva took a cup from the shelf above the sink.

"Yes, ma'am."

"Ah, call me Eva. I don't much look like a ma'am." The housekeeper smiled and poured the coffee.

"Then please call me Rory. I haven't been a missus in a year."

"*Bueno*."

Rory sat at the table and breathed a sigh of relief when Benjy sat down as well. Eva set the cup in front of Rory then turned to Benjy.

"I have fresh milk from Daisy." She didn't push or rush the boy.

166

After a minute, while Rory sipped her coffee, he finally nodded.

Eva poured a cup from a cloth-covered bucket by the sink, then set it on the table for Benjy. Rory could see the housekeeper wanted to ruffle his hair or hug him or just touch him to make sure he was real, yet she held back. It was hard for his family to have him back, perhaps harder than having him missing.

"Let me get the eggs cooking." Eva turned back to the stove and Rory tried to relax.

It was harder than she thought to sit at the table while a sleepy, sexy Caleb waited for her in the other room. In truth, the time here with Benjy and Eva saved her from acting on her impulses with the ranger. She wanted to do much more than sit beside his bed and that was dangerous. Rory had already been married and knew what it was like to be with a man day in and day out.

Was she ready to make that kind of commitment to Caleb? Or was she in love with him because he saved her life and they'd had an incredible experience together? She didn't know and that worried her.

Eva whipped up eggs quickly and set down plates of food in front of both Rory and Benjy. The boy pushed the food around the plate and ate a few bites. Eva sat down with her coffee and Rory did her best to eat normally although her stomach was tight with emotion.

After ten minutes, Benjy set his fork down. "May I be excused?"

Eva sighed. "*Sí, hijo*. You need to eat more."

He got up and went back outside, alone in a family of eight siblings. Rory's heart ached for him and she wished there was something she could do.

"You knew him when he lived with this man?" Eva asked the question casually but Rory heard the underlying emotion.

"A little. He never spoke, and I'm still surprised to hear words come out of his mouth."

Eva sipped at her coffee. "Was he happy?"

Rory considered her answer before she answered. "I don't think he was unhappy, but I can't say if he was happy. He was a shadow of a boy and I think he spent his time finding new places to hide."

A small sob escaped from the older woman's house. "*Pobrecito.* If we knew he was two hundred miles from here, I would have crawled there on my knees to get him."

Rory put her hand on Eva's, her own throat tight. "Sometimes I wonder why God does things that hurt people but then something else

167

happens. If Caleb hadn't come to my property, I wouldn't have climbed the tree and gotten hurt, or gone to Garza's hacienda for help, or found Benjy."

Eva was silent for a minute. "You climbed a tree?"

Rory smiled. "It's a long story. I was trying to show the ranger I wasn't going to go quietly."

Eva chuckled and patted Rory's hand. "I like you. You will be good for him."

"What if he changes his mind about me?" The question burst out of her mouth before she could stop it.

"I do not think you need to worry about that. He already wants you. I saw it in his eyes when you held his hand." Eva's grin grew wider. "Now we need to make him want you more."

"How do I do that? I don't know anything about being a woman." Rory had trouble thinking of herself as something other than a blacksmith.

"Then I help you. Hannah will help too. We will make you irresistible."

Rory didn't know what that meant but she was encouraged by Eva's confident tone. "How do we do that?"

"First we make him sit in there alone until he can't stand another minute of it. Caleb was the most selfish of the boys growing up. He was so busy thinking about himself, he didn't see everyone else. For the first time, he sees you." Eva got to her feet. "Now let me bring him breakfast while you find other things to do."

"But he's recovering from a bullet wound." Rory wasn't sure she wanted to keep away from him.

"We'll take care of him. Look in at him once a day but no more. We want him to wonder what you're doing and why you aren't in there with him." Eva put her hands on her hips. "It will be good for him to realize he has to work for the love he has for you."

"You think he loves me?" Rory's heart leapt at the thought.

"*Sí, hija*, I know he loves you." Eva pointed to the plate of half-eaten eggs. "Now eat up. We've got some planning to do."

Caleb was grumpy. It had been three days and he was damn tired of lying in the bed. His stitches itched, his mood was sour and he missed Rory. She'd barely even said hello, letting Eva and Hannah take care of him. Crazy as it was, he had been in her company for a short time, but every minute of every day in that week. They became connected through an intense experience, through death and life, and everything in between.

He was trapped in his childhood bedroom and none too happy about it. Coming home to the Circle Eight had been what he wanted, wasn't it? However now that he was here, he wanted something else.

It took him two days to figure out that something was Rory. She was the reason he looked to come back. She reminded him of what he'd left behind and he contemplated sharing with her. That was the crux of the problem.

He lay there considering asking her to marry him, which was the craziest thought to ever enter his head, and she didn't visit him. It was the last nail in his coffin of grumpiness. If anyone came in other than Rory, he snapped and snarled at them. A foolish man with a foolish heart. What he needed to do was tell her how he felt and ask her that question tumbling around inside him.

She had to actually enter the room for that to happen.

When the door opened he snapped to attention, making his side hurt. Matt poked his head in and Caleb growled. His older brother frowned and stepped in, taking his hat off.

"I heard you're acting like a bear and scaring the children." Matt sat in the chair beside the bed, apparently not intimidated by the snarling beast in the bed.

"So what?"

Matt raised one brow. "You've been gone for four years, with a handful of visits lasting no more than a day or two. Now you show up with Benjy, a lady blacksmith with a deadly hammer and an attitude that could flay the skin off a beeve."

Caleb told himself not to lower his gaze. He was a grown man, no longer a young 'un who had to bow his head when his brother chastised him. It was hard, but he kept his head up and his shoulders back.

"I left because I had to."

"I can appreciate that." Matt nodded. "I stayed because I had to. But I love it here, the land, the sky, the cattle. Most of all I stayed because of family."

The implication of Matt's words were clear but Caleb wasn't his brother.

"My life had a different path than yours. Not better or worse, just different." Caleb folded his arms. "Am I not welcome here?"

"Hell, that's not what I meant." Matt blew out a breath through his teeth. "I never knew what to expect outta you, Caleb. You were a pain in the ass as a boy and worse as a teenager, then you disappeared at nineteen to join the Rangers. I don't know who you are as a man."

The bald truth was hard to swallow but Caleb recognized it as such.

"I didn't know who I was either. I do now." He ran his hands through his hair, knowing he probably looked frightening with four days' worth of whiskers, dirty hair and a snarl on his face.

"Sometimes it takes a while to find your way." Matt waited for Caleb to continue.

"I won't regret being a ranger. It was a worthy profession and I did many things to keep Texas safe."

"Was?" Matt's mouth quirked up at the corner.

"Yeah, was." Caleb found a matching grin for his brother. "I decided to stay on one condition."

"Don't ask me to call you Mr. Graham."

Caleb laughed then clutched his side when his wound sang a sad song. "No, you fool. I will stay if Rory stays here with me. As my wife."

Matt's mouth dropped open. "Wife? Truly?"

"You have something against her? She's not a typical female but she's got so much—"

"That's not what I said," Matt interrupted Caleb's thoughts before he got too far. "I like her. She's the toughest woman I've ever met, and that includes Eva and Olivia. I'm surprised that you want to get married. Weren't you the boy who said he'd never take a wife?"

Caleb made a face. "I was ten."

"You never changed your mind."

"Until now. Until Rory." Caleb held up his hands. "I can't explain it but I know I want to marry her, wake up next to her, fight with her, avoid her hammer swings and make beautiful babies with her."

The very idea of seeing her face every day, her smiles and her scowls, and kissing her each morning and each night was enough to make his heart clench. Oh he had it bad, really bad.

"That's how I feel about Hannah, except for the hammer part." Matt smiled broadly. "Well, hell brother, you're in love."

"Yeah, I am." Caleb returned the smile. "Will you help me?"

"Sure I'd be happy to. What do you want me to do?"

"I have no idea." Caleb's scowl was back. He more or less had never sparked with a girl. The women in his life were paid for or widows. He'd had no time for proper courting. Now he needed advice on what to do. "How did you woo Hannah?"

"I didn't. I asked her to marry me when we were strangers, remember?" Matt looked perplexed. "I eventually found my way, bumpy and foolish but I got there."

"That's not helpful."

"I'm not one who had lots of experience with females, Caleb. Maybe we ought to ask Hannah for advice."

Caleb looked at his brother with horror. "No. No. No."

"You want her to say yes? Be your wife? Then you're going to have to ask someone who can actually help." Matt was right. Dammit.

"Okay, I give in." Caleb didn't look forward to admitting to his sister-in-law he needed her assistance. The first time they met, he'd called her a heifer. That memory made him cringe. "I can't woo her if she's avoiding me. Maybe Hannah can help get her in the room with me."

Matt nodded. "Agree with you on that one. She's been shoeing horses."

"What?"

"Said your horse had a nick in his shoe so she set up shop for Justice. Next thing you know, folks heard about a farrier on our ranch and started coming by for shoeing." Matt shrugged. "It's two hours to town and having a smithy here on the Circle Eight is convenient. She said it made her feel useful, refused to accept any money. Instead people have been bringing food to pay for her work."

It was Caleb's turn for his mouth to drop open. "She's been shoeing horses?"

"Damn good at it too. Keeps complaining she doesn't have a proper forge or anvil to do anything else, but she swings that hammer with something like grace. I ain't never seen the like."

Caleb pulled the blanket back and swung his legs to the edge of the bed. "There is no chance I am staying in this bed. I've been waiting for her to come see me and she's been working? I'm done waiting. That woman is going to be wooed, dammit, whether or not she likes it."

EMMA LANG

CHAPTER TEN

Rory walked through the entrance to the barn, leading the gelding back into the building. He'd been one of the most even-tempered of the equines on the Circle Eight. He belonged to Javier, one of the handsome Vasquez men. Both he and his brother had wide smiles to go with their wide shoulders and impeccable manners. They had been nothing but polite to her.

Everyone was polite. It was driving her mad.

Three days of staying away from Caleb and pretending she was happy shoeing horses. Not that she didn't like taking care of the beasts, but it wasn't what she needed or wanted. They were coming together, those needs and wants stuck in her heart and gut, pulsing with their own life. It took every ounce of willpower not to run in the house and confess to Caleb that she loved him.

It had taken every ounce of strength she had to accept her feelings as real. If she told him, she opened herself to another man, another potential loss in her life. She had lost everyone and everything she loved. Using the hammer helped her get rid of her frustration most days. She couldn't quite do that at the Graham ranch.

No anvil, no forge, and only some horses to shoe. It left her antsy and grumpy. Javier had nearly run off when he dropped off the gelding to her half an hour earlier. She expected the snarl on her face had something to do with it.

She secured the gelding in his stall and closed the door. Leaning against it, she wished for the millionth time she was back home with all her familiar things. She was out of place and lost, nothing to anchor her but the hammer and tongs. They were nestled in the sack she'd carried them in, hanging off the side of her saddle, which sat unused on the saddle stand in the corner. The Grahams were so unfailingly nice. They had retrieved the rest of her belongings and took care of Cora for her.

The next person who asked her if she needed anything might get a right-hook to the jaw.

"What the hell are you doing?" Caleb's voice cut through the air, throwing up a storm of dust motes around the barn.

She turned to find him in the doorway, his hair sticking up in a hundred different directions, dark whiskers on his chin, clothes buttoned wrong and a fierce scowl on his face.

"I could ask you the same question, Ranger." She put one fist on her hip. "You're supposed to be in bed recovering."

"I'm done lying in that fucking bed." He stepped into the barn, his movements more like stalking.

She stood her ground, excitement curling in her belly. "Your language is appalling."

He waved his hand in dismissal. "I've heard worse out of your pretty mouth."

Her lips twitched at being called pretty. "What do you want?"

"You." He bit off the word. It hung in the air, dancing with the dust motes while she tried to think of how to respond to him.

"How nice for you." She turned her back and walked deeper into the barn. If he came after her, it would be slow going. Truthfully, his injury gave her time to get her thoughts together. What if he asked her to stay? Could she and would she?

He snatched her off her feet before she'd gotten more than a few steps in. A squeak burst from her mouth as he pushed her up against the barn wall. A very hard male body kept her in place.

A shiver of excitement raced through her. Rory wasn't the type of woman to be ordered around by a man or enjoy it, but this side of the ranger thrilled her. Deep inside where she told herself no one could see, she shivered in arousal.

"You've been ignoring me, Aurora."

Aurora. Her given name rolled off his tongue like a caress. She closed her eyes as her body warmed, thumping with heat.

"You were shot. I didn't know I was supposed to entertain you. Didn't your family take care of you?" She didn't try to escape his hold, although she knew if she pushed back, he would let her go. She was safe but held in place at the same time. It was just as strange as their relationship had been since the moment she'd laid eyes on him.

"They fed me and changed my bandages, even emptied my piss pot. It wasn't them I wanted." He ground his cock against her ass and she was instantly wet and ready. For the first time in her life, she wished she wore a skirt so he could toss it up and bury himself inside her. Yet she had donned her stained trousers to work in the barn.

Perhaps she needed a dress or two after all.

"What do you want, Caleb?" She didn't recognize her own voice, breathy and high.

"I want to hear my name on your tongue when I take you against this wall." He nipped at her neck, kissing and licking his way to her ear.

She had never heard or experienced anything as arousing. A small moan escaped her throat. He stilled, his breath gusting on her ear. Her entire body was tight as a bow string, her nipples ached and her pussy throbbed. She needed him to make good on his threats. Now.

"All talk." Rory pushed back against him. "Show me."

This time he growled and she shivered at the sound. He stepped back, and the loss made her body follow him. She would describe his resulting chuckle as evil. At the moment, she wanted nothing more than to have him up against her, pushing into her, making her call his name like he wanted.

Oh God, she wanted, so badly.

"Take off those damn trousers. I never even thought about how sweet a woman's ass was until you paraded around in front of me with those on."

She grinned at the wall, pleased to know she drove him as mad as he drove her. Made her feel feminine. Powerful. However, she still also needed to strip before her body imploded from need.

Rory made quick work of her trousers, pushing them down and yanking off her boots. A sudden thought struck her.

"What if someone walks in."

"I'll shoot them." He grabbed her hips, his callused hands sliding down her skin to her thighs, then back up on the inside. She held her breath until his fingers dipped into her moisture. "You're wet. I think you like this, Aurora."

"Shut up and get busy, Ranger. I'm not standing here naked so you can tell me what I already know." She wiggled her ass to emphasize her point.

He sucked in a breath and then a very hard, hairy, and naked male body pressed against her. She opened her hands on the wall, pushing against him. He felt good, more than good, perfect.

His knee crept between her knees and moved her legs apart. He kissed her neck again and reached around to cup her breasts.

"I dreamed about these, you know. Your tits are flawless, round and ripe, perfect for my mouth and my hands. One day I might try my dick between them." He pinched her nipples and she gasped in pleasure. "You like that?"

"Better than coffee."

He chuckled against her skin. "I can't wait any longer, Aurora. I need to fuck you."

She tightened at the naughty words, her body more than ready to receive his. "Then fuck me."

He drove into her body in one stroke. She let loose a scream that spooked a few horses but he didn't shush her. No, he pinched her nipples again.

"Next time I want to hear my name."

Her eyes about rolled back in her head as he thrust into her, again and again. Harder. Faster. The wall rocked with the force of their joining. Her body tightened around him with each moment, her slick passage welcoming his hard cock. She scratched at the wall, her breath coming in short bursts.

A coil of pleasure tightened in her belly each time he pulled out completely, then filled her again. A moan built inside her as her release approached.

"I won't last long, honey. You need to come for me." His voice was rough and breathy.

"Close, so close." She spread her legs a bit farther, pulling him deeper.

They both groaned at once. His pace increased and she knew he was about to find his release. To her surprise, he reached between her legs and pinched her clit. Her orgasm ripped through her with the force of a twister, pulling her this way and that, pure ecstasy, sweeter than any moment in her life.

"Caleb!"

He gripped her hips and drove into her, touching her womb, her heart, her soul. She shuddered with shocks of pleasure as her body accepted his. Her heart thudded hard enough to block out all sound but her blood rushing around her body. He laid his forehead on her shoulder, his breath hot and heavy on her neck.

"Holy shit."

She chuckled, joy and satisfaction warring for control of her. "I second that."

"I came out here to ask you something but now I've taken you against the wall." He pulled away and his warm seed trickled down her leg.

To her consternation, he was also pulling away from her emotionally. "I wanted you to."

"Doesn't mean I should have done it." He buttoned up his trousers and moved back a few feet. "You should get dressed."

She whirled around, furious with him. "No."

His brows went up. "If you want to sashay around half-naked, that's your business." His tone said something entirely different than his words.

"I am your business and you are mine." She approached him, poking at his chest with her finger. "You came in here to tell me you loved me and ask me to marry you but you're too much of a chicken to do it."

His eyes widened. "Pardon?"

"You heard me." She cupped his whiskered cheek. "If you're going to be a coward, then I'll do it. I love you, Caleb Graham. Marry me."

He threw back his head and laughed, a gut-busting guffaw that made him double over, hand on his still healing wound. "Woman, you… I can't…"

Rory had made a terrible mistake. One of epic proportions. Her body ran ice cold, every sliver of pleasure frozen in the wake of his rejection. As her heart broke into a thousand pieces, she yanked on her clothes and ran from the barn as fast as her legs could take her.

The shaking started in his legs, then traveled up to his gut and soon he trembled from head to toe. What the hell had just happened? He staggered, bracing his hand against the same wall the woman he loved had just been scratching while he fucked her. His fingers traced the marks she'd made in the wood while he tried to stop himself from wobbling around like a newborn calf.

He dropped to his knees and took a deep breath before he landed on the floor face first. What kind of fool was he? Apparently the jackass she had accused him of being. He had treated her like a whore, then let her walk away.

She might even walk right off the Circle Eight.

Caleb had done some dumb things in his life but this was the worst. Matt had tried to tell him to do the right thing. Yet Caleb had done the opposite, letting his dick lead him around instead of his heart.

"Are you yanking at your pecker?" Nicholas's voice came from behind him.

Caleb glanced at his brother. "I'm trying not to puke."

"Shouldn't you be in bed? I thought you got shot." Nicholas stood with his hands on his hips, pants tucked into shit-covered boots. Maybe if Caleb asked, his little brother would kick him. He sure as hell deserved it.

"I was trying to, well, I fucked it up good." He got to his feet carefully, swallowing back the bile that coated the back of his throat.

"Fucked what up?" Nick pushed his hat back.

"My marriage."

"Your what?" His brother's eyes almost popped out of his head.

"I have to find her and make her understand." Caleb took a deep breath and spotted Cora's saddle. "You went back for her things?" He ran his hand along the old, smooth leather.

"Of course we did. She helped find Benjy didn't she? Besides, we wasn't gonna leave her things for someone to grab." Nicholas gestured to the saddle. "We took care of the mule carcass too. Damn, she ran that thing into—"

"Remember you're talking about my future wife, Nick." Caleb's voice was more of a growl, his protective instincts jumping up and down on his heart.

"Jesus, fine. I won't talk about it then." Nicholas held up his hands. "I came to find you since Eva about had kittens when she found you gone from the bed. Olivia had the baby."

Caleb blinked at the rapid change of subject. "What?"

"Liv, your sister, she had the baby. It was a boy. Brody sent over one of his farm hands to let us know. The girls are fixing to head out in an hour." Nicholas turned to leave the barn. "Eva was worried to leave you alone. I'll tell her you're acting like your normal self and not to worry."

"Wait, what's my normal self?" Caleb knew the answer before his brother spoke.

"Like a jackass."

Caleb stood there and stared at the saddle, his mind whirling with the possibilities of what he could do to convince her he wasn't the jackass he had been. Then he noticed the burlap bag and knew she wasn't really gone. Rory wouldn't leave without her hammer and tongs. She'd told him more than once how important they were to her.

He still had a chance.

With renewed determination and an idea, he left the barn and out into the bright sunlight. He headed for the creek. Rory would have wanted to clean up and not out by the well. No, she was half-naked when she ran off, so the creek was the likely place.

He kept telling himself she would listen and he would grovel. For the first time in his life, he would do the apologizing and hope like hell she forgave him. No woman had received so much as an "I'm sorry" from him. Now he needed to do much more than simply apologize.

She sat on his favorite rock, knees up and arms wrapped around them. Rory looked small and alone as the water burbled merrily past her. His heart twisted at the sight. It was his fault she ran and he knew it.

"When you first called me jackass, it annoyed me." He spoke aloud and she started, whirling around to glare at him. Her amber eyes flamed and her mouth tightened enough to make her jaw clench.

Caleb's heart thumped as he knelt in front of her, literally now on his knees seeking forgiveness. "I know now you were right. I am a jackass, a big one. I'm sorry, Aurora, so sorry." He took her hand and to his surprise, she didn't pull away. Her skin was clammy and hot, limp in his grasp. So unlike the strong Rory he knew.

"I know you won't forgive me that easily and I don't blame you." He swallowed the fear stuck in his throat and took a step he didn't expect to ever take. "I love you and I want to marry you."

She snorted and frowned at him. "You love me, hm? Then why did you laugh in my face when I told you how I felt?"

"Because I'm a fool. You did the proposing part that I'm supposed to. I wasn't thinking and when you asked me, I reacted badly."

She pulled her hand back. "You're still a jackass."

"I'm apologizing to you. Can you give me a chance?" He couldn't possibly lose her. Not now. Not after he finally accepted he loved her and wanted to marry her.

"I just did and you showed me what a mistake that was." She jumped off the rock and stomped back toward the house, her arms swinging.

"Wait! I need your help." He searched his brain for an excuse, any excuse, to keep her at the Circle Eight.

She didn't even break stride. "You do not need my help."

"I meant, Benjy needs you." Caleb jumped on the idea, crafty and sneaky as it was. "The girls are getting ready to go to my sister's farm. She had her baby and she doesn't know about Benjy yet. He will be more comfortable if you go with him."

She stopped and her head dropped to her chest. Triumph danced beside him. One more opportunity to make up for his mistakes.

"That's a dirty trick. You know I would do anything to help him." She didn't sound pleased with him, but her words told him she would give in.

"They're leaving within the hour." He sure as hell hoped that was right. Nick's words were a blur in the middle of Caleb's self-pity.

"Find. I'll do it for your brother, but not for you." She started walking again, leaving him on the damp ground with wet knees and regrets.

Caleb would drive the wagon to Olivia's home. It gave him two days to woo her or really make a fool of himself trying.

When he got back to the house, Captain Williams was waiting for him. It wasn't a happy expression on his commanding officer's face.

"You look like shit, Graham."

"Thank you, sir. I feel like shit." He gestured to the rocking chairs. "Care to sit? I'm sure you're not here on a social call."

The captain was a big man, with curly black hair and shoulders as wide as the door. He carried a knife as large as his forearm on his back and had the speed of a predator. No one messed with Cap if they valued their life.

He sat down and waited for the captain to do the same. Whatever it was, it wasn't good news or the Captain would have sent word, not come in person.

"I heard about Garza and his men. I brought a wagon to take care of the bodies. They were pretty ripe but still recognizable." The captain was originally from Kentucky and he had a thick country accent.

"Are you here to arrest me?" It was Caleb's worse fear. The idea of a man of the law being imprisoned for kidnapping his own brother. He wouldn't regret it. Ever.

"No, I'm here to tell you that you found a wanted man. The man you met as Pablo Garza was a war criminal. His real name is Ephraim Cunningham. He sold weapons to the Mexican Army during the war. He disappeared after Mexico lost and has been wanted since." Williams might have told Caleb that Garza was a woman in disguise. He wanted to pinch himself to make sure he wasn't lying on his bed dreaming.

"A wanted man? You mean I'm not being arrested?" Caleb had to be sure. No matter what part Rory played in their deaths, he would take all the blame for the killing.

"No, you fool. In fact if you want it, there was a five-hundred-dollar reward on his head." Williams raised his dark brows. "You did the Republic of Texas a service and closed the case of Benjamin Graham."

Caleb took a moment to absorb what his captain said. Not only was Caleb free of murder charges, but there was a reward to boot, plus Benjy was home with his family. Everything was perfect, if only he hadn't completely made an ass of himself with Rory.

"Thanks for coming to tell me." Caleb's voice was rough with the emotion that bounced around inside him.

"How are you feeling? You're walking around but you look half-dead." Williams didn't believe in telling anything but the truth.

"I'm healing. Sore but I'll survive." He came to a decision and needed to follow through on it before he changed his mind. "I was going to come see you when I was healed."

"To get your next assignment?" The captain's expression said he already knew what Caleb was going to say.

Caleb took a deep breath and took a chance on his future.

Rory wanted to curl up into a ball and nurse her wounds, but she didn't. As a strong woman, one who could hammer molten iron, she would never cower when her heart hurt. No, she would stand tall and show that jackass what she was made of.

She believed him when he apologized, but he still didn't quite understand she didn't fit into the idea he had about what a woman did. She never would. Caleb had to accept her as who she was—a blacksmith who did what needed doing, with no pretenses or preconceived notions about what was proper. Until he did, she wouldn't allow herself to give into his proposal.

Although if she thought about it too much, she might give in just to have him in her arms. It had been difficult to be cold to him, give him her back and refuse the love he offered. She had to be sure he was looking at her, and seeing the real her. Not a woman he could mold in to what he wanted her to be.

She found the house in chaos, with the Graham women running around getting things together to leave. There was shouting, laughing, pushing, shoving and all around silliness. They were all so excited over the new baby, no one seemed to notice Rory standing in the middle of the room.

"I am not changing," Catherine yelled as Eva chased after her wagging a finger. The slender blonde was faster than the housekeeper. "I want to ride my horse, not in the wagon."

"*Hija*, you listen to me." Eva and the girl disappeared into the back of the house.

Benjy appeared at her side, startling her. He moved silently, like the shadow he pretended to be. She made no move to touch him although she wanted to pull him under her arm and protect him from the madness that was his family.

"Where are they going?" He spoke softly and she barely heard him.

"To see your sister Olivia. She had a baby."

Benjy's mouth opened into the shape of an O. "Liv had a baby?"

"Yes, she had a little boy. She's married to a man named Brody and lives on a farm." It was strange to be telling Benjy about his sister's situation. Rory wondered if anybody had told him or if he hadn't listened when they did.

"Why don't we go with them and you can visit Olivia?" Rory felt awkward asking him but the women were distracted enough they likely didn't have time to consider it. They might assume he would come but Rory knew what it was to be a stranger in her own house. Asking seemed to be the right thing to do.

Benjy turned to look at her, his blue-green eyes haunted by shadows she wanted to help chase away. "Do you think she will want to see me?"

"Yes, I think she will. Do you want to see her?" Rory spotted Eva walking up toward them and she must have overheard at least part of their conversation.

"I miss her." It wasn't the answer Rory was expecting, but Eva seemed to understand.

"*Hijo*, she misses you too." Eva held out her hands. Benjy hesitated but he took one of her hands. The housekeeper's took a breath and managed a shaky smile. "We have all missed you but Olivia looked for you until she couldn't ride any longer because of the baby. She never gave up."

Benjy blinked rapidly. "I want to see her and her baby." He swayed toward Rory. "But Rory has to go too."

"*Bueno, hijo, bueno.*" Eva glanced at Rory. "You will come, *no*?"

It wasn't as though she had a choice, but Rory wanted to go. She would appreciate being away from Caleb for a day or two. Plus she might find out tidbits from his sisters and sister-in-law. Women did like to gossip but most days, Rory was too busy to participate, not that she had anyone to chat with besides her neighbor, Eloise.

"I'll go. How long will we be gone?"

"Two days, perhaps three." Eva waggled her finger at Rory, and it made her feel as though she was part of the family. Being chastised by the housekeeper was a silly reason to make her feel welcome, but that's how she felt. "You need to keep the dress Hannah gave you. It does not fit too well after she had the babies."

Rory was going to refuse the gift of the dress but Eva had already moved on, leaving Benjy with Rory again.

"I don't have anything to pack." Benjy left with only the clothes on his back.

Rory tucked her arm in his, taking a chance on touching him. "Then let's go find some clothes your brothers can lend to you."

He wasn't quite as big as his brothers, but she was sure they could find something. Within a few minutes, she had plucked a pair of trousers and two shirts from the bedrooms in the house. Hannah approved and came up with a traveling bag for Benjy to use. By the time they made it back into the kitchen, the girls were ready to leave.

Caleb stood by the door, watching her. She told herself not to react to his presence, but her entire body tightened at the sight. He nodded but she ignored him, choosing to speak to his sister-in-law instead.

"We're ready to go. Anything I can help with?" Rory could see Caleb out of the corner of her eye. He was too damn big not to see.

"No, I think we are finally ready." Hannah smiled at the Graham sisters. "Not that any of these girls were anything but excited."

The girls all looked affronted and the noise level crept up again. Rory had always wondered what it was like to be amongst a big family. Now she knew—it was a churning mass of noise and confusion, but also love, acceptance and life. There was a pulse to this house and it was because of the Grahams. She didn't know what she would do in the crushing silence after she left the ranch.

Eva herded everyone out the door, with Meredith and Margaret bouncing up and down. Rory found herself smiling despite Caleb watching her. When she made it outside, most of the girls were already in the wagon, and Elizabeth was holding out her arm to help Benjy up. Rory was pleased to see him accept his sister's hand. This trip would be good for him.

She set her bag along with Benjy's into the back with the other bags and assorted baskets of food, then climbed into the wagon. As she settled in beside Hannah, Meredith popped onto her mother's lap while her twin sister landed on Rory's. The three-year-old snuggled under her chin, the fresh smell of little girl permeating her nose.

Rory's heart caught and a lump formed in her throat. She would admit to herself she wanted a little girl of her own. One she could teach how to be strong and smart. Yet Rory couldn't have children. After being married to Horatio, she never missed her courses, no matter how many times he liked to leave his seed within her. A little girl would not be part of Rory's life. She put her arms around the child and decided to enjoy the experience for as long as she could.

Then Caleb climbed into the wagon seat wearing his pistol and picked up the traces for the horses. Rory stared, unable to reconcile the sight.

"What is he doing?" she whispered furiously to Hannah.

"Caleb? Oh, the rest of the men had too much to do on the ranch to spare the time to go to Olivia's. Eva was against it at first, but he convinced her that he was hale and hearty. Besides, he needs to explain to Olivia and Brody how he found Benjy. That's a story none of us want to tell Liv." Hannah chattered on as though she hadn't just told Rory that she would have to endure the man's company for four days in close quarters.

Damn.

"Don't squeeze too hard or you'll make me fart." Margaret squirmed from her perch on Rory's lap.

Hannah gasped and tut-tutted at her daughter. "You spend far too much time with your father."

Rory eased her grip on the child, her cheeks warm from embarrassment. "Sorry, sweetie."

"Mama, how long until we get there?" Meredith looked up at her mother. "I want to see the baby."

"It'll take a while. Uncle Caleb has to drive slow since there are so many of us in the wagon."

Catherine trotted alongside the wagon, her face wreathed in smiles as the wind caressed her skin. She was stunning at age eleven, natural on a horse, with grace and beauty to spare. When she grew up, her brothers would have a hard time keeping the boys off the ranch. All of the Graham girls were attractive, but Catherine was gorgeous.

Benjy watched her, longing on his face as he watched the horse. Other than riding alongside Caleb and Rory, she guessed the boy hadn't been on a horse since he'd been taken from the Circle Eight. She would have to mention it to Eva and perhaps get the boy a mount of his own to ride.

The girls demanded a story, and Hannah set to telling one about a princess who lived in a castle. Fanciful stuff, things Rory had never heard. Hannah was a good storyteller, with lively expressions and different voices. The girls were enraptured, their gazes glued to their mother.

After Hannah finished, others took turns, weaving tales from sweet to scary to funny. Rory thoroughly enjoyed each one, her envy over the Graham family growing. It was a wonderful way to pass the time. The little girls finally succumbed to the rocking motion of the wagon and fell asleep.

Rory closed her eyes, the exhaustion of the last week and her recovery from the wound and fever catching up to her. She dreamt of Caleb's touch, his mouth on hers, waking up beside him. Then there was a little girl with amber eyes and Caleb's brown wavy hair. She laughed as Caleb swung her around in a circle, her little feet pointing like arrows in the wind. Joy swept through Rory. It was a perfect moment.

"Aurora?" Caleb's voice startled her and she woke, gasping. He frowned at her. "Are you okay? Your face is flushed."

She glanced around and saw everyone preparing to jump out of the wagon. A small white house sat against a clear blue sky, fields of symmetrical lines of plump green plants dotted the landscape behind it. Rory heard an infant cry and her confusion sharpened.

"We just got to my sister's place. You were sleeping pretty hard." He picked her up out of the wagon and set her on her feet. "Stand there and get your bearings for a minute."

A tall man with black hair and blue eyes stepped off the front porch, grinning. The twins jumped on his legs and he laughed, dragging his steps as they squealed. The older girls gave him a brief hug before Eva took over and squeezed him so hard, Rory thought she heard a bone crack.

"*Hijo*. I am so happy for you. A boy!" She cupped his cheek. "How is she?"

"She's good. The midwife is still here. Liv will be glad to see you all." The man looked at Caleb and his brows went up. "Ranger Graham."

Caleb glanced at the ground and toed the dirt. That was by far the most interesting response she'd ever seen from the rough ranger. He obviously respected this man a great deal.

"Brody. I, uh, brought all the women." Caleb grinned. "You are a lucky man to have a boy. We've got females coming out our ears at the Circle Eight. You're not wearing that fancy pistol of yours anymore?"

"Nah, Liv doesn't want either of us carrying weapons anymore since we're parents now." The man laughed.

Either of us carrying weapons? Did that mean Caleb's sister carried a gun too? The Graham family was still an unfolding puzzle Rory had yet to figure out.

Caleb laughed too. "That sounds like a reasonable argument to me. Besides I was always afraid she'd find a reason to shoot one of her brothers."

The man called Brody shook Caleb's hand. "How did you get this assignment? The captain run out of jobs for a Texas Ranger?"

"Nah, I got shot. It's a long story." Caleb watched Benjy climb down out of the wagon. "I have a surprise for Liv and for you."

Brody's expression changed from amused to serious in a blink. If

186

this was Olivia's husband, the ex-ranger, Rory was suitably impressed by his ferocity. She'd thought Caleb was intimidating, but this man had his brother-in-law beat.

"You found him." Brody's voice had dropped to a husky whisper.

"Through a series of accidents, yes, we found him." Caleb turned to his brother. "Benjy, this is Brody, Olivia's husband."

Benjy stared at the black-haired man with something like awe mixed with fear. Brody held out his hand to the boy.

"I'm very happy to meet you, Benjy." The ex-ranger swallowed loud enough for Rory to hear it.

After a brief hesitation, Benjy shook his brother-in-law's hand. Briefly, but he did shake it. She thought she saw the boy tremble a little but he stood with his shoulders and back straight. He was a hell of a person.

"Sir."

"Call me Brody. I am married to Liv. She will be so happy to see you, Benjy. She never gave up hope." Brody picked up the twins, one on each arm. "You two go to the barn and take a look at the piglets the sow just hatched."

"Piglets!" The girls squealed and wiggled their way out of his grasp, running for the barn.

"Don't climb up in the loft!" Hannah called after them, shaking her head with a small smile.

"Are you ready?" Brody asked the boy.

Benjy nodded and they walked into the house together. Rory followed, her heart beating fast for the reunion that was to follow. She barely noticed Caleb taking her elbow and leading her into the house.

It was a modest place with one large room to the left with a few pieces of furniture. A kitchen tucked into the right side with a homey appeal, including a table and two chairs with a square lace tablecloth on top, a vase with black-eyed susans in it.

Ahead lay an open door with the sound of an infant crying emanating from it. Hushed voices of the girls also came from within. Rory didn't know Caleb's sister or this dangerous looking man with the black hair. She was uncomfortable and out of place. If she'd known Caleb was driving the wagon or how she would react to the new baby, Rory would have refused to come. Her gut twisted with what she might call fear.

Brody walked through the door in front of them and his

expression changed again. His entire face softened as he looked at whomever was in the room. It was pure love, unfiltered and unrestrained. It made Rory's heart pittypat. She wished Caleb would look at her like that.

Then she wanted to smack herself for the thought.

Yet it was the bald truth and she couldn't deny it. This hard man, Brody, loved his wife with a ferocity she recognized. It beat within her, waiting to be set loose. Caleb's rejection had wounded her ferocious core, but she never lost its depth.

"Liv? Caleb is with the girls and he brought you a surprise." When Brody turned to look at Caleb and Rory, his eyes were suspiciously wet.

Rory's heart pounded hard now, the impending reunion between brother and sister, and fear of what she would witness, made her feel itchy and odd. She wasn't used to so much emotion. It was overwhelming.

"Caleb came? What happened, did they want to punish him?" A woman's soft, tired voice came from inside the room. The girls giggled.

"Come on. You deserve part of this." Caleb stepped through the door and pulled Rory in with him.

A woman lay on the bed, her long brown hair in a braid on her shoulder. A tiny baby was bundled up beside her, an angelic face with a loud pair of lungs. He had quieted when they stepped in, blinking his owlish baby eyes at them.

The woman cocked her head and looked at Rory, making her feel self-conscious and foolish. She almost left the room but Caleb had a death grip on her arm. Benjy hovered behind her, his discomfort greater than her own.

Brody walked over to the bed and picked up the baby in his big hands. The infant waved his arms, instantly recognizing his father. "I'll let your brother tell the story."

"Liv, this is Aurora Foster, the woman who finally put a twist in my tail. Rory, this is Olivia Armstrong, my sister."

"I'm pleased to meet you, Rory. I knew there would be a woman one day who could do it." Olivia smiled at her and Rory found herself smiling back. Caleb's sister made a body feel at ease.

"And one more visitor for you." Caleb pulled her to the side, exposing Benjy to his sister.

A hush fell over the room as Olivia's amusement faded. Her face blanched and tears sprang to her eyes.

"Benjy? Oh my God. Benjy?" She crawled out of bed, ignoring her husband's protests.

Olivia was shorter than Rory but she was taller than most of her sisters. She shuffled toward Benjy with her hands out, wearing a long white nightdress and an expression of disbelief and joy. She opened her arms and Benjy fell into them.

"BenjyBenjyBenjyBenjy." She crooned as she rubbed his back, rocking back and forth with Benjy in her arms. Her voice crackled with a mixture of pain, joy and disbelief. Tears streamed down her cheeks unnoticed and unheeded. "I never gave up hope. Never."

The other Graham sisters wept at the reunion, using discreet handkerchiefs from their sleeves. Brody let a few tears fall unchecked, which surprised and humbled Rory. Caleb sniffed beside her, wiping his eyes so no one would see he cried too.

Rory held the tears back, the emotion in the room pummeling her with the urge to let them loose. She didn't know these people well but she knew what loneliness was. To be Benjy and have his family welcome him back, no matter what, that was worth a thousand days of mediocre with Horatio. Her marriage had been convenient but never full of love.

The Grahams showed her what true family was again, what she'd lost when her parents died. She wanted it again, bad enough she could taste it on her tongue. Even though they'd been separated for nearly half of Benjy's life, the love was still there. Rory wanted to hug all of them, to absorb some of that love.

"How?" Olivia cupped her younger brother's face. "Where?"

Benjy used his sleeve to wipe his eyes. "Rory and Caleb found me."

Olivia looked at Rory. "Then I have another reason to thank you."

"I didn't do anything but get myself banged up." Rory didn't deserve the gratitude. Without Caleb, nothing would have happened. "Your brothers were the brave ones. I was along for the ride."

"Don't listen to her, Liv. Rory has brass balls." Caleb's bald statement made Eva gasp but his sisters shook their heads as though they expected it.

"*Hijo*, your language." Eva snuck the baby out of Brody's grasp and snuggled the little boy. "In front of the baby too."

Olivia hugged Benjy again. "This is the best gift I could have received. A new child and my Benjy back in my arms." She started weeping again, this time silently, and sat down on the bed, pulling him down beside her.

"I hope you can stay for a while." She gripped Benjy's hand as though he would fly away if she let go.

"We can stay a couple of days. After that the men will come after us." Hannah smiled. "We took all the girls. None of those men can cook anything more than boiled water. We left two loaves of bread and a hock of ham."

"They can figure it out. I want you to stay at least a week." Olivia ignored her husband's frown. "I can't bear it if you leave sooner than that."

"You have a new baby to take care of. You can see us anytime." Eva cooed at the baby, as though she would leave a moment sooner than absolutely necessary.

"We can talk about all that later." Caleb motioned to his sisters. "Let's give Liv and Benjy time alone and you girls can make fools of yourselves over this little boy."

"What's his name?" Rory couldn't help the question. It just popped out of her mouth.

Olivia smiled. "Stuart Armstrong. After our father."

Caleb's expression changed and Rory knew he'd been deeply moved by the baby's name. If Rory ever had a child, not that she would, she would do the same thing Olivia did and name a boy after her Pa. It was a fitting tribute for a lost father.

"That's a good name." Caleb opened the door and shooed his sisters out, followed by Eva who didn't appear to be giving up the baby soon, and Brody. He held out his hand to Rory. "C'mon, honey, let's get some coffee."

Rory looked back at Olivia and Benjy, heads bent together, and the longing for family hit her again. Hard. She wanted that for herself, that unconditional love. Unless Caleb accepted her as she was, and what she was, she wouldn't get what she desired.

She joined the Grahams in the kitchen. Hannah already had coffee on the stove and was busy coordinating the baskets of food the girls were carrying in. Catherine ignored Brody's raised brows at her trousers, while Elizabeth and Rebecca quietly worked to assist their sister-in-law. Eva found a rocking chair and was currently snuggling little Stuart.

Rory wasn't sure what to do. Not only as she wearing trousers too, she was out of place in this house, in this family. She was about to leave for a breath of fresh air when Brody spoke to her.

"Tell me how you found him and how you came to tame this foolish man." He sat down at the table and pulled out a chair for her.

Rory sat down, her discomfort with the black-haired man not completely gone. His blue eyes were intense, and would have been cold if she hadn't seen the true love he had for his wife and child.

"I haven't tamed anything and I didn't really find Benjy. I knew him as Marcello. Your, uh, brother-in-law and I ended up at this man Garza's ranch. Caleb recognized his brother and we managed to get away." She looked at Caleb, who was currently hauling in baskets and burlap sacks from the wagon. "It was a rough time but we made it almost to the Circle Eight before Garza caught up to us."

The memory of their mad flight, the fear and the blood washed over her. She shivered and Brody put his hand over hers. She almost snatched her hand back but hesitated at the sympathy in his gaze.

"Life sometimes forces us to make hard choices that can haunt us. Liv can talk to you about what she went through." He glanced at Caleb. "I hope he didn't do anything stupid to ruin things."

Brody was a very perceptive man. She wasn't going to talk to him about what did occur between them that morning. She could barely think about it herself considering how it ended with her marriage proposal rejection.

"I'm glad Benjy made it back to his family. He is a sweet boy." She needed to change the subject from her relationship with Caleb to something else. Rory wasn't prepared to talk about her feelings with a virtual stranger.

"I've never met him but he was the baby of the family. Liv was near obsessed with finding him. It about killed her we never did." Brody shook his head. "No matter how many lost were found, she always searched for him. She was like his second mother, did you know that?"

"No, but it doesn't surprise me. The Grahams seem to be a close family." It was an understatement and she hoped he didn't hear the need in her voice.

Brody narrowed his gaze and stared at her intently enough to make her squirm. "I know you."

Her stomach clenched. "I don't think so." She didn't know what it was about this man that made her nervous, but his question made it worse.

"You're a smithy from north of here, right? Foster?" He nodded as though he was agreeing with himself then he smiled. "I think you shoed my horse once about seven or eight years ago. You were a bit of a thing, almost swallowed by the apron you wore, but you did the work while your father watched."

She couldn't have been more surprised. "I am a smithy." Rory found herself smiling back at him. "I can't believe you remember me."

"How could I forget a lady blacksmith?" He shook his head. "You impressed me. Not too many women swing a hammer like that. How did you meet Caleb anyway?"

Rory finally relaxed, pleased this man remembered her, Rory Foster, as a smithy. She might be an ordinary woman, but she was a damn good blacksmith. When Caleb returned, he stopped and stared at her, then he smiled. This man's smile made her feel all puddly inside, warm and liquid.

"Don't flirt with my girl, Brody. You've already got your own." Caleb set down the basket where Hannah pointed and the spell was broken.

Rory looked back at Brody and he raised one brow. "He might get on your nerves now and again, but he's a good man."

She knew he was a good man. What she didn't know was if he was meant to be her man and whether she would she take a chance and find out.

CHAPTER ELEVEN

Caleb watched his sister sleep, the baby tucked in beside her. It was a beautiful sight. One that made his ranger heart melt. He had told her the whole story, from finding Rory, to discovering Benjy and their wild escape from Garza. She wept again, to know only the barest of what their brother had gone through.

She insisted that Benjy stay with them, until he wanted to go home. He would leave it up to the boy where he stayed. Although he wasn't even eleven, he had the right to choose. Hell, he might decide to stay with Rory.

The thought of his lady blacksmith made his gut clench. He thought the time together would help his situation, but it was so damn busy and cramped in the house, there had been no opportunity to do anything but nod good morning.

"You're thinking about her, aren't you?" Olivia's soft question startled him.

Caleb scowled. "She really does have my tail in a twist."

His sister smiled. "Do you love her?"

"Yes." No hesitation at all. It surprised both of them.

"What are you going to do about it?" Olivia caressed the top of her son's sleeping head, the downy soft hair sticking to her fingers. Even now, Stuart was attached to his mother. Caleb wanted to see Rory with their child, and feel the sweet softness of a baby with his mother's amber eyes.

"Marry her."

"What about the rangers?" Her question wasn't unexpected and for once, he was prepared with an answer.

He had done a lot of thinking the last three days. The entire experience had reminded him what was important in life—family, home, love and all the moments they brought. He'd been chasing his own shadow for four years and never catching it.

The truth was his shadow had been waiting for him on the Circle Eight. Being a ranger had been an experience he wouldn't trade, but Caleb was ready to come home.

"I'm going to give it up. Stay on the ranch, maybe build a house for us."

"Good. I like her. She's strong too." Olivia raised one brow. "Why is she avoiding you?"

Caleb sighed. "I did something stupid and I need to fix it."

"Then why are you sitting here with me? Find her and fix it." His sister smiled. "I want to my son to grow up with lots of cousins."

"But I haven't seen you since Christmas and—"

"Shut up and do what I tell you to." Olivia shooed him with her hand. "Get out."

Caleb shook his head and chuckled. "You won't ever change, will you?"

"I'm allowed to boss you around. You're my little brother." She snickered and pointed at the door. "Now get."

He got to his feet and bent down to kiss her forehead. "Love you, Liv. Don't tell anyone I told you that."

She smiled and touched his arm. "Love you too, Caleb. Good luck." She yawned and closed her eyes, snuggling up with her baby again.

Caleb went in search of his quarry but she was elusive. He couldn't find her at all. They were leaving for the Circle Eight in a few hours and he was running out of time. When Hannah asked him to load the empty baskets into the wagon, he snapped.

"Jesus Christ, Hannah, am I a goddamn pack horse? They're empty. Why can't you girls put them in there yourself?" He wanted to cram the words back in his mouth as soon as they escaped.

Hannah's eyes widened and Meredith ducked behind her mother's legs. "That was unnecessary."

"I'm sorry. I don't know what the hell I'm doing. I've been looking for Rory and she's missing." His chance with Aurora was slipping through his fingers. When they got back to the ranch, it would be his every last chance. What if she still refused to marry him? He was a little nauseated to think he had thrown it away because of his foolishness.

"She went for a walk with Benjy. He decided to stay with Liv and

Brody for a month." Hannah took Meredith's hand. "I'm going back in the house. When you're ready to be polite, you can join us and finish packing the wagon." She walked back into the house, her head held high.

Caleb refused to blush but it was hard. He deserved a dressing down but it didn't mean he had to enjoy it. Hannah wasn't his mother but she was the female head of the family and she took her responsibility seriously. Cussing in front of one of the twins and yelling at Hannah was a mistake and he knew it.

Elizabeth walked past him with an empty basket on each arm. She raised one brow at him. "I heard you have a filthy mouth. Meredith is going to shock her Pa when we get back."

Caleb cursed under his breath. "I didn't mean to do it."

"Children that age absorb everything that touches their ears. She'll be cussing like her uncle in no time." She set the baskets in the front of the wagon beneath the seat. "You mad at Rory?"

"No, I'm mad at myself. I need to talk to Rory."

Elizabeth put her hand on his arm. "Be patient and tell her how you feel. Women don't need fancy talk or displays of manliness. We need honesty, love and respect."

He stared at his younger sister, wondering how he missed her growing up. "You're a woman already. How did that happen?"

She snorted. "A lot has changed since you ran off to be a ranger."

Elizabeth left him standing there, feeling more foolish than he thought possible. The women were going to make his head pop off, or possibly explode. He needed to be calm when he finally talked to Rory or he could make another stupid mistake. Hannah was right, he should help load the wagon and then hope what he planned at the ranch would be enough to convince Rory he loved her.

His future depended on it.

Within an hour, everyone was ready to leave. Rory still avoided him but at least she was there, returning to his family's ranch. He had a chance to woo her if he made the right choices. Benjy stood between the house and the wagon, hands in his pockets, looking at the ground.

Everyone waited to see if he would stay with Olivia or change his mind. Caleb tried not to stare although everyone else was doing the same thing. Averting their gaze and trying not to let him see them looking at him. It was the wrong thing to do.

"Benjy, you still fixing to stay with Liv and Brody?" Caleb asked

EMMA LANG

what everyone was thinking.

He nodded. "I don't have anything to wear though."

Brody shrugged. "I'm sure we can fix that. Neighbors have been throwing clothes at us to make into baby duds for Stuart. Hannah taught Liv how to sew real good. We'll have clothes for you in no time at all."

"Okay. I'll stay." Benjy toed the ground with his boot. He wore Matt's old clothes, but the shoes on his feet had been provided by that bastard Garza. He couldn't let his brother continue to wear them.

Before he could change his mind, Caleb took off his boots and handed them to his brother. "Keep these. Burn the ones on your feet."

Benjy glanced down and started, as though he realized what he had been wearing. He sat down and yanked off the old shoes then pulled on Caleb's. Brody took the rejected footwear and tossed them in the side yard.

"We'll build a fire tonight so you can finish that." Brody held out his hand and helped Benjy to his feet.

"Thanks." Benjy's mouth nearly turned up into a smile. That was the first sign he was beginning to heal. The tension in the air dissipated and the good-byes began. Rory stayed by the wagon, speaking quietly to Benjy. A good-bye from one survivor to another. The boy had a special place in his heart for the blacksmith, but Caleb didn't blame him one bit.

Olivia stood on the porch with the baby, kissing and hugging everyone in turn. Eva wept openly for having to leave baby Stuart so soon, but she promised to return next month. Catherine stood by looking bored, while Elizabeth and Rebecca cooed all over the baby before they climbed in the wagon. Hannah let the girls plant sloppy kisses all over Stuart, their baby cousin, before herding them away.

Caleb kissed Olivia's forehead, then her son's. "Take care of him. He's fragile."

"Don't worry, Caleb." She smiled, a mature wife and mother, so unlike the hellacious bossy wench he'd grown up with.

Caleb shook Brody's hand. "Send word if you need anything."

Brody laughed. "You can stay and wash the diapers."

"No, thanks. Too many of bad memories of those." He chuckled at his brother-in-law's sour expression. Being a father came with shitty diapers and no sleep, along with the joy of holding the baby.

Caleb walked to the wagon, making sure all the ladies climbed

196

into the wagon safely before turning to Benjy. This was the hard part, saying good-bye after only having him back for two weeks.

"If you want to come home, let Brody know. He can send word to us or bring you back. Are you sure you want to stay?" Caleb secretly hoped his brother would say he changed his mind.

"Yep. I want to be with Liv for now." Benjy stuffed his hands in his pockets again. "Don't be mad."

"I ain't mad. Not even a little." Caleb pulled his brother into a quick hug then let him loose before he wiggled away. "I'll see you soon. I promise."

"Okay. Bye, Caleb."

Caleb climbed into the wagon, he didn't look back at Benjy but he did glance at Rory. She stared off into the distance, not bothering to even blink at him. He would change her mind no matter what. As they pulled out of the yard, he glanced back at his brother and Benjy raised his hand in salute. This time, there were no dark times ahead. This time only good things waited, he wouldn't accept anything less.

The ride back to the Circle Eight was more sober than the ride to the Armstrong farm. The twins were subdued, choosing to whisper to each other rather than chatter with their aunts and mother. Caleb's sisters were quiet, dozing or simply watching the trees go by.

Everyone noted Benjy's absence either by look or word. Rory had known the boy a short time, but his silent presence was one she missed. They spoke of the future before she left. He was a brave boy, choosing to stay with his sister, away from the rest of his family. Rory was proud of him although the parting was bittersweet. She would miss him.

Hell, she would miss all of them. Being with the Graham women had been lovely, more than she had ever expected. Her mother hadn't been an affectionate woman, but she'd been a good mother. Rory never knew how much fun she would have with sisters. They laughed, bickered, argued, talked and loved, all at the same time. She wanted to keep them.

More than that, of course, she wanted to keep Caleb. He hadn't spoken to her since they arrived at the Armstrong farm. She would tell herself it didn't hurt her feelings, but that would be a lie. His behavior had been erratic and she heard Hannah complaining about his cussing in front of the twins.

Rory didn't know what she would do after they returned to the Circle Eight. She would find a way to get a new mule and make her way back to the forge. No matter what the Republic of Texas said, she had nowhere else to go. A blacksmith was a profession she could take anywhere, but she didn't want to wander or find a new place to be.

If she couldn't have Caleb, then she would return to what she had before. Perhaps luck would be on her side and she could take back her business without the government noticing. Although in truth, she didn't expect it.

The hours passed slowly, leaving Rory to her thoughts. It wasn't pleasant. They whirled around and around, making her sick and dizzy. When the ranch came in to view, she breathed a sigh of relief. Helping out the Grahams with supper would take her mind off her uncertain future and the husband she wouldn't call her own, the children that would never exist.

Self-pity was not palatable and Rory was tired of it. She jumped out of the wagon after it stopped to help unload it. Matt walked out of the barn wiping his hands on a rag. Rory had to look away when he greeted his daughters and wife. Their love for each other was pure and sweet, too beautiful to watch.

Caleb got down and waited until Matt stopped long enough to notice him. "You about done?"

"No, I'll never be done." Matt grinned.

"Did you get everything taken care of?" Caleb's gaze slid momentarily to Rory, then skittered away.

What was going on?

"We did and you owe me a hell of a lot of sh—dirty jobs and sweat to pay me back." Matt tipped his hat to Rory with a secret smile on his face before he scooped up his girls and carried them to the house. They squealed the entire way, their mother shaking her head and chuckling as she followed at a more sedate pace.

Catherine rode toward the barn, no doubt to groom the horse she insisted on riding. Eva left with the Elizabeth and Rebecca, chattering on about supper. That left Rory alone with Caleb. She turned to escape, to follow everyone into the house when his voice stopped her.

"Please don't go, Aurora."

"Why not?" Her hurt still burbled inside her.

"I need to show you something and ask you a question." He held out his hand. "Please."

She didn't remember the ranger using his manners before, and he had rarely said please to anyone, much less her. Rory had the choice to follow him, take another chance with her heart. A last chance. She tended to hit back when she was hurt.

Yet the honesty in his beautiful eyes told a story. Her heart did a funny flip and she took his hand. This was it. The last time she would take a chance on Caleb Graham. He smiled, a beautiful grin that took her breath.

"This way, honey." He walked her around to the side of the barn, to the grassy area that led to the creek.

She liked holding his hand more than she should. The warm, wide palm, the calluses, the sweet way he held her hand as though he would hurt her. She was a blacksmith and had as many calluses as he did. It was another piece of the puzzle of whatever he was up to.

They walked around to the back of the barn and she stopped in her tracks, overcome and overwhelmed.

Somehow in the short time they'd been gone, Caleb's family had retrieved her anvil. It sat in the middle of a newly cleared back stall. A stone forge had been built, its mortar still wet from whomever had built it. Her hammer and tongs lay on top of the anvil, while the rest of her tools from home were lined up against the stall door. Her leather apron hung from a nail on the wall.

Her throat closed with emotion and she fought like hell not to cry. He had done this. Caleb had made arrangements to make a place for her. He reached in and pulled out a sign that had been painted with whitewash to read "AURORA'S SMITHY."

She burst into tears.

Caleb looked horrified and she shook her head. It took another minute of snuffling like a foolish female before she found her voice.

"I can't believe you did this." She wiped her eyes on her sleeve. "Why?"

He shook his head. "I had to show you I love you. Words weren't working. I want to marry you, Rory, stay here and make babies with you. I want you to be a smithy and be happy here."

She stared at this man, who had been an arrogant ass pushing her off her land. So much had changed in a few weeks, she had changed. No longer the blacksmith who hid behind the fire, existing but not living. Their relationship had been fraught with arguments, danger, injuries, intense emotions and in the end, love.

"I can't have babies." A sob worked its way up her throat.

He pulled her into his arms and she breathed in his scent, the now familiar smell of the man she loved. "I don't care. We can adopt some babies then. Or spoil our nieces and nephews then send them home to drive their parents crazy."

She laughed against his shoulder. "Are you sure about this?"

He leaned back and cupped her face, his kiss softer than a spring breeze. "I've never been sure of anything in my life until now. Until you. This is where I belong, with you, on the Circle Eight. I quit being a ranger before we went to Olivia's. I'm going to go back to ranching and sleep every night beside a wife I love. Aurora Foster, will you marry me?"

Rory looked into his eyes, and saw the love and hope shining there. She had nothing to lose but so much to gain.

"You don't mind that I swing a hammer?" She had to ask or she would regret not doing it.

"I love that you swing a hammer. Your body is beautiful to me, sleek and muscled. Enough to make me hard all day every day."

She barked a laugh. "Jackass." He was crude but he was hers. "Yes, I'll marry you."

"Thank God." He squeezed her so hard, she didn't know where he ended and she started.

Joy bubbled up inside her, that elusive emotion she had never found. Who knew the appearance of a pushy Texas Ranger would change her life forever? She closed her eyes and held onto her love, her life.

The blacksmith and the ranger found what they had been looking for in each other's arms. Love, respect and joy. Another circle joined in the circle of eight.

ABOUT THE AUTHOR

Beth Williamson, who also writes as Emma Lang, is an award-winning, bestselling author of both historical and contemporary romances. Her books range from sensual to scorching hot. She is a Career Achievement Award Nominee in Erotic Romance by Romantic Times Magazine, in both 2009 and 2010.

Beth has always been a dreamer, never able to escape her imagination. It led her to the craft of writing romance novels. She's passionate about purple, books, and her family. She has a weakness for shoes and purses, as well as bookstores. Her path in life has taken several right turns, but she's been with the man of her dreams for more than 20 years.

Beth works full-time and writes romance novels evening, weekends, early mornings and whenever there is a break in the madness. She is compassionate, funny, a bit reserved at times, tenacious and a little quirky. Her cowboys and western romances speak of a bygone era, bringing her readers to an age where men were honest, hard and packing heat. For a change of pace, she also dives into some smokin' hot contemporaries, bringing you heat, romance and snappy dialogue.

Life might be chaotic, as life usually is, but Beth always keeps a smile on her face, a song in her heart, and a cowboy on her mind. ;)

www.bethwilliamson.com

CPSIA information can be obtained at www.ICGtesting.com
Printed in the USA
LVOW08s2156240516

489818LV00004B/203/P